ANOTHER
October Child

ANOTHER
October Child
RECOLLECTIONS OF

ELEANOR SPENCE

Collins Dove
Melbourne Australia

Published by Collins Dove
60-64 Railway Road, Blackburn, Victoria 3130
Telephone (03) 877 1333

Designed by Liliana Hustwayte
Typeset in Times
Cover illustration by Dianne Vanderee
Printed in Australia by The Book Printer

National Library of Australia
Cataloguing-in-Publication data:

Spence, Eleanor, 1928- .
    Another October Child.

    ISBN O 85924 638 8.

    1. Spence, Eleanor, 1928-   - Biography.
    2. Authors, Australian - 20th century - Biography.
    3. Women authors, Australian - 20th century -
    Biography. I. Title.

A823'.3

Contents

	Page
Chapter I	1
Chapter II	11
Chapter III	21
Chapter IV	31
Chapter V	44
Chapter VI	57
Chapter VII	71
Chapter VIII	84
Chapter IX	98
Chapter X	111
Chapter XI	119
Chapter XII	132
Chapter XIII	144
Chapter XIV	156
Chapter XV	169
Chapter XVI	184
Chapter XVII	199
Chapter XVIII	212

I

October is more than a month. It is a time, and a tide, and in our country it has a nature which owes nothing to the autumnal harvest glories and threshold-of-winter melancholies of that country which, in my childhood, my elders called 'home'. In the late twenties and the thirties, there were many traces still of the British colonists' tendencies to impose northern-hemisphere patterns even upon the Australian landscape; as yet they were unaware of the incongruities of trying to make our wayward and stubborn seasonal displays into a tidy English pageant of spring, summer, autumn, winter.

Even as a young child I knew that October was a doorway to summer. Indeed, there were days in October when summer was no longer drawing near, but had emphatically arrived. The bush smelt of dry leaves and paperbark blossom, the sky was an eye-aching blue, and the cooee bird, back from that impossibly far Siberia whose existence I had recently discovered from a picture book, became the harbinger of Christmas and holidays and trips to the beach and all manner of precious things.

October is also my birthday month. As a family, we did not make much of birthdays, nor a great deal of Christmas, for my mother was Scots, reared in the tradition of Hogmanay, but October had the added advantage of being my brother's birthday month, too.

It is also my daughter's. And for me it has that extra connotation of my best-known and best-selling novel,

1

The October Child. While not astrologically minded, I rejoice in these small and delicate webs of connection. That events and associations should fit so nicely together, strung between one's own life and the lives of others, and decorated by the imagination, suggests the reality of Stevenson's 'Brooches and toys for your delight'.

It is October again, and yesterday I had another birthday — my fifty-sixth. It seems as good a time as any to indulge in recollections of childhood, girlhood, family and friends, and a particular set of places, and to trace those connecting strands which were woven into a pattern of one person's life, as viewed from a present standpoint, which is simply another part of the landscape.

I have even returned literally to the district of my growing years, but to the south of our family home, and with wide stretches of water between. Stretches of water — creeks, lagoons and the ocean — were so much a part of our childhood landscape and climate that they must have shaped the banks and coastlines of our dreams. All three of us now live within a few kilometres of the sea — my brother at Buderim in Queensland, my sister at Lewes, in England's Sussex, and myself on the New South Wales Central Coast.

Though I can no longer physically hear the sea at night, as I used to in my Erina childhood, the sense of its nearness is always here. The tide that came uninvited across the marshes and into my back yard a few months ago was salt and sea-scented; my old iron fence, partly restored, has a solemn row of maritime images — starfish, coral, seaweed, lighthouses and one quizzical seahorse. And I have no doubt that the cottage itself once belonged to a fisherman.

For some people, the place of one's childhood has a pull as strong as that of the tide.

Family history grows into a kind of folklore, and often steps over into the neighbouring territory of myth. There can be family myth, and a separate myth for each individual. My father's side of the family tended to embellish its history, while my mother was more of a stickler for fact. Even today my romanticism is anchored, so to speak, by a kind of semi-detached respect for reality inherited from generations of independent and down-to-earth Scots ancestors.

Yet way back in their ranks was a poet. That, as far as I know, is fact. In my young adult life this struck me as romantic indeed, especially for a budding novelist. His name was Robert Henryson, and he died at the beginning of the sixteenth century. I have to admit that his poetry was, at first glance, rather disappointing. It was hardly in the manner of Keats or Shelley, and the ancient Scots vocabulary was even more baffling than that of Robert Burns. I have since reinstated him in my affections, if only because he was a schoolteacher. It seems to have become a Henderson family vocation. And the name Robert likewise became a hand-me-down. It was that of both my grandfathers, and is my brother's.

Summer apparently came early in the October of my birth, and it was a month of bushfires on the Central Coast. Eighteen months previously my sister had been born in an autumn of floor rains, when the waters covered the Punt Road between Erina and Gosford. Such snippets of family history are not, I think, intended to be omens. My father was more taken with the fact that Dorothy was born close to Anzac Day, and he always maintained that he wanted to call her 'Anzac Dardenella'. Because I arrived on the anniversary of the Battle of Trafalgar, I was threatened with 'Horatia Nelsonia'.

That our birth dates should be linked with the distant drums of wars was not without meaning. In our history books the victories of Trafalgar and Waterloo were

3

given more weight and prominence than the exploration of Australia, and the shadows of Gallipoli and the Somme stretched far across our family life in a very real way. My mother had lost her first fiancé, who in civilian life would have been a doctor, when he died in a hospital behind the lines in France two weeks before the Armistice. My father was wounded in one leg by shrapnel, and also suffered from what, for want of a more formal word, was called 'shell shock'. The effects of the events of World War I upon both of them lasted, in different ways, for the rest of their lives, and inevitably shaped the lives of their children, too.

It was a common enough family history in the twenties and thirties. Nor, when for four days one October my mother found herself with three children under the age of three would it have been considered in any way remarkable in the district. To have a new baby every year or so was accepted as a woman's lot, and only families with more than half a dozen children could really be termed large. Local myth proclaimed that those with the biggest families had to be Catholics; in reality, they were more likely to be Protestants. Catholics were in the minority, because most of the settlers in our area were of English and Scots origins. Many of the latter were Gaelic speakers, and to listen to them when they did speak English was just as baffling as trying to read my ancestor's poetry without a glossary. By comparison, my mother, coming from Edinburgh, was a lowlander. Later, all my romantic attempts to claim kinship with adventurous, kilted highlanders fighting to the death for Bonnie Prince Charlie had reluctantly to be abandoned.

(I would have liked to have laid claim to Mary Stuart too, but my mother said firmly that as far as the ordinary Scots people were concerned, she was a disaster. So was Bonnie Prince Charlie. Some of my forebears — Presbyterians all — had been Covenanters, but to me

4

that was about as romantic as cold tapioca pudding.)

Families round the district might boast of ten or twelve children, but to my mother and father, having three in as many years was just as great a triumph. They were forty and forty-one when I was born; again, it was World War I which had brought them so late to marriage and parenthood. And decreed, too, that I should remain the youngest, much as I later wished — or thought I did — that I could have had a romantic younger brother or sister.

The floods of April and the fires of October threatened to interfere with my mother's lying-in arrangements because they might have barred the way to Sydney, where all of us were born. There were three private hospitals in Gosford, and some excellent doctors, but my paternal grandmother and aunts decided, perhaps because of my mother's advancing years, that it would be altogether safer if the children were born in the metropolis. So instead of arriving in a private hospital in Gosford, we were born in a private hospital in North Sydney, not far from Grandma's home in Waverton.

By the time it was my turn, the journey must have taken on the nature of an almost-annual pilgrimage. Of course my brother and sister had to go too, and come flood, fire or anything else, all had to be transported to Gosford railway station and bundled onto the train. Fortunately, my mother (who had travelled alone across half the world to marry my father) survived it all, including the return trip with the new baby.

When I hear the phrase 'five miles' (ignoring any mention of kilometres), I always automatically envisage the road between our home and Gosford station. That was the length of it. It doesn't take a lot of imagination to travel along it as it must have been in the late

5

twenties. My father drove a sulky then; if you did not own one, you walked, or begged a lift in somebody's truck, until the bus service started a few years later.

Our house was on the main road, and had the odd distinction of being sometimes on a corner and sometimes not. At the time of my birth, the dirt road took the shortest way between two points, and dived down a very steep and stony hill towards the village of Woodport. When traffic increased, the hill was abandoned, and bypassed with a tarred road known grandly as 'The Deviation', or, to us children, 'the divvy'. With the coming of the new road, our property turned into a corner block.

But the horse and sulky and passengers, born and yet unborn, would have negotiated Pengilley's Hill, and no doubt would have reached in some relief the flats where Erina Creek wound away, diminishing (except in the year of the flood) into the scrub to the east. Then came the rise to the Terrigal Road turnoff and the little grey weatherboard Anglican church, and another, gentler descent to Woodport and the Punt Road and the bridge. Gosford would by then be on the horizon.

Across a distance of five miles, in those days and nights of deep rural silence, from beyond Mount Elliot and the Ridgeway and the north end of Brisbane Water, the confident and imperative whistlings of steam trains entered into the background of our listening even as the thudding of surf came to us, on still nights, from the beaches. Train journeys were always part of our lives; perhaps we acquired a taste for travel before we were born.

Now I can hear the train whistles more clearly still, as electrically driven wheels pound the tracks between the viaduct and the Woy Woy tunnel that in our childhood was so mysteriously long, and so stuffy and redolent of soot and dankness. Nor do I lament because the whistles of electric trains have a different sound; that's

6

the way it is, on this middle-aged side of the water.

My mother came back from that last childbirth pilgrimage to the house called 'Gibraltar', where my father had been all along, taking care of the livestock and the orange trees and the fifteen acres of land. Such whimsies as 'hobby farms' were unheard of; though my father had a war pension and a small share of his mother's family investments, the farm still had to be very much a paying proposition. With the Depression looming, its productivity was to be even more vital.

The house had been built by a retired English naval man — hence its name, which was apt enough anyway, for there was rock aplenty on those coastal hills. But it was not ungenerous land. For every scrubby ridge there were two well-watered valleys; and the slopes, when cleared, had good brown soil where citrus trees thrived, and beans and peas could be made to grow, and cows and horses pastured. Later we had poultry yards shaded by plum and peach and nectarine trees — further images and waymarks of the seasons.

Our amiably eccentric naval architect had designed the cottage to resemble a ship at sea. At the back, where the foundations were high because of the fall of the land, he had placed his quarterdeck, with a great tilting window facing south across the valley to the next ridge, which was called Conroy's Mountain. It was the first 'mountain' I ever saw, so my personal image of such eminences is of something a few hundred feet high, which seems to bear little relation to Everest or the Matterhorn. A couple more windows were landlocked portholes, and at the front door the threshold was raised in nautical fashion, making entry into the hallway a bit of a hazard for small feet and unaccustomed visitors. There was less allowance for such landlubberly distractions as domestic conveniences, and the bathroom happened to be between the living room and the kitchen.

My parents defied the seafarer by adding on a

7

verandah. My mother always said it saved her sanity. Railed in by wood-framed fibro, gated at front doorstep and side stairs, it was long and broad enough to serve as a cricket pitch in wet weather and, at various times, as sleeping quarters, tea room and breakfast room, day nursery, playground and roadway for a kind of tricycle known as a 'flivver'. I remember it also as being furnished with a beloved rocking horse, a big wood-and-canvas chair with arms that folded into a writing desk, and a couple of huge crates we called 'cupboard boxes'. The biggest crate of all, in which my mother's piano had been brought from Scotland, did duty as a feedbin under the house . . . for chooks, not children.

A further important piece of family history records that it was here on the verandah that my three-month-old life was almost extinguished, when my sister, herself about twenty-one months old, tried to smother me with a pillow. I suppose I was making too much noise. But I was rescued, and no sinister motives were imputed to Dorothy. The kind of psychiatry which puts infant behaviour under the microscope was then in its own infancy, which for my mother's sake was just as well. Ever conscientious, she must have had trouble enough even feeding us on time according to the mothercraft principles of the day.

Yet, paradoxically it seems, at a time when every family in the neighbourhood was in some kind of financial difficulty, ours included, home help was readily available. There always seemed to be women or girls who would do the washing or other chores to eke out their own family's incomes. They came by the day, and were more like temporary members of the household than paid servants. They had their pride, and an independence to match my mother's own.

I cannot claim to remember anything of the first two years of life, but my mother and I both later took some pleasure in the fact that at the age of twelve months I could repeat the last words in four lines of verse, a ditty beginning: 'Little drops of water . . . ' It would be romantic to think that this bore promise of a literary career, and realistic to add that it indicated a certain innate tendency to play to the gallery and earn applause. And as the poem made reference to 'water', 'sand' and 'ocean', it may have been an early introduction to some of my favourite, and readily available, images.

Shortly afterwards, a temporary stop was put to such entertainments when all three of us got whooping cough. For me, it was followed by a bout of gastroenteritis, which in those days stalked through the summers of infancy as a genuine potential killer. The combination of my mother's nursing and the faithful visits of a local doctor ensured that I would survive to quote more poetry, and indeed attempt one day to write it, among other things.

Convalescence from whooping cough alone was very lengthy. One usual remedy was a change of air, but my parents could not afford a holiday for the three of us. Instead, by somebody's happy inspiration, we were given a giant sandpit — not so much a pit, as a great golden crunchy pile of sand, at the top of the slope near slip-rails which led to the main road, under a huge old coral tree to which our first swing was attached. It may not have provided a change of air (which was fresh enough, anyway), but it gave healthy, happy and safe occupation. We had it for some years, and it became the venue for imaginary games such as 'going to the beach' and 'trains'. We would push around toy trains made out of my father's old pipe tobacco tins. The brand was 'Temple Bar', and they came originally from McGee's in Sydney. The tins had hinged lids, which could be taken off or replaced according to their pretend function, and they had a pleasant lingering aroma. They were one of my father's few luxuries, I think.

I can remember playing in the sand when I was about three. Our family sulky was kept there by the slip-rails, but already its days were numbered, like those of the horse, called 'Girlie', who had shared the shed with a cow or two. On one side of me my mother's garden was already taking shape, and she often worked in it while we played. On the other side was a fowl-yard with the huge old plum tree that in spring resembled the Snow Queen of Hans Andersen's story. Stories were already part of my inner world, for they were read and told to us along with nursery narratives such as 'The House That Jack Built' and 'Who Killed Cock Robin?'. In response to that question, for it seemed to demand a response, I once answered with my sister's name. It was preferable to having to own up to such a dreadful deed myself.

In the coral tree, the gillbirds carried on with their raucous gabblings. Their relations do the same now, in my own backyard coral tree, hung about with spring green, heart-shaped leaves.

II

The other day I watched from my kitchen window the little girl next door playing an imaginary game with a trio of soft toys. And an eternal cry drifted through the bright spring morning:

'Mum! Look at *me*! Look what *I'm* doing!'

It's reassuring to hear it still. Maternal responses haven't changed a lot, either.

'Yes, I see, dear. I'm watching.'

So she is, with at least half an eye and ear, while she deals with loads of washing, wonders whether there's time to clean the windows, and plans what to have for dinner; and no doubt gives more than a passing thought to a few more personal and private problems which she doesn't share with anyone.

I think I was probably born with that traditional child's cry of 'Mum, look at *me*!' upon my lips. My own mother was set squarely and constantly in the centre of my life all through my childhood and beyond. I deeply resented being parted from her in my infancy, and would howl at the kitchen door until I was let in. No matter how busy she was, she seems to have yielded, in spite of those child-rearing dogmas which declared you must let your child cry at times, lest it become spoilt. She preferred peace at any price, a principle I later adopted myself.

11

So, spoilt I no doubt became, and rejoiced in it.

Many years later she told me quite sincerely (for she was not a pretentious woman) that she believed it was better for children to be a trifle indulged than to be too severely treated. A happy childhood, she said, was the richest legacy she could give to us. It was one gift which could never be taken away, no matter what happened to us all in later life.

I believe her.

My mother was born in Ormiston, in the County of Haddington, east of Edinburgh, three days after Christmas in 1887. (As a child, she felt keenly the injustice of having no real birthday celebration of her own; it became part of the Christmas–New Year festivity, and was overlooked. By contrast, more was made of the birthdays of her two younger brothers.)

Her name was Eleanor Mary. The Christian name was an unusual one in a Scots family where 'Jeans' and 'Margarets' and 'Elizabeths' were the norm. It was perhaps the choice of her father, Robert, the schoolteacher who loved books and history. My mother's best friend in her secondary schooldays, a girl called Evelyn, declared that the name 'Eleanor' did not suit her; rather did it go with a vision of someone tall and stately, if not queenly, and apparently my mother was none of these things.

As a child, I listened in fascination to my mother's reminiscences of her schooldays, and Evelyn was a leading character. She was, it seems, devastatingly clever and witty, and belonged to a large family endowed with charm, good looks and brains. I often wished I could have met her.

My mother was not allowed the distinction of 'Eleanor' for long. At some stage in her childhood it became 'Nennie', and that stuck for the rest of her life.

When she passed on her proper name to me, she made sure it was never abbreviated, and I grew up being rather proud of it. It had such romantic possibilities, even though there were problems with the spelling.

I never knew my maternal grandparents, except from hearsay and one or two photographs. Grandfather, a pleasant, bearded, dark-eyed fellow, looked friendly and gentle, and I was sure I would have liked him. That could have been because my mother was so fond of him, and gave only good reports. If she liked him, I was prepared to like him too. He shared with her his literary tastes and encouraged her to gain the best possible education at a time when few girls, even in Scotland, could think realistically of tertiary education.

He was one of a large family, mostly brothers with names such as 'John' and 'James' and 'George' — although George, I think, was a black sheep, such as every big family tends to have. He embezzled money from the bank where he worked, and may eventually have gone to Canada. Not that that was unusual — many Scots seem to have had a natural taste for emigration, although it may have been economic necessity rather than a fondness for adventure, or — as in Great Uncle George's case — the requisite new start in life.

Though the Hendersons could claim some kinship with the clan Macdonald of Glencoe, my grandfather's family seem to have been lowlanders for many generations, and produced numerous schoolteachers, civil servants and Presbyterian ministers. They set great store by a sound education, and the schools to which my mother and uncles were sent were of the moderate-fee-paying, public-foundation kind which seem to have been peculiar to the Scots education system, and remarkable for their high standards of teaching.

As a village schoolmaster, my grandfather was

13

transferred at intervals, and my mother remembered at least part of a childhood spent in a small mining town near Glasgow, which from her description might have been the inspiration for Harry Lauder's songs, with special reference to the joys of the Lanarkshire miner's Saturday nights. My mother recalled mostly the miseries of the wives who sat at home waiting for the inevitable brawls. It gave her a lifelong distaste for any form of alcohol, and may also have fostered her interest in women's rights.

She went from Grandfather's school to the Edinburgh Ladies College, which name (since changed) she maintained was snobbish and inaccurate. It was not, she pointed out, a private school in the accepted sense — but she did not deny that it was a very good school, and she enjoyed it. She insisted that she was not really clever, like her celebrated friend Evelyn, yet she had a special gift for languages — French and German — and a talent for piano playing.

By the time I was old enough to listen, she was a good pianist still. She played in the evenings, sometimes after I was in bed, and the strains of Mendelssohn, Chopin, Schubert and Schumann entered as comfortably into my half-sleep as ocean sounds and train whistles. None of us inherited her musical talent, though we all had lessons, but she lived long enough to see a grandson take promisingly to the keyboard.

Sometimes she departed from the classical, and chose pieces from the *University Songbook*, which gave me my first introduction to 'Gaudeamus Igitur' and similar pieces. My favourite in her repertoire, was a deliciously melancholy setting of Walter Scott's 'Coronach': 'He is gone on the mountain, He is lost to the forest . . .'

I found it so touching and inexpressibly sad that I could never have enough of it. It hinted at highland mists and moors and landscapes that I had never seen, and mysterious historic tragedies. When, as an adult, I visited Culloden Moor on a wet, sombre, late-summer afternoon, with rowan berries glowing like candles, I recognised the land of the 'Coronach', and the ancient lament for the fallen. But what at ten I'd seen as romantic, I later accepted as tragic reality. My mother was firm on the matter of 'lost causes'; she had suffered enough from wars herself to see them as nothing but a senseless, shocking waste of young lives.

There is something about 'Scottishness' (the word 'Scotch' was outlawed, as being an English invention) which has a powerful pull upon the emotions — another paradox, for the Scots seem generally an unemotional race, at least in public. As a child, my sister was quite electrified by the sound of bagpipes; my daughter, after a brief trip to Scotland in her teens, accepted it as a second native land; and a nephew tramped all over it, wearing a Henderson kilt and collecting bits and pieces of ancestral history. And I admit myself to finding Edinburgh one of the most charming of cities.

As a child, I tried hard to envisage it as it must have been for my mother in her growing years, but it taxed even my extravagant imagination. While the luminous blue of an Australian winter sky was spread over orchard and garden, or a pretty, spiky frost clung briefly to grass stems, and we made a few concessions to winter such as sleeping indoors instead of on the verandah, I struggled to see my mother, the girl (and that is effort enough for a child — how *could* one's mother ever have looked like a fourteen-year-old?), practising piano scales with fingers frozen as icicles, then setting off in the dark to catch the train to school, past tall, grey stone buildings and banks of snow.

I had seen pictures of snow, of course. And of holly and sledges and carol singers at Christmas time. We were sent comics from Britain. The series I remember best was *Chick's Own*, which had as a magnificent extra a fat, colourful Christmas annual. I knew all about plum

15

puddings long before I tasted one.

The comics were sent by Grandmother. If Grandfather seemed a distant and invisible yet benign figure, Grandmother — in spite of the comics — was even less well defined, and less well disposed. She and my mother seem to have been temperamentally opposed. From a few photographs, she appears as a rather handsome, well-built woman with a lot of long, fair hair and an unsmiling countenance. I may have acquired early a suspicion that it was not done for grandmothers to smile. My father's mother, in her photo, has an expression of stern detachment not unlike that of the late Queen Mary. It could have been a simple distaste for being photographed, especially in old age.

My mother's mother was called Jessie, and she seems to have been a person of moods and tenses. She was often displeased for reasons the rest of the family could not fathom, and both my grandfather and my mother were convinced that her displeasure had in some way to be their fault. This had the effect of bringing father and daughter even closer together, which no doubt increased Grandmother's displeasure. She seems to have been quite open in her favouring of the younger son, Martin, leaving the unfortunate Harry stranded in the middle. In photos, Harry has a doubtful and worried look; Martin, on the other hand, resembles Little Lord Fauntleroy, even to the golden ringlets and lace collar.

My mother, in buttoned boots and white frilled pinafore, is, if not quite glaring at the camera, at least giving it a thoughtful, considering stare. Her large, very dark eyes are like those of her father and my sister. Her long waving hair is dark too. Her mother hoped her daughter would be fair and sweetly pretty, so Martin's blond curls had to compensate. Years later, when I met my Uncle Martin, I found him a most delightful man, with a keen sense of humour and an ability to tell a beguiling story for every landmark in Edinburgh. Harry

16

I never knew; he died comparatively young.

It was an orthodox Presbyterian household, with church-going two or three times on Sundays, and no Sunday recreational reading except what was available in the Bible. My mother resented having her hair fiercely curled and brushed for Sabbath appearances, and there must have been vast stretches of juvenile boredom, especially as sermons could last up to two hours. But it was by no means a static and desiccated form of religious observance. Matters biblical and theological were there to be discussed and argued about with energy and intellectual discernment, and children's questions do not seem to have been discouraged, at least not by Grandfather. All this, plus regular Scripture readings at home, gave my mother both sound Bible knowledge and an appreciation of the Bible's poetry and literary treasures. Her favourite psalm, 'I will lift mine eyes unto the hills . . . ', was one day to become my own.

They had rich resources, too, in their family connections. There was much visiting of uncles and aunts and cousins, and gatherings to celebrate births and marriages and anniversaries in a small, close clan. And I imagine that at some of these events, my mother, in white muslin dress and coloured sash and hard-won curls, played the piano when it was her turn.

Beyond the family circle was the wider milieu of Edinburgh's culture, and that also was rich. My mother saw both Anna Pavlova dancing, and Sarah Bernhardt performing in *L'Aiglon*. I remember her description of the latter, because Sarah played Napoleon's ill-fated son, the King of Rome, although the actress was quite elderly by then. Anything to do with children dying in tragic circumstances was bound to appeal. To match the content of some of my favourite storybooks, *L'Aiglon* would have gone one better had he been an orphan — which, poor child, he emphatically was not. But the

17

memory gave a special piquancy to an adult visit to Schönbrun, where the King of Rome actually died in suitably palatial and romantic surroundings.

My mother also went to the opera, but in spite of her fondness for music, she was unable to suspend her disbelief when 'Mimi', dying tunefully of consumption, was in reality a plump soprano almost bursting with health, or Wagner's 'Brünnhilde' leapt about the stage so heartily that the scenery tottered. I think this scepticism must have been a family trait: she once went with an uncle to *Lohengrin*, only to be distracted by his plaint of 'Here comes yon blethering bird again!'

I'm afraid I inherited it. Especially concerning Wagner.

An acute domestic crisis arose when my mother finished school and sought to go on to Edinburgh University. Grandmother believed that the place for an only daughter was in the home, helping with the housework, entertaining visitors, sewing and the like. It was a natural enough assumption, closely connected with that other traditional belief — that a girl would soon marry, and further education would therefore be wasted.

That my mother had her way seems to have been almost entirely due to Grandfather. He braved storms of wifely anger, and it was arranged that my mother should combine an Arts degree with teacher training.

It must have been like a door opening. She loved her university years, and the friendships thereof. Travel now became possible, in student groups, and she spent some time in Paris, caring for some French children in an early version of the *au pair* system. The Scots have always had strong historic links with the French, and even pronunciation of the language seems to have been easier for a Scots tongue. She studied German, too, in a Rhineland university town, but was less than attracted to

18

some of the local male students, upon whom the mantle of Prussian militarism seems to have descended. I suppose it was a prophetic experience, in a way.

Photographs of her in those days show her as an attractive young woman with fashionably cropped hair and a rather shy smile. It's a little reminiscent of the theme song from the movie (and the book, with its Scots educational setting) *The Prime of Miss Jean Brodie*: '. . . You're young and alive, And the grass in the meadow is green. So run, if you will, to the top of the hill . . . '

She looks young and alive, indeed, and quite ready to climb in confidence her own special 'hill' of chosen career, love and marriage, and the life of a Scots doctor's wife. And children — she always wanted children.

She was twenty-six when war broke out in August 1914.

After her fiancé's death she seems to have come full circle, back to being the useful daughter ready to care for ageing parents. She never spoke much of those times, but the bitterness must have seemed impossible to swallow. It might not have helped much, at first, when her brother Martin, himself an ex-soldier, brought home an Australian friend convalescing from wounds. It was not until a few years had passed, and Bill was back in New South Wales, that the possibility of marriage was discussed, by letter, of course. She still called him 'Mr Kelly' when she agreed to come out to Sydney and marry him.

To a youthful listener like me, it all had the true romantic ring. Rather like the plot of a novel. And I had a keen vested interest in it, because, as I kept telling myself in egocentric wonder, if it hadn't happened, I

19

would never have existed.

Years later, I wonder in a different way. When my mother left Scotland, she became cut off, for the rest of her life, from a whole series of vital relationships: from the place she could never cease to call 'home', from the landscape and people of all those precious early dreams. What she felt of the emigrant's deep loneliness and alienation, she kept to herself.

She never went back to Scotland, but until her death the small tricks and intonations of the Scots tongue stayed in her voice. And the last person she ever spoke of was her father, just before she died.

III

The World War I recruiting slogan 'What did *you* do in
the War, Daddy?' was not only blatantly loaded, but
also ignored the nature of young children, who are not
given to asking such cute, pertinent questions of their
elders, especially their fathers. We accepted, as part of
our landscape, our father's limp and his sometimes
irascible temperament, along with his old A.I.F. hat and
leggings, the annual importance of Anzac Day, with its
marches and reunions, and the way he whistled, on the
way down to the orchard, Sousa military airs and
'Mademoiselle from Armentières', 'There's a Long
Long Trail A-Winding', and 'Keep the Home Fires
Burning'. Other children had fathers and uncles who
had been at the war; why not ours? We knew that his
reference to a man in the neighbourhood as 'an old
Digger' was a tribute, and that if such a man was in
trouble, as so many were during the Depression, he
deserved help.

But to this day I don't know precisely what he did in
the war. He told tall tales in which he featured as a
mythical military hero defeating hundreds of Germans
single-handedly. We recognised and enjoyed that as
fiction. I see it now as a kind of self-defence; he didn't
talk about his actual experiences because there was too
much he did not want to recall. He was a romantic, too,
in his way, and his tendency was to enlarge upon and
glorify the very real mateship he experienced in his

21

Army days, and leave the rest. In this he differed markedly from my mother, who believed that in order to prevent wars, you had to accept that their reality was loathsome and insupportable.

His father is the unknown quantity in the paternal family history, as symbolised by the 'X' with which he signed his name on Dad's birth certificate. Robert (the name keeps cropping up on both sides) was an illiterate miner from Enniskillen, in Northern Ireland. He was forty-five when my father, William, was born at Rix's Creek, in the New South Wales Hunter Valley. And that is about all we knew of this mysterious grandsire; he died when his children were still quite young, and I suspect that his Irish descent and his lowly status were covered up by some of his descendants, for his wife belonged to a family which definitely struck it rich. Ironically, their fortune came from the Hunter Valley coalmines where Robert had worked.

With Grandma Rachel, a streak of Lancashire hardheadedness enters the scene, along with an aggregation of relatives. She had three brothers and six sisters, which explains why the family fortunes had dwindled somewhat by the time the shares reached the second and third generations. Each sister, plus sister's children, were generously provided for, except that a convoluted disagreement — always spoken of in hushed voices in front of the children — led to one sister getting rather less than the rest.

Rachel — of course; my grandmother. Her connections tended to be the poor relations.

I inherited her name — my middle one — and remember her as an autocratic and rather unapproachable old lady, presiding over my aunts' household. But there is much more to relatives than meets the infant eye. Not long ago, one of my aunts told me that Grandma, in her hours of sitting in her Waverton garden, made up stories for herself, about flowers and other things. She died when I was about five or six, and when, a little later, I took to scribbling stories myself in the same garden, I curled up in the old basket chair she had always used.

The women on my father's side of the family seem to have been long-lived and physically strong and tough. They needed to be. Grandma Rachel reared three daughters and two sons (the younger of whom was my father) in Hunter Valley towns where a widow's lot could not have been a happy one, even though her older brothers were amassing capital. Girls as well as boys went to school until they were fourteen, and both my father and at least one of my aunts became pupil-teachers, under a system which allowed older students to teach the younger ones while getting on with their own education. Eventually, I think, they went on to become fully fledged primary schoolteachers. My father certainly did so. I have a photograph of him as a young man, looking dashing and affluent in three-piece suit, watch-chain, starched white collar and cuffs, one hand negligently in his pocket. He has a small book in his other hand (not, I think, a New Testament, but rather an address book), and carefully placed in the right foreground is a fine new panama hat. A note on the back of the photo is to his oldest sister, Alice; it finishes: 'Am in a deuce of a hurry — [signed] Will'. He is quite remarkably handsome, with a beguiling air of youthful confidence — as if it were life in general that he was in such a hurry to get on with.

At some time in the pre-war years his family moved to a house called 'Ellesmere', in Gordon Road (now the Pacific Highway) in Chatswood, Sydney. My father gave up schoolteaching to study wireless telegraphy, which occupation took him eventually to Thursday

Island. He later moved south to Queensland (perhaps when war broke out), and enlisted at Rockhampton as a signaller in the A.I.F. in 1915.

He would have been twenty-nine by this time, and surely that fine young fellow with the panama hat must have had a few lady friends. My mother hinted that there may have been one called Dorothy, the name given to my sister. It was also the name of a musical comedy star whom my father had admired. He enjoyed such entertainments, and while my mother tackled on the piano the works of Chopin and company, my father played Strauss waltzes, Gilbert and Sullivan pieces, and a waltz called 'The Pink Lady', which attracted me both by its title and by its colourful cover.

He would have visited some of the theatre shows while on leave from the A.I.F. training camp on Salisbury Plain, before going over to France, where he remained as a sergeant until January 1920. I don't know where, when or how he was wounded; place names such as 'Villers Bretonneux' and 'Ypres' echoed distantly through my childhood. A book called *The Wipers Times* drew my attention at intervals (but I found it lacking in my kind of human interest; it had no apparent story line, and World War I battlefields humour was beyond me).

He owned, besides the Erina property, an orchard at Coorenbong, north of Gosford, where he installed a manager. Yet he was not at heart a farmer. It was just that, after the war, there seemed to be little else for him to do, and he had enough capital with his war service payments, to become a property owner in a modest fashion. He had a fondness for detailed historical research, and belonged, until not long before his death in 1956, to the Royal Australian Historical Society. On the shelves in his little study at one end of the verandah, the Society's journals kept company with a growing collection of C. E. W. Bean's Official War Histories, and — witness to another keen interest — Wisden's Cricketers' Almanacs. I think he was happier in that room of his own, with his books and papers (he was a meticulous keeper of accounts, enjoyed totting up figures, and wrote in a beautiful italic script), than he was at work in the orchard or fowl-yards.

He was the kind of father who was more comfortable with small children than with half-grown ones, with whom he tended to be impatient. When I was under school age, I sought him out for singing games and stories, or followed him about while he worked. If he was not always talkative, then I had enough conversation for two, having taken up verbal expression with a will ever since my poetry recitations at age one.

Perhaps he was, in some ways, a shy man. I know so little of his deepest feelings because he didn't speak of them to anyone — not even my mother. Almost to the day of their marriage they addressed each other formally; it was for both of them a kind of marriage of convenience, a last chance for matrimony and parenthood before they became respectively confirmed bachelor and spinster. The relationship, undemonstrative and at times austere though it was, endured. Each had separate interests (my mother was unimpressed by cricket, and my father could not abide visits to the beach, which she loved), but they had much in common, too. Reading and discussion of ideas and of travel, and a liking for theatre and cinema.

It might have been expected in such a marriage that a common interest in their offspring would be the greatest bond between them, but I don't believe this was so. Both, for instance, had a good old-fashioned sense of involvement with, and responsibility towards, the community in which they lived. As a result, we children grew up with an important feeling of belonging in a particular place, in a neighbourhood where a nucleus of people stayed put. We were known to all of them, and they to us. It was like that, in the Erina-Wamberal-Terrigal districts of the thirties.

When, after a sea voyage which was apparently tedious and comfortless in the extreme, my mother arrived at Darling Harbour towards the end of 1924, she was taken at once into the household of her future mother-in-law and two unmarried sisters-in-law. They had moved from Chatswood to Waverton, which suburb — a leafy, leisurely, well-to-do place — was liberally sprinkled with my father's relatives. A third sister lived with her husband and two children on the North Sydney fringe, one aunt was at the bottom of the hill near the station, a cousin at the top of the same hill, and an aunt just up Hazelbank Road. Another aunt had a mansion at Mosman, while the uncles (the rich ones) had boldly opted for Point Piper.

I imagine my mother was on perpetual display before and even during her wedding.

She had brought her wedding dress with her, in the massive, humpy brass-bound cabin trunk which later became a combination of treasure chest and dress-up box for us children. The dress was charmingly suitable for a New South Wales December wedding — sleeveless, with dropped waistline and much embroidery around the serrated knee-to-calf-length hemline. I think there was a matching cloche hat, and certainly buttoned-strap shoes of extreme pointedness.

She always liked good clothes, and some of the outfits she brought from Scotland lasted for many years. Our favourite was a fox fur stole, complete with gleaming glass eyes; for me, it became confused later with images from one of the first picture books I clearly remember. It may have been special because it was my own, or perhaps because I was old enough to read the words myself. It was called *The Tale of the Tail of the Little White Fox*, and was of Russian origin. The heroine was named Olga, and the little white fox of the title had the kind of adventures bound to touch my five-year-old susceptible heart. Not only did it lose its tail, but it got lost itself, in strikingly pictured Siberian-Arctic wastelands that imprinted themselves on my imagination. Fortunately, it had a happy ending.

My mother brought many books with her, as well as clothes. I can't tell how much she was prepared, mentally, for the new life that lay before her. There must have been considerable culture shock. I know that on her arrival, that first Christmas, the relative-by-marriage she warmed to most was the youngest of my father's aunts, Emily. She was the one who lived in Hazelbank Road. Only last year I revisited Hazelbank Road and found it — despite its new conglomeration of home units — still one of the most attractive of suburban streets, with the plane trees that have grown so big since, as a child on holidays at my aunts' home, I trailed up its apparently marathon-type length to go to morning service at St Thomas's church. I have to admit that it did not seem so long or arduous on weekdays when Auntie Lil took us to the Zoo or Balmoral, and we caught the tram at Crow's Nest after buying mouth-watering eatables for our picnic lunch. Which only goes to show that the nature of one's destination, and its imagined delights, can greatly influence the enjoyment of one's journey.

Great Aunt Emily was a friendly, handsome and charming woman, well-travelled, but with that broadness of mind without which travel can lack any but superficial meaning. She had, also, four lively and attractive daughters of similar tastes. She seems to have been kind to my mother, with the true kindness of understanding, and was a favourite with my father, too.

My parents were married at the Crow's Nest

27

Presbyterian church, not at the Anglican church of St Thomas, which Dad's family all attended, and where later we were all christened. It must have been my mother's decision, to have been wed in her own ancestral denomination, although since the war, and its catastrophes, she had had many second thoughts about matters of faith and formalised religion. My father's sisters seemed to have had no such doubts; they were convinced Anglicans, and must have been relieved to find that their new sister-in-law had the decency to be a Scots Presbyterian as the next-best-thing to being an Anglican. Had my father dared to choose a Catholic bride, I cannot imagine what would have happened. I often wonder about the official religion of that forgotten Irish coalminer, Robert. Could *he* have been a Papist? To some of my father's family, it would have been a skeleton in the closet even more shameful than illiteracy. Fifty or sixty years ago, one needed no particular justification for being rabidly anti-Catholic; sectarianism was at its worst, fuelled by official intolerance on both sides.

So, there were my parents on their wedding day, two days before Christmas, and the church overweighted considerably on the bridegroom's side. My mother's bridesmaid was, I think, a personal friend she had kept in touch with, and the groomsman was Great Aunt Emily's son Tom. Grandma Rachel and her three daughters would have been in the front row, but I am not so sure about my father's elder brother, another Robert. He too was a creature of distance and mystery. As children we hardly knew him, or his wife and the four children, although the last were our first cousins, and because half our relatives were on the other side of the world, we were singularly short of cousins. They were much older than we were, and the only one I

28

actually met was Cousin Joe, who distinguished himself by becoming a Member of the New South Wales Legislative Assembly — only on the Labor benches, which may not have been so acceptable in some family quarters. I found him most likeable.

Only one of Dad's sisters married, and thereby considerably provided us with two cousins of suitable age, girl and boy. They would have been small children at my parents' wedding. My mother was particularly taken with Ted, who was somewhere between two and three, a most fetching age in a brand-new nephew. His mother, Jane, and her husband, a retired Army colonel, lived on the North Sydney side of Waverton, overlooking Shore School; comings and goings between that household and Grandma's and my aunts' in King Street, opposite Waverton Park, were constant.

It seems never to have been questioned, in those times, that at least one unmarried daughter would be available to care for a widowed mother. It just seemed to work out that way, conveniently. Where an ageing relative was unmarried, or childless, it was usually a single niece who took over the caring role. This was certainly the case in my father's family, where his aunts Alice, Jane, Annie, Sarah, Mary and Emily each had her own household, as did Grandma Rachel at Waverton. Almost all of them, I think, died at home.

It was in my own generation that the pattern was first broken, when for economic and social reasons women took up paid employment outside the home and became increasingly independent as the traditional family togetherness crumbled round the edges. It had to happen; with it went the widow's own household and attendant relative, and there grew upon the horizon the nursing homes, the retirement villages, and a new question: 'What shall we do with Mum? Or Dad?'

Grandma Rachel and her sisters would not have heard that question; it would have been irrelevant. Grandma had her sizeable and well-appointed house, a modest but sufficient income from capital invested, and not one daughter, but two, living with her. There was Aunt Jane, as well, just around the corner, and at some time there was also a paid housekeeper. That's the way her world was; she had worked hard for most of her life, and comfort and financial security in her old age were the fruits of it.

My aunts did not have to work outside the home, and opportunities for matrimony apparently had not come their way. They were spinsters, but it would be too easy — and less than kind — to see them in archetypal roles of frustrated, lone, middle-aged ladies who had devoted themselves to an elderly parent, and thereby wasted their lives. They had their own dignity, and their own pursuits and consolations. Perhaps most importantly, they had numerous family connections, and a devotion to their nephews and nieces. Family *mattered*.

So my parents went to live in the cottage called 'Gibraltar', and, in the following October, Robert (the Fourth) was born. Then my sister and myself in rapid succession. My mother made no secret of the fact that she wanted as many children as possible, and my father appears to have had no objections.

It is no small thing to have been a truly wanted child.

IV

It is All Saints'. No November mists, nor coming Guy
Fawkes' fires to help consume the autumn leaves, nor —
for which we may be thankful — Halloween high jinks.
Instead, the Christmas-bush blossoms are already
touched with pink, and soon the jacarandas will be
colouring the hills. And, if the voice of the turtle dove
is not precisely what we hear in our land, the wood
pigeons are doing their best, competing with the fanatic
squawks of the plovers guarding their young, while the
'cooee bird' keeps on with what sounds more like a
complaint (possibly to do with the hazards of long
migration) than a mating call.

It's the time of year when I started school.

As far as I can remember, I did so with confidence.
My brother and sister had been setting out for some time
with packed lunches (which I saw as proof of
independence) and leather satchels on their shoulders.
They duly returned unscathed, and kept on going back,
so school could not be too awful.

So, in spite of my enduring devotion to my mother,
from whom I was to be parted for some six or seven
hours, I went off optimistically. I knew she would be
there at home when I returned. So would my father. As
far as I was aware, no fathers ever left their farms to go
to work, except to go 'on the roads', which meant
working for the Council.

The walk to school was an uphill quarter of a mile. It

31

would hardly have been new to me, because it was also the way to the only shop, and as young children we were often taken for afternoon strolls. There was a kind of British orderliness to our upbringing; each day had its recognisable shape. In the mornings we played around the garden or on the verandah; then came lunch and a rest, then walks, sometimes with a picnic afternoon tea. Before dinner, my mother somehow found time always to play with us, usually 'let's pretend' games, which require no props other than furniture and dressing-up clothes. A more vigorous and highly exciting game was 'Jack Above Ground', which, with its twin, 'Puss in the Corner', involved the part-frightening, part-challenging risk of getting caught. As peaceful aftermath, we had stories read or told to us. Dinner, baths and bedtime by candlelight followed in sequence. Even had my mother been able to afford to employ a nanny, she would not have done so. It wasn't a Scots custom, and in any case she wanted to share herself in our daily occupations, no matter how taxing it may have been.

It was a pleasant walk to school. On either side there were still acres of bushland with tracks here and there, inviting exploration, though they went nowhere in particular, except down the ridge on either side, to the village of Matcham or the still uncleared valley below the Terrigal Road. On some of the slopes there were orchards like our own, and what houses there were stood close to the main road. We knew all the people who lived in them.

Nor was the school unknown to me. Its tennis court was used by the grown-ups at weekends, and its classrooms for Parents and Citizens meetings and euchre parties. My mother disliked the card games, but I think my father sat in, sometimes. They were played with fierce, competitive zeal. The tennis matches could likewise turn serious on occasions, whereupon my parents would have retired more or less gracefully. My father was handicapped by his lame leg, and my mother lacked the competitive spirit.

I can remember clearly being placed at a front desk, nearest the door, for that was the bit of the classroom belonging to First Class. My sister was on the other side of the room, beside the windows, in the Third Class rows. As for my brother, he had disappeared into the 'big room', presided over by the headmaster. The child next to me was no stranger, either. She was Gwennie, the fifth daughter and sixth child of the family that lived up on the hill beyond the school; at home she had three little brothers, and another sister on the way. Her grandfather had been headmaster of the school for many years, and had lost his own three sons in the war.

Dorothy and I wore navy-blue tunics — cotton in summer, serge in winter — and white blouses with round collars. And socks and shoes. It was of no sociological importance whatsoever to me that many of the other children didn't wear shoes to school; I rather envied them. And school photos show that on the whole, and in spite of the Depression and the size of some of the families, the children were wonderfully well turned out. Most of our clothes were home-made; a 'bought' dress was an intriguing extra, associated with Christmas and birthdays, and often supplied by our Sydney aunts. My mother's hand-operated sewing-machine seemed forever on the go.

'The cat sat on the mat.'

It hardly seems a meaningful line with which to begin a literary career. It did not bear much relation to the printed adventures of Peter Rabbit, or Winnie the Pooh, or characters from Andrew Lang's Fairy Books, which I knew from my mother's readings. But words fascinated me, and so did books. The first reading primer had a red cover, and inside the cupboard opposite me were other

33

books with stiff, shiny covers of olive-green, blue and dull chocolate. The last seems to have been a standard colour in Department schools; as trim, it went with gallons of wall paint of yellowish hue.

The statement about the cat was underneath a bright picture in which the animal was without doubt sitting on the mat. It was an oval mat with stripes to rival Joseph's coat. I can't remember spelling or sounding out the letters, but as teaching aid there was beside me a frieze showing the alphabet. Further along were the multiplication tables, which later explained the mysterious chant coming from my left, where Second Class sat. At the back of our row was a sandtray with miniature animals and other figures, and on the wall were nature study posters.

I can't recall being disappointed on the one hand, or over-excited on the other. This was it — school. It was friendly enough, and there was plenty to do. Even when the teacher, the daughter of another old Digger, an acquaintance of my father's, was busy on the other side of the room, you could dip further into your red primer, or make marks on your slate in preparation for getting a real writing book. I had my eye on the exercise books, too; they were kept in the cupboard along with the primers. In fact the cupboard, from which later came crêpe paper for making Christmas decorations, and cardboard and coloured pencils for making Christmas cards patterned with Christmas bells copied from the real flowers on the teacher's table, soon seemed like Aladdin's wonderful cave.

Meanwhile I learned to read, then to write; and began to develop a fascination with all forms of stationery. It was for putting words on.

Storybooks, however, can exert a two-sided power. I must have been aware of it before I started school. On the one hand, they were entertainment, and food for thought, and extensions of, and adjuncts to, all those games of 'Let's pretend'. You could laugh with them, and even cry with them.

But sometimes they could be frightening. There was one book in particular, one of the Lang Fairy Books, illustrated, I think, by skilful Arthur Rackham. He was altogether too graphic for me. One especially gruesome picture sent me into screaming fits, but I couldn't leave it alone. I kept sneaking a look, and screaming some more. My mother, understandably, finally hid it in the top of a cupboard, whence it disappeared. She decided the rats must have eaten it. That didn't sound a comforting suggestion, either; I preferred to think possums were the culprits. Possums might go bump in the night, on our iron roof, but they were furry and featured in storybooks as well-disposed creatures.

I was, in a word, impressionable. In another word, susceptible. And not only to pictures in books.

My mother used to tell how I was terrified out of my infant wits by the appearance of two entirely benevolent nuns collecting for charity. I must have been sitting near the front doorstep, absorbed in some pursuit of my own, when between me and the sunlit garden arose two figures clothed all in voluminous black, with faces enclosed in stark white. As they bent to offer kind words of greeting, it must have been my personal encounter with the Apocalypse.

My Protestant aunts would have approved my reaction, I'm sure. (*Of course*, those Papist nuns went about terrorising little children. It was a prelude to dragging them in . . .)

My mother welcomed them in and sat them down, and they were full of apology for causing such distress. I suppose I calmed down when they had gone — but I did wait another forty-five years before becoming a Catholic.

That may not have been all comedy. C. S. Lewis, in *Surprised By Joy*, muses on the premise that those who suffer from nightmares and similar terrors as children often do not come to full acceptance of spiritual faith until middle age. (He himself was both nightmare-prone child and middle-aged Christian convert.) It may be that the child has experienced too much of the negative side of the supernatural; I know, for instance, that I was made uneasy by mention of such a being as a 'Holy Ghost'. I heard only the second word. (It was away from my own home that I heard it, in St Thomas's church, where a large, loud-voiced minister towered in the pulpit preaching on sin, damnation and hellfire.)

I had no desire to be reminded of ghosts. They existed. I had seen one or two, and recognised but one way of escaping them — diving into my mother's bed. To be told that you didn't really see anything, that it was all your imagination, or that you had been dreaming, was little comfort. A young child, to whom the whole world is new, has no way of distinguishing what is 'real' (in adult terms), and what is not, as far as its own perceptions are concerned.

There seemed only one remedy, and that was to grow out of it. One could not go on forever taking refuge in one's mother's bed. But for a long time, the night terrors were associated for me with another 'bug-bear'. (Interestingly enough, bug-bear is derived from the same root as 'bogy-man' and the old English ghost term, 'bogle'. My mother would not have used such casual teasing adult phrases as 'Watch out for the bogeymen', and so forth, but other relatives and acquaintances may have done so.) Twin to the nightmare was acute and intense homesickness. These days it would probably be called 'separation anxiety', an apt description for the abysmal despair of going to bed in a strange place, a long way from mother and father and the family rooftree.

I think my mother took a sensible course in letting me stay away on occasions with my aunts, or a close family friend, though I imagine they were warned in advance. I was quite happy in the daytime, for I genuinely enjoyed changes of scene, other people's homes and gardens, and in particular the company of one aunt who related well to young children. It was at bedtime that the misery descended. On one occasion I was alone in the Waverton house with the eldest of my aunts, Alice, and put to bed briskly in the middle bedroom which in darkness became suddenly quite unfamiliar and stocked with shadows that simply could not be looked upon.

The problem could have been easily enough solved by the provision of a night light. But there seemed to have been no such concession in my aunts' house, and in no time I was convinced that part of the washhandstand beside me was a villainous creature aiming a weapon at my head. (I think I was at high-school age before I stopped sleeping with the bedclothes over the back of my head and neck. I apparently feared execution by beheading.) I eventually went into near-hysterics, and I think I was sent home next day.

Nowadays I feel much sympathy for my Aunt Alice. And for my mother. While I could get to the throwing-up stage through terror and too intense an involvement in such things as movies (which helps to account for the fact that until our teens, almost, we went mostly to Shirley Temple films), my sister could do the same simply by setting foot in any kind of conveyance — train, car, bus or tram. Sometimes, as the Sydney train pulled out of Gosford and my mother could not help casting anxious looks in Dorothy's direction, I would start feeling sick too, probably from a sense of rivalry. My brother seems to have maintained an admirable detachment.

Such behaviour can rightly be called attention-seeking, but that's hardly the end — or the beginning — of it. In a family of three young children, close in age, there was bound to be much jostling for places in the sun of parental affection. My mother understood that, though at times my father was less tolerant. She refused to let us be treated with any kind of violence of harshness, or with any form of cold repression. That this was achieved at some cost to herself, and her own feelings, did not become apparent to me until I myself was well into adulthood.

Somehow we missed being obnoxious. We were taught manners beyond the etiquette of how to eat correctly at table (something at which I was particularly inept). Manners, said my mother, were based quite simply on consideration for other people's feelings. My father, perhaps with memories of Army training, seemed to stress deportment; I can still hear his voice ringing from the verandah as I set off for school: 'Head *up*, Eleanor! Put those shoulders back!' I was no sooner out of sight than I was slouching again.

With my mother's encouragement, we grew up as distinct individuals. We didn't even look much alike. By contrast, there were families in the district with such strong resemblances to one another that the relationship was unmistakeable. Perhaps it was our mixed ancestry that produced such varied colouring — fair hair and blue eyes for my brother, auburn with brown eyes for my sister, dark and olive-skinned for me. It was an era when adult comments on children's looks were free and frank, and based on family likenesses. I got used to hearing that I had a 'Longworth nose', or 'Kelly eyes', or that my fringe (I had a Buster Brown haircut) was getting too long. Like our cousins, we simply put up with the ways of our elders. But our mother said such personal remarks were uncalled for, and didn't constitute good manners.

My First Class career was cut short when I developed impetigo, a rather nasty skin complaint, which was contagious, and, in those days, banned the sufferer from school. I think my brother and sister might have had to share my exile for a while, and it might have been then that Bob invented an absorbing game played with marbles, all around the garden. He must have picked up the post-war atmosphere, because the marbles were marshalled in battalions and other military groupings and we were the opposing commanders-in-chief, strategists and deployers of troops. (His favourite song at about this time was 'Onward, Christian Soldiers', his requested piano-piece a thunderous drawing-room solo called 'The Battle March of Delhi', and for reading and recitation he preferred 'The Charge of the Light Brigade' and Macaulay's 'Horatius'.) I imagine my round, glassy soldiers were decimated in the end, but for me the joy was in the terrain, where rockeries became mountain ranges complete with caves, a bed of annuals a whole forest, and puddles were lakes and streams. It was a new, inspired version of 'Let's pretend'.

Our best walks were along the valley road below our orchard. It was a flat, gently winding road of soft fawn-coloured dust, and once through the orchard slip-rails, you had a pleasing choice of right or left. The latter led to Lathams' bridge, which crossed a modest creek, brown and boggy and lined in spring with arum lilies. It was an excellent place for playing with toy boats, and when we were older, and had become film fans, we re-enacted there such favourites as *Beau Geste*. (Perhaps it was a drought year, and the dried-up creek bed sufficed for the North African desert.)

When the military and naval faction (my brother) was outvoted, and Dorothy and I were pushing the fine blue and pink toy prams given to us one Christmas, it was usual to turn right, and follow the road to a place I especially loved — though it was known locally by the peculiar and prosaic name of 'Blackfellows'. There must have been a house on it at one time; there were the remains of a chimney, and an old quince tree still bearing fruit and the grass, bounded by ti-tree scrub and swampy vestiges of Erina Creek, was thick, green buffalo. It was a wonderful picnic spot, although apt to be rather mysterious late in the afternoon, when the grass was darkened with shadow, and the slanting sunlight played at random on reed and fern and trunks of paperbark.

To me it was a meadow, such as I read about in English books. I looked in vain for ruined castles, stately manors, and thatched cottages to go with it. The local landscape, beautiful though it undoubtedly was, lacked romance. Or so it seemed to me.

But in the summer, when we went to the beach, the duality of my landscape-viewing fell away, and I was more than satisfied with what I could actually see, hear, smell, touch and taste. Here was no call for 'Let's pretend'; the beach was one great playground, of the true 'Adventure' kind.

At first we came and went by bus. That meant enduring the pre-expedition excitements of packing lunches, bundling costumes inside towels, and each being responsible for his or her inflatable rubber lifebuoy. Then there were hats. We girls had coloured, cotton models that tied under the chin; the starch put into them dissolved in the sea air, whereupon they flopped. But we never went to the beach without them, and the cry of 'Put your hats on!' followed us around the sandhills and down to the edge of the lagoon.

We took lunch, pullovers and sundries in an old suitcase. On one unusually dramatic occasion the bus, having set us all down at the top of the beach road, sailed on towards The Entrance with our case still aboard. Seeing our distress, a kind, passing motorist gave chase, and the bus driver duly pulled up and returned our provisions. I remember it as rather alarming; I enjoyed drama in books and my imagination, but in reality it made me uneasy, and threatened to disrupt what had seemed like a perfectly good day.

It was an easy walk down the hill, past the Wamberal hall (every village had its hall, usually not far removed from its church), onto the flat, where excitement grew as the reedy headwaters of the lagoon appeared. Then the landscape opened out like a cardboard pop-up in a book, and — it seems — just as vividly coloured. Gold sand, blue sky, olive green lake were all there, waiting, as we had left them the week before.

There were days when we had the place to ourselves. A few families came and went in the afternoon, but our mother said mornings were the best time to start out, before the wind freshened, or changed from summery nor'easter to intrusive southerly, or, least pleasant of all, the heated westerly that flattened the surf and drove sand into faces and legs and luncheon sandwiches. There was one spot in particular that was ours — a grassy hillock under banksia trees, where our mother could watch us all and enjoy the shade. While she loved the Australian outdoors, she never took kindly to the glare of the unprotected shore.

The day, like most of our days, had its accepted pattern. The best swim was the first, the before-lunch one, and that was always in the lagoon, not the surf. That promoted keen appetites for lunch, after which there was no swimming for a whole hour — an unbreakable rule. But there were sandhills to play on, the lagoon to circumnavigate while paddling, castles and cities and bridges to build at the damp, crunchy lagoon-edge, where now and then there surfaced humps of black rock, according to the level of the water. It was momentous indeed to be there when the lagoon had

41

recently been let out, and the sea rushed in and back again, in a gloriously energetic confusion of little waves and eddies, unexpectedly chilly.

We never went into the surf alone. Wamberal Beach had a deserved reputation for being treacherous, and it was only too easy to be swept by the undertow into holes and over sandbars. My early relationship with the ocean was one of love and fear; I was fascinated by it, yet knew the terror of being suddenly engulfed just when I thought the coast was clear. It featured sometimes in my nightmares, complete with a mysterious, huge, dark ship, looming out of nowhere, close in shore.

Later we walked north along the beach to the rocks, where I could follow my favoured occupation of discovering worlds in miniature, in tidal pools that at some point became associated with *The Water Babies*, and in the crevices and tiny caves and little cliffs and beaches decorated with shells and starfish and the dark-red, jelly-like 'plum puddings' that came alive and tried to digest one's daring finger. Then it was back to the ancient, grey weatherboard dressing sheds, set alone on the sandhills, and to tugging on clothes over salt stickiness and socks over feet where sand clung in spite of requisite washings-off.

To be sure, reality broke in now and then upon our summer paradise. My sister was stung by a jellyfish, and we had to rush off to the accompaniment of her (quite justifiable) screams. Then, too, there were bluebottles on the ocean shore, and sometimes storms came up so violently that we had to seek shelter on the verandah of an unoccupied holiday home. But that was something of an adventure — I loved to explore empty houses, and speculate on who had lived there, or who would one day come. It was all the more agreeable when my mother was there both to provide security and to share in my romantic imaginings.

And sometimes we missed the bus home. To wait for the next one would have meant sitting around until dark, so we walked. It was a long way, made more tedious by the climb up Brooks' hill, an escarpment which, we later discovered, defied the efforts of even the strongest, biggest boy to scale it on a bicycle. It was a mean hill — you no sooner struggled up to a promising curve than another steep slope arose before you. When we had breath enough, we sang ragged choruses to our mother's songs, such as 'Old Macdonald' or — with a nice sense of the fitness of things — 'One More River To Cross'. By the time we reached the top of the hill where the old Oak Road took its starboard turn towards Matcham, hope began to bloom again. It was a downhill walk, then, past the school and on to the house where, if the evenings were drawing in, our father would have the lamps lit.

V

I have always appreciated a celebration, and occasions marked with names and dates on calendars. It's a taste I acquired as a child, and one which grew with me. One of the small but keen delights associated with my anticipated entry into Sydney University was the discovery that its three terms had *names* — Lent, Trinity and Michaelmas. Had there been a 'Hilary', I would have adopted that, too, because it derived from the very word meaning 'festive' and 'joyful'.

Our schooldays were rich in celebrations and commemorations. As I grew older, they gave shape and order to that barely conceivable length of time — a whole year. In the beginning, they were mysteries, with rituals and words the First Class children viewed, so to speak, from afar, without joining in — such as the morning pledge to God, king and flag.

Easter was perhaps the most baffling occasion, being a movable feast. We drew Easter eggs on cards long before we had actually tasted such luxuries; chocolate was something bought, if you had the money, from the shop across the road from the school, and came in small slabs accompanied by cards to collect and put into an album. One year the theme was the discovery of Tutankhamun's tomb, and the pictures of mummies and gold headdresses and jewelled caskets were enough to raise the youthful imagination to fever pitch — to say nothing of adding a new dimension to nightmares.

Such secular matters inevitably became mixed with matters religious. The once-a-week lesson called 'Scripture' was of itself a mystery. One's regular familiar teacher was suddenly replaced by the Anglican minister, or his wife, and our attention directed to pictures and stories of people in robes and turbans, while the sandtray was transformed (with little difficulty) into a desert, and miniature camels and donkeys were much in demand. I enjoyed it all, because of the stories, but I found the account of the Crucifixion too harrowing for my taste. The only image that lingered, for some years, was that of the 'green hill far away, without a city wall', which was confusing enough. Similar bits of information were collected from Sunday School, both in Erina, at the little weatherboard church by the Terrigal Road turnoff, and during holidays with my aunts in Sydney.

When I was older, and began to pay attention to the gospel verses my mother quoted, I could barely equate this friendly Jesus she seemed to admire with the mistily vague yet oddly haloed person we had sung about in Sunday School or been sketchily introduced to in school Scripture. My overall impression seems to have been that he wasn't really one of us, being closely related both to a white-bearded old man who lived in the sky (or beyond it, which gave me to wonder anew about why sky was made of) and to the afore-mentioned ghost I so meticulously avoided.

If there was uncertainty about Easter, Anzac Day was unequivocal. At least to me. My father left home around dawn to go to Sydney, wearing a three-piece suit, felt hat and his medals, and we children went to school wearing red paper poppies. My mother, whose Scots lover (a legendary figure) actually lay buried in one of those fields where the poppies grew, had little to say about Anzac Day. The school service had a solemnity palpable to even the youngest child; it was held outdoors, often on the most balmy and serene of mid-autumn days, and there was usually a visiting adult to talk to us of Gallipoli, about which, in any case, we had been learning in class. And one of the older children would read Binyon's 'For the Fallen', the only part of which I could understand was 'At the going down of the sun, And in the morning, We will remember them'. Sunsets and early mornings were recognisable aspects of life; death and mourning were mysteries. My favourite Anzac Day hymn was probably 'The Recessional' (a baffling name). Kipling I had already met, through hearing his *Just So Stories*, and the words were set to a fine rousing tune. The 'Lest We Forgets' recalled Binyon's instruction to 'remember', which, as I got older, I conscientiously tried to do, at least for five minutes each Anzac Day, and again on Armistice Day. And, unconsciously, I was noting that God came into these ceremonies, too, for He was frequently addressed, more in the nature of protective overseer than of the militant leader in 'Onward, Christian Soldiers'. I was of course quite unaware that back at home my mother was probably questioning, as she and many of her generation had been questioning for years, why God allowed wars to happen at all.

May sometimes had two celebrations. The big one was Empire Day, but on at least one occasion, we held a May Day festival as well. From where I stand now, the notion of holding in a small New South Wales country school a ceremony derived from pagan spring rites in Old England seems odd — but charming nonetheless. After all, many of our elders, including my mother, and even my aunts (all Australian born), still referred to Britain as 'home', and 'Mother England' was a name heard every Anzac Day, and in history lessons. So we dressed up and danced around the Maypole in the playground, and parents and younger brothers and sisters came to watch and applaud. As with much in my life, my vision of myself as performer collided with the actuality. And, in this case, 'collided' was the appropriate word. The whole thing required a co-ordination that was beyond me; to weave a pattern with ribbons while dancing and prancing in limited space in various directions was asking of me that which I could not give, however willing the spirit. My sister would have done it beautifully, along with several of my classmates, for many were naturally graceful dancers. I can't remember whether the boys took part; if so, most would have been under duress. Sexist roles were clearly defined. The usual reasons for staying away from school were twofold — the boys had to help Dad pick oranges, or beans, or peas, and the girls had to help Mum in the house (often when there was a new baby). A few boys grew up to become adept on the dance floor, but the majority didn't — something that was evident a few years afterwards, when they wore Army boots. All was forgiven, however, when they were in uniform.

Empire Day, with further references to Mother England, and pointings to maps of a world lavishly splashed with the red of dominions and colonies, offered not only a half-holiday but much breathless excitement; its theme song was 'Land of Hope and Glory'. One year we shared a bonfire with friends and neighbours on a vacant bit of scrub across the road from our house. I imagine the stock of fireworks was communal too; certainly, on our own, we could not have bought the sky rockets and catherine wheels and bungers the size of elongated teacups that delighted my brother. I think I observed from a respectful distance. The extraordinary fact of being out in the dark so late (about seven or eight o'clock) was enough to mark the occasion.

Then there were the minor commemorations, not involving half-holidays but marked by our all crowding into the big schoolroom at some point during the day. They had names such as Arbour Day (tree planting — but we already had a playground full of grand old pines and, down the hill towards the creek, towering gums where the cicadas gathered in summer); Red Cross Day (when some of the girls had enviable white veils and red capes); and Gould-League-of-Birdlovers Day. For the last mentioned we were all given cards with shiny bird pictures — rather like coals to Newcastle in a district rich with bird life.

The first of August was Wattle Day. One year I almost got to be the Wattle Queen, only to be ousted by a girl called Lois, which for a short while put quite a strain on our friendship. With only seven or eight girls in each class, we were all more or less friends. However, I was appointed Lady in Waiting, and allowed to carry the wattle crown on a cushion. Having read so many storybooks, I accepted that attendants did have some importance.

The last ceremony before Christmas was Armistice Day, when we wore rosemary and observed a two-minute silence so intensely still that one hardly dared to breathe, let alone shuffle a foot. The phrase 'the eleventh day of the eleventh month' thereafter had an almost mystic importance; forever associated with the end of a war that had cut so deeply into our parents' lives and beings it seemed to have been imprinted also into our own dreams and memories.

The end of the school year bore a happy profusion of events, to be deliciously anticipated, experienced, then recollected. My own long suit was anticipation; in imagination I lingered during a week of bedtimes over the glories of school parties, prizegivings, breakups, the beginning of the summer holiday, then Christmas. The parties were held in the classrooms, and involved the intriguing pooling of each child's festive goodies, so that you could actually see and wonder at what Marjie or Irene or Tommy or Stan ate when they were at home. Most of the mothers were excellent cooks, and even at the height — or depth — of the Depression there seemed to be no lack of the cream-filled sponge cakes, Christmas cakes, and home-baked biscuits that appeared on every festive occasion, and on the stalls at school fetes. Those children who for economic or other reasons could contribute little were amply fed from the communal table.

There was usually a concert, too, around break-up time. My first public appearance on stage was as Snow White, not, I am sure, because of dramatic talent, but rather because I could manage to remember the lines. Verisimilitude flew out the window when having achieved a thumping collapse on the boards in apparent death throes, I at once sat up and finished eating the poisoned apple. (I did like my food, as the saying went in family circles.)

Then there was the prizegiving. Our mother did her best to make us non-competitive, but she was battling both the system and — in my case — natural temperament. There being little else to compete for, as organised and inter-school sports were almost unknown, the Parents and Citizens provided prizes for places in class.

And the prizes were books. Moreover, winners sometimes were allowed to choose their own, from one of those magnificent, full-colour, pre-Christmas catalogues that we all loved to pore over. Once arrived, the books were kept in that capacious cupboard until the prizegiving; one could glimpse the bindings, and even a word or two of title, and it was all most tantalising. I wanted a prize, without a shadow of a doubt.

Perhaps in First Class we all got a small tribute just for being starters. In Second Class, however, matters became more serious, and we had real tests. I was full of confidence, being well into a Primer ahead of the standard one for the class, but probably lacked dedication concerning arithmetic tables. In any event, I came second (which merited only a small, thin book), and the glittering first prize went to a boy called Tommy, a nice little boy with whom I had always been on the best of terms. Here was chagrin of an unexpected kind, but by the end of the following year Tommy's family had left the district, and I came top, having never at that time heard the phrase, 'big fish in a little pond'. Some understanding of what it meant awaited me in my first year at Gosford High School, a very large pond indeed.

At about the same time, we went to a Sunday School prizegiving as well, and here was competition of a different nature. It was not to do with material rewards; indeed, the three of us were given a lovely tin of toffees, which was generous in view of our rather erratic attendance record. (It was a long walk from our home to the church and back again.) It was probably the first time I took conscious note of physical appearances and comparisons between them. Our mother was adamant, throughout our growing years, that one's looks did *not* matter, nor one's clothing (which was not an excuse for being grubby or having unbrushed hair). Unfortunately, other people thought differently. The age of Shirley Temple had dawned, and curls, ribbons, frills and silver-frosted shoes were breaking out all over a small girl's world. It was as seductive as the tin of toffees and the Christmas catalogue. At the Sunday School gathering were a number of children from the Woodport side of Erina, comparative strangers, and although I had the reputation at home for being a tireless talker, I was shy enough amongst unfamiliar faces. The scene stealer that day was a little girl called Judy, with thick curls (genuine, not the product of rags or curling tongs), dimples, a beautiful smile and a frilled dress with a sash. The grown-ups, including my father, were much taken with her.

We were ourselves a well turned-out bunch, and that day my sister and I were probably wearing the liberty-print frocks (one green, one pink) given to us the summer before by our aunts. Our brother wore white shirt, tie, navy-blue shorts and even, on occasions, a school cap. Our resemblance was certainly more to young Britishers than to the offspring of America, a country barely heard of until Shirley Temple came along. But neither Dorothy nor I had curls, and our short hair wouldn't hold ribbons for five minutes. And if I was shy away from my own setting, my sister was even more so. On this particular occasion, all three of us were probably standing about feeling displaced and looking — to say the least — reserved. Watching the charming Judy, I was becoming aware for the first time of such things as social graces and the seeming importance of being outgoing and attractive, to say nothing of being put out because some other child was stealing the limelight.

There was a sad sequel to this encounter. Not long afterwards, the beautiful little girl called Judy caught poliomyelitis, and spent the rest of her life in a wheelchair. Polio was generally known as infantile paralysis, and I already knew the term because my best friend, Dotty, had been a victim, and walked with a limp. Another close friend was to die from it in his mid-teens.

Another salutory lesson on the nature of competition came at a school picnic. Like Easter and May Day ceremonies, the picnics were movable feasts, happening, I imagine, when the hard-working Parents and Citizens were able to raise the funds. In my recollection, it seems to have been in the Depression years, or towards the end of them, that so many treats and diversions were provided for us children. And that may have been no coincidence — the children's enjoyment was, I suppose, a treat and diversion for the grown-ups, too.

The picnic was held at Chinaman's, hardly ever referred to by its proper name of Toowoon Bay. It was new territory to us, being close to that other place, of sometimes doubtful repute because it was infiltrated by so many summer visitors, The Entrance. Our ambit was restricted; while The Entrance, to the north of us, was apparently out of bounds, that other place to the south, called Woy Woy, was even more dubious, because, during the late twenties and early thirties, those who boarded the Sydney trains at Woy Woy seemed to have a tendency to carry, either within or without, plenty of strong liquor to while away the hour or so of the journey. My mother had an imbred horror of drunkards, and we were hurried past the doorways of Gosford's three hotels when we went shopping.

Chinaman's, therefore, had the excitement of the unfamiliar, without being at all threatening, for not only were all my classmates present, but my mother came too, and the whole school complete with staff and helpers. Even the red and yellow bus was 'our' bus, one of the regulars that went to and fro past our front gate.

As at break-up parties, we were constantly eating. Sandwiches and cakes came in paper bags, brown as distinct from the white ones that held boiled lollies, and there were bottles of Margins' soft drinks of vivid hue and encouraging names such as 'Cherry Cheer'. Then — most wondrous of all — we had real icecream. It was a rarity in our lives. Occasionally, on summer days of special magic, a travelling icecream man came by our house, pedalling a tricycle with van attached, and ringing his bell. Never since have I tasted icecream as delicious, and that is not all imagination. He must have had a secret formula. (I suspect he was also known, in some quarters, as 'the dago', being Italian.)

Our mother must have kept a rather anxious eye upon the picnic feasting, knowing all too well the limitations of our digestions. It was always dismaying to her that while so many of the local children could thrive on green oranges, bread-and-dripping sandwiches, raw onions and unrefrigerated milk, her own offspring turned pale and queasy after one small bottle of Cherry Cheer. That — plus excitement. At some stage, which must have been before lunch, we all ran races. This too was new to me, for our P.T. breaks at school seem to have consisted mostly of circle games, or the more stimulating 'Fire on the Mountain' or 'Sheep, Sheep, Come Home'.

A foot race looked pretty easy, when you'd already mastered the rules of 'Farmer in the Dell' and learned the proper procedures of 'counting out' to the chant of 'Eeny, Meeny, Miney, Mo', and the rather grander 'Elby, Delby, Ripty, Rah . . . ' I watched the older ones, and saw my sister actually win a prize (more lollies). I lined up with my usual confidence, and came last.

My mother probably spent the rest of the day, when not checking on how many more drinks and pieces of cake were being handed out, telling me that coming last didn't *matter*. She might, when pressed, have gone so far as to maintain that coming last was a good thing, because it allowed other people to win. Here was conflict indeed. It was as plain as the nose on anyone's face that winners were highly thought of — they were applauded, patted on the head, and given extra things to eat. Coming last was mortification, and onlookers actually laughed. I should think it was my initially cheerful and lackadaisical approach to the whole thing that amused them — I was rather chubby, and definitely no athlete.

Could it be that the world outside home was not quite as I imagined, or expected?

Then there were the fancy dress balls. Nothing could quite approach these in splendour and anticipatory excitement, which began weeks before the events when our mother brought out the pattern books, and looked through the fancy dress sections to puzzle anew over making three costumes out of inexpensive materials, without duplicating last year's models. She set her own standards, and bravely went for the 'Most Original' class for each of us. Her imagination went beyond the fairies and pirates, clowns and ballerinas that sprang up on all sides, with the result that the judges (yes, there *were* prizes) didn't know immediately whom we were representing, and when told were not always any the wiser, so that awards tended to go to the fairies and princes Charming after all. My brother and sister once went dressed as the Pearly King and Queen of Cockney fame, their costumes sewn with buttons from our mother's old tin buttonbox (a treasure trove in itself), and on other occasions Dorothy was a Hebridean fisherwoman and then Mary, Queen of Scots, in black dress, widow's cap and veil, all of which I greatly admired as the trappings of romanticism. I remember being 'Folly', with jester's frills and pointed hat, and an eighteenth-century boy, with suit of geisha silk and paper ruffles — my favourite, I think. It went with my fringed hair.

On these occasions, prize-winning was not for me of primary importance. In fact, my first experience of a fancy dress ball turned into a survival exercise. I was barely school age, and economically attired as 'Peace', with white gown, a headdress with a cardboard dove, and a sheath of the white flowering plum that grew in the garden. It was not altogether a fitting role, for not long after the affair had begun, I was terrified into screams by the sight of a Sixth Class boy dressed as a giant black spider. I hope he got a prize — it was a most realistic costume.

But thereafter, until I left primary school, those balls, fancy dress or plain, were the height of my social season. On the day itself, we were sent home early from school, in order to rest and presumably compose ourselves before the event. In our family it was necessary in case one or other of us started feeling ill with excitement. Then came the putting on of the costumes we had watched emerge gradually from the sewing machine, and the reluctant donning of coats over the finery. As the years went by, we sometimes got a lift with neighbours, but I can remember walking, too, taking the short cut down the old road, past the Seventh Day Adventist church, onto the flat, up and then down Ducker's Hill. It was usually springtime, and there was enough light left in the western sky for us to see our way, until the new electric lamps of the Erina hall shone out through the dusk. Sometimes the piano was being warmed up with a few enticing tunes. Ever since, the sounds of piano music from a distance in the evening has always attracted me.

Not all our school friends wore costumes, but most came anyway. I think my father was in attendance, too, somewhat on sufferance because he would rather have been at home with a good book, or, a little later, the radio. That, in itself, made the occasion special. He did not always share in our outings, but I can hardly wonder at that; he was at various times busy with the district Packing House Co-operative, the Returned Soldiers League, and the Gosford District Cricket Association, as well as supporting the Parents and Citizens.

It was again the last-named body that provided our fancy dress ball suppers. This came towards the end of the evening, when costumes were a bit ragged and smaller children were asleep on the wooden chairs that lined the walls. The show opened with a Grand March, which we had been practising at school beforehand. The pianist worked hardest of all, pounding out the appropriate march tunes from *Aida* or *Carmen*, or both. Then the floor was polished with candle grease for dancing, and teachers and other grown-ups were here, there and everywhere, trying to bring order from chaos in the progressive barn dance. It was not necessary to have a boy as partner; I think I was in Fifth Class before I discovered that mixed dancing had its own attractions, once you got used to it.

Sometimes, after one of the festivities and outings, you had to write in class a composition about it. Far from developing a style of my own, I stuck mostly to the tried and true formula — 'As we set out happily for our school picnic, the sky was blue . . . ' to 'And so we went home, tired after our pleasant day . . . ' If your handwriting was legible, and your spelling and grammar correct, you got high marks for this sort of thing.

That there was a different and more interesting way of writing I had already discovered. But it belonged to home, not school.

VI

This morning I was listening on radio to a broadcast from A.B.C. Archives of the U.S. space travellers landing on the moon in 1969. It consisted of excited cries, some mumbling, and comments that sound, at this distance, banal. But it was real. Without any visual accompaniment, it immediately challenged the imagination. Reality emerged through the actual, very human 'voice overs' combined with the listener's inward reconstruction of what was happening.

We grew up in an era when the visual, and therefore what seemed to be the 'factual', was something of a rarity. Even many of the books I read were without illustrations, and you could guess nothing of their content from their plain drab bindings. You were challenged to explore within the covers, forming your own pictures as you went, or as was the case with many books on my parents' shelves, abandoning a particular volume altogether, for the time being. If you wanted to know, as I invariably did, what the characters looked like, or what sort of landscape they inhabited, you relied on the author to tell you. I can remember feeling disappointed and somewhat deprived when a writer failed in this duty, but it was more in sorrow than in anger — authors were grown-ups, and for much of my childhood I regarded adults as close to infallible. But I could always fall back on my own imagination, and picture the heroes and heroines as I fancied.

Picture books, of course, had their own set of laws, as did those 'reading aloud' books which had much print and fascinating contents, but needed a parent or another adult to bring them to life. From some of these I derived visual images that have stayed with me all my life. For instance, when I see today, across the marshes, a particular stand of slim young she-oaks, I am at once reminded of an Ernest Shepard picture of Christopher Robin's 'enchanted places' at the top of the forest. And the image and symbol of both aloneness and independence — and wilderness — is Kipling's cat, walking by himself along that bare road between black and leafless trees. (That particular copy of the *Just So Stories* is named and dated: 'Eleanor M. Henderson. 1912', and has a few pencil scribbles throughout — my own, I regret to say.)

At our aunts' house in Waverton there was an unexpected half-shelf of children's books, which had probably been outgrown by our cousins. I can remember meeting Peter Rabbit there, and Leslie Brooke's Johnny Crow, and Ameliaranne and her Green Umbrella. She was a great favourite — I found such stories and pictures of real children in plausible predicaments most satisfying, provided all ended happily. A little later I identified similarly with Milly-Molly-Mandy. I also enjoyed my encounter with Blinky Bill, and found the real koalas at the Zoo a bit lethargic by comparison. I felt ambivalent about Snugglepot and Cuddlepie too, because their adventures involved those nightmare figures of the thirties, the Bold Bad Banksia Men, and loathsome Mr Snake.

'Adventure' is probably the right word to describe my experiences with books. It's a term I would have associated with a mythical inner landscape where I — naturally — stood in the centre, surrounded by woodland paths, flowing streams, castles ruined or intact, caves and cliffs with secret passageways (useful for escape from rising tides, which were constantly threatening so many of my storybook heroines), hidden treasure, mysterious gardens, and all manner of jolly, exciting, but not too alarming things. The other people who lived there seem to have been a fairly cheerful lot, always ready for a bit of adventure. There could be unworldly creatures flitting among the trees, but they were required to be friendly! It was a happy pagan world, with glimpses of the unexpected and usual — akin to Rat's encounters with The Piper At the Gates, in *Wind in the Willows*. And always with a secure home base to return to.

That this special place could have been at odds with my actual life and surroundings was no great problem. Only in dreams, and the occasional nightmare, did the two get tangled. Otherwise, it made for a certain absentmindedness, and a tripping over things (I was a child with a tendency to fall over wherever I went) and a fondness for staring out of windows, in the classroom or elsewhere, gazing at clouds and wondering whether something truly exciting would happen on the way to or from school. Nothing seemed impossible, and adventure was forever imminent.

In the present climate of ponderings on the psychology of children, preoccupation with books and reading can at times be considered as withdrawal from a less than happy real world. In the case of fiction-reading, it can still also be termed a 'waste of time', an attitude common in my mother's day, when *her* mother objected to children who 'always had their noses in a book'. This seems to ignore the fact that reading, for many children, is delightful entertainment, and no more a withdrawal from reality than riding a bicycle or going fishing. And just as much an exploration as either.

I suppose there is some element of escapism in any kind of recreation, including that of adults. I may have tried to put this to practical use by disappearing with a book when it was time to set the table or dry the dishes. But I could be lost in a book one minute, and back in the actual classroom, or the family circle, the next, without much of a jolt. Whatever else I may have been, I was hardly withdrawn. I did not like being ignored, nor was I ever at a loss for words — reading added a new dimension to mealtime conversation.

If I had a reading problem, it was probably a scarcity of material. When we visited other people's homes, I cast an eye around for children's books, and now and then came upon riches indeed, as when a whole family had been storing up their books for years. Perhaps more often I discovered that homes could be completely without books, or that the term applied only to magazines.

I soon found that not every small girl had dolls, either. I was a collector of these — not so much the infant kind as the more sophisticated models that could be called upon to act as characters in ongoing stories. But many of my friends and acquaintances didn't have indoor playthings at all — then it was satisfying enough to switch to outdoor pursuits such as swinging from trees, exploring bits of bushland, clambering around storage sheds, or helping to bring in the cows or feed the bantams.

At school we had a few classroom books, the School Magazine, and of course the reading primers. As we advanced through Third and Fourth classes, the primers offered less advice on cats and mats, and more proper stories, although some seem to have been of a rather gloomy nature. I can remember especially one, 'Pretty Dick', where the little boy was lost in the bush with sad consequences; and a tale of a mother koala parted from her baby by heedless human hands — a narrative guaranteed to fill me with horror and distress. Another heart-tugger was the story of a plover which pretended to have a broken wing in order to lure intruders from its nest. Where I am now, the plovers don't bother with such subtleties. On the assumption that they own the entire fifteen hectares of swampland, they adopt a demented divebomber approach to every unwary intruder.

On a grander scale was the story of Grace Darling, who rowed a lifeboat to rescue the shipwrecked. I had great admiration for her, because as a coast-bred child I appreciated the difficulties of her undertaking.

Our school 'library' was a book box, a grey wooden receptacle which came and went once a month in a mysterious process of exchange. It arrived on a carrier's truck, and had to be carried into the school by two big boys from Sixth Class. It was my first encounter with any kind of library; the second came when my parents, recovering slowly from the financial problems of the Depression, began subscribing to Dymocks' lending library. I think it was on Friday afternoons that we were allowed to dip into the box. Friday afternoons had a different quality from other afternoons; in the lower classes we coloured in, or cut out and pasted up shapes from shiny, brilliantly coloured paper, or made things out of plasticine, while higher up the school we had spelling bees, and listened — mostly in stupefaction — to required reading from a book on Morals. The chapters — on Honesty, Courage, Patience, and the like — were of that deceptive kind which any listener over the age of six can immediately recognise; they began, hopefully, with real narrative, then rapidly sank into abstractions concerning the desirability of good behaviour. I was already familiar with this trickery, for at home we had a supply of such books, paper-bound, with rather attractive covers, bought from a travelling salesman connected with a certain religious sect. They were collectively called 'Bedtime Stories', and our mother found it easier to buy them than to stand about listening to the sales talk. The school book, however, didn't even have the benefit of illustrations.

All this, morals and all, was forgotten in the excitement of choosing library books. It was here that I learned not to select a book by its cover, as I did with Christmas catalogues. The only way was to take a quick look at Chapter One, applying certain rules of thumb. For instance, I would take any book that on the first page or so introduced a family with members around my own age, give or take a few years. Equally desirable were orphans — the more the merrier. Than came girls' school stories. As these, with the exception of Louise Mack's *Teens*, were uncompromisingly British (upper class, at that), they entered the category of 'Romance' from the moment jolly Fenella bounced into the Junior Common Room (whatever was that?) with a cry of 'I say, girls! Have you seen that new kid in the Remove?' I think I was quite dashed to find later that our local high school had only grades unimaginatively labelled 'One' to 'Five'.

Boys' school stories I could tolerate, but even an enthusiast such as myself was exhausted after reading *Eric, or Little by Little*. *The Fifth Form at St Dominic's* was better, but the library box did not yield Kipling's *Stalky*, whom I discovered several years later. The adventure tales my brother liked — *The Coral Island*, *The Last of the Mohicans, King Solomon's Mines* and the rest — I did not much care for, any more than I enjoyed the adventures of Fireworks Flynn of the R.A.F. in his copies of *Champion*. I did try to appreciate these, and later the doings of 'Biggles', because I held my brother in high regard, but I found the military jargon boring, and regretted the absence of girls, orphans and proliferating families. Animal stories were acceptable provided they had a few human characters thrown in, even if they lacked moral fibre, as some adults in *Black Beauty*, which I can remember weeping over one summer afternoon. Perhaps I felt this was expected of me, because I had the same feeling about *Uncle Tom's Cabin*, another novel written with didactic intent.

I was also willing enough to read stories about children in faraway places with strange-sounding names — with the usual proviso, that they had some interesting adventures. Geography was never my long suit; I can recall in primary school drawing maps of the British Isles, but chiefly we seemed to draw, or trace, a series of maps of Australia, either for geographic purposes, or in order to mark in the tracks of the explorers. Consequently I remembered best those adventurers whose tracks failed to turn round and come back, such as Burke and Wills, and Kennedy and Jacky Jacky. Their stories at least had *some* sort of ending.

And I loved historical novels. These all seemed to be British, and were full of family trees, in which I rejoiced. At one time I knew considerably more about the Yorkists and the Lancastrians, the Tudors and the Stuarts, and even the Plantaganets, than about captains Cook and Phillip, and governors Bligh and Macquarie, who were all, I thought, quite unromantic. Indeed, the library box was deficient in Australian stories altogether, for the excellent reason that there were so few of them. I liked *Dot and the Kangaroo*, and two other stories by Australian writers which seem to have disappeared entirely — *The Adventures of Melaleuca*, and a fantasy by Irene Cheyne called *The Golden Cauliflower*. My favourite among Ethel Turner's books, after *Seven Little Australians* (which I constantly re-read), was *The Ungardeners*, a romantic piece combining orphans with family affairs. The 'Billabong' books of Mary Grant Bruce I steadily devoured, but I still preferred her *Anderson's Jo*, which had one orphan, a dying mother and a mystery concerning a father.

There were some oddities, too, in that library box. I was hardly ever subject to parental censorship in my reading, though my mother might occasionally venture to criticise a book on literary grounds. She took it for granted hat I would grow out of an addiction to Hilda Richards' stories of the doings of Mabs and Babs at Cliff House School. She was right. But I had a lingering fondness for works by certain old-fashioned writers of girls' stories, one of whom was L. T. Meade. A book of hers, called *Beyond the Blue Mountains*, was a kind of romantic, feminised version of *The Pilgrim's Progress*, and I loved it. The four children in the story were, naturally, orphans, and had names such as Primrose and Buttercup. They had to make a journey (another motif I liked) to some place that was evidently Heaven, and on the way encountered enough dangers, physical and moral, to startle even Bunyan's Christian. Again, it had a happy ending, although, like most stories with religious–allegorical themes, it failed to give me a satisfactory picture of what Heaven was *really* like. I suppose I considered that grown-up writers were in a position to know.

Another allegorical favourite from the library box was George Macdonald's *At the Back of the North Wind*. Today it would probably be considered both sentimental and long-winded, but I was not put off by a bit of emotion, and I was used to reading long books with lingering descriptions. The hero, Diamond (I was certainly drawn to characters with eccentric names), was an English, late-Victorian child of the poorer classes, who at intervals was carried off by the mythical woman, the North Wind. It was the kind of fantasy that appealed most to me, because it combined imaginary adventures with real life, and thus reinforced my secret belief that it was entirely possible to step from one world into another. The ending, where Diamond is borne off by North Wind permanently, did not alarm me; I didn't consciously equate it with death, for Diamond, like Little Eva in *Uncle Tom's Cabin*, and Beth in *Little*

Women, had been in decline for some time, and was clearly not long for this world. I found the last chapters of *Seven Little Australians* much more disturbing, for Judy's accident was so sudden, and she had been so very much alive immediately beforehand.

My overwhelming interest, in both reading and writing, was in people, real and imagined. For a short time I gave a bit of thought to fairies, and looked for them now and then in likely spots about the garden or the bush, but soon gave up. I had nothing against them; they were just so boringly elusive. My favourite fairy story, which again is more of an allegory, was Andersen's 'Snow Queen'; the vicissitudes of Kay and Gerda (flesh-and-blood children, so to speak) I found both exciting and touching. And the classical myths and legends which I enjoyed had only too much flesh and blood in them. They gave me my first introduction to the nature of drama.

I was an observer of people and places long before I realised it. From there, and from my reading, it was a natural step to making up stories of my own. I can remember quite well the feeling that went with my putting down on paper my first ever story (*not* a composition). In my recollection the process had — as the unfolding of all big events should — a definite sequence. It began with a shopping trip to Gosford, and that in itself was a happening. Much of our household buying was done at our own front gate, or the kitchen door. Meat (usually corned beef or a leg of mutton) was delivered from a butcher's in Terrigal, whence came also the fishmonger, on Fridays, with his covered basket of mullet and bream and flathead, cosily arranged among ice chips and fern fronds. Such fruit and vegetables as we did not grow ourselves were likewise sold door to door, and there was also an informal barter system, which had its own protocol — 'n return for tomatoes, you gave so many eggs, and even a cup of sugar, borrowed on a baking morning, could come back as a pot of jam. Groceries could be bought at the shop near the school, and a child sent on such an errand generally had a halfpenny or a penny to spend, which meant a delightful poring over boxes of lollies conveniently priced to suit our purses.

Then there were the occasional hawkers, plentiful during the Depression, and sometimes of Indian extraction. My mother once bought a dress for me from such a caller; she did not like to send anyone away empty-handed, and she could never dismiss from the premises the tramps who came by. Often they asked no more than water for their billies, but a bit of tea and a scone or two were generally added. Very few actually begged; they had their pride, and explained that they were out and about looking for work.

We went to Gosford, in the years before the attendances at movie matinees, only to buy such things as could not be bought or made or grown at home — such as shoes and hats and towels and hardware. Or, on not so cheerful occasions, to visit the dentist. This, for me, became fraught with terrors that I have never quite forgotten. Once, after having a tooth out, I went into a prolonged and delirious fit of nightmarish hallucinations, which my mother decided must have been brought on by an overdose of dental anaesthetic. I had similar, though less dramatic, reactions after my tonsils were removed, in an operation that then seemed obligatory for any child under the age of six or seven.

The first buses to Gosford were of the toast-rack variety, with wooden seats across the width of the vehicle, and canvas side-screens for wet weather. Their bumpiness on ill-made roads must have been an additional hazard, given our tendency to travel sickness. And once you arrived in Gosford, you were stranded until the bus set out for home again, so it was no expedition for the fainthearted. Our father usually had business to attend to at the Packing House at the north end of town, which left the rest of us to explore from the station up to the courthouse and the post office, if the youngest pairs of legs could stay the course.

The shop I remember best was Cannings' Cash and Carry, opposite the Royal Hotel. It was especially appealing around Christmas time, for we did not yet have decorations at home, and the long, narrow shop was transformed into a magic party-hall with streamers and silver tinsel, Chinese lanterns and coloured balls, from the two sandstone steps at the entrance to the dim recesses at the back, where a very important employee sat in a kind of pulpit to count out the change and send it whizzing back to the counters on a kind of miniature flying-fox wire.

It was here that I first spent my pocket money on scribbling pads and pencils. We had pencils at school, of course, but they were not personal property. I think I might even have been far-sighted, and financial, enough to buy a rubber as well. You didn't need pencil sharpeners if you had a father like mine who delighted in keeping pencils wonderfully keenly pointed with the aid of a kitchen knife. Learning how to write without breaking off the lead was an art. I at once sat down on the steps with my booty, and started to write. It was not the most convenient place, but having begun, I then had a great deal to look forward to — going on with my story when I got home.

It was a feeling akin to exultation, and something all my own. The growing awareness that by putting words on paper I could create people and happenings and places that only I knew existed was a wonder, a mystery and a source of power. I was perhaps seven or eight, and full of creative confidence. As time went by, I abandoned the scribbling blocks and used exercise-book

67

paper cut and folded and sewn to make real book shapes. I did my own illustrations, of course; the time had not yet come when I understood that I was not 'good at drawing'. My sister was the artistic member of the family, but one Christmas we were given a communal paintbox we all dipped into. It was seemingly enormous, with such exotic colours as gold and silver, burnt sienna, and yellow ochre. The little trays of crimson lake and prussian blue emptied first, being much in demand.

That first story I ever wrote was about a family living in, of all unknown places, Canada. Either I had been reading a book with such a setting, or I had been listening to my mother's news of some of her Scots emigrant relatives. I have no recollection of the plot, which was probably shamelessly borrowed from my reading, but I can recall my pleasure in lining up my characters, so to speak — endowing them with names, ages and physical attributes. This sort of thing tended to occupy most of the story space. One early creation, to which I devoted extra care because I wrote it for my mother (who had been explaining what 'dedications' at the front of books actually meant), was entitled 'Bush Margery' [sic] — I had a friend called 'Marjorie', but my mother said she liked the old English spelling. It may have been this story which secretly entertained her in a manner quite unintentional, for the heroine (a rather moral child) was one of a family of ten children, *all* of whom had been born after poor Mother's husband had been killed in the war. I assumed that if there were such creatures as orphans, entirely without parents, then there could also be children without any fathers. Babies, I thought, just happened. Although I had visited the homes of friends at a time when the mother was pregnant, I merely noted her increased size, and didn't connect it at all with the arrival later of Eunice's or

68

Lois's baby brother or sister. I asked no questions until my pet cat produced her kittens on my own bed.

The most important, the most vital thing about my writing was that my mother, in particular, did not laugh at it. My father may have teased me now and then about my 'scribbling', my sister may have been sceptical and my brother unimpressed (because he was writing sagas of his own, all about flying machines, space wars and logistic details concerning number, style and deployment of troops), but no one attempted to dissuade me from my chosen literary career. I was convinced, from the beginning, that an 'authoress' was what I was going to be. My mother approved, but pointed out that as writers did have a tendency to starve in garrets, it would be a good idea to get a sound education in the meantime. Starving, in or out of garrets, definitely did not appeal to me.

I didn't mind at all that my stories had a readership of one — my mother, of course. I didn't show them to my friends, or wave them about at school. The joy was in the creating, and the whole atmosphere of the writing — the gathering of the paper, the sharpened pencil, the sitting down (usually after school) at the solid mahogany desk which had belonged to my mother's father, and the setting to. As encouragement to thought and inspiration, I had on one side a window overlooking bush and orchard, valley and fields, friendly mountain and wide open, arching sky. To my other side was a recess where the piano stood, and bits of living-room furniture beside a wall which on winter evenings was coloured by flickering firelight — all images of homeliness and comfort and of belonging. I was in a place where I was myself, writing and all.

Of course, it was not always so serene and joyous. There were times when I had nothing to write about, no books to read, and lapsed into boredom, or when I fought with my sister and went off in sulks, or when I had to eat loathsome vegetables such as parsnip and sweet potato. Or when — tragedy indeed — it rained on a day when a beach outing had been in the offing.

But at bedtime (especially after electric lighting came to banish the shadows that had lurked beyond the orbit of candles and lamps) there was generally a fairly good day to look back upon, and a tomorrow that held no threat. And when the rain fell on the iron roof, and the occasional light of a passing car slid across the verandah onto the bedroom wall, there was a wonderful feeling of being gathered safely in, with everyone and everything that I loved securely held under that one roof. Even the dog had his place on the verandah, the cats downstairs on the sacks in the feedbins, the cow in her shed, and the hens (I didn't like to think any creature was left out) roosting in ample housing of their own.

There was no reason for a child to believe that that kind of peace would ever end.

VII

Midway through the thirties, changes big and small were taking place around me, but I found them mostly agreeable. If my parents had more and more to discuss concerning world affairs and the state of the nation, then that seemed a natural consequence of the arrival of our first radio, and their attention to incomprehensible news broadcasts. They had, in any case, always been given to reading from cover to cover the daily newspaper (which came with the mailman), the *Sydney Mail*, and the *Bulletin*, as well as the Dymocks' books, so they had plenty to talk about. Their tastes in books were rather different; my father liked war histories, cricketing books, outback and pioneer reminiscences, and the romantic historical novels of Dumas and company, which my mother said were all fiction and no history at all. She liked Australian novels among others, and later introduced me to such writers as Kylie Tennant, Eleanor Dark and Dymphna Cusack, but I still shared with my father a taste for historical romance, inaccurate or not.

To us children, the radio was a grand acquisition. When there was not too much static, we could listen in the late afternoon to the serials. These were irresistible combinations of story and live drama, and had names such as 'The Search for the Golden Boomerang'. I was also a devotee for a while of an unseen but very audible woman called the 'Fairy Godmother', and later joined a listening group known as 'The Smiles Club'. This entitled you to a fine little dark-blue badge with gold trim, and once, while we were holidaying at Waverton, we were taken to meet the Club compère, who was known, I think, as 'Auntie Pat'. As with many of my keenly anticipated experiences, there was little romance about the occasion, and much reality. The studio was small and crowded with other children (I think I expected a private, personal reception), and Auntie Pat, though nice and friendly, looked the same as any other woman.

For us children, however, the most exciting changes of the thirties were associated with the cinema. I saw my first movie in Sydney, and here was an outing to outdo in splendour even fancy dress balls and break up prize-givings. We were taken by our Auntie Lil, efficient organiser of all our holiday outings, and no doubt wore our best dresses and white socks and shiny black shoes (both our aunts were most particular about cleaning shoes; it was a ritual in itself, carried out in the scullery behind the kitchen). And we were never late for anything, because Auntie Lil always allowed so much time in which to catch train, tram or bus that we invariably caught the one before it. (I seem to have inherited this foible; I still secretly believe that unless I arrive at the station at least fifteen minutes before a train is due, it will sneakily depart without me.)

So we marched briskly along King Street, round the corner, and down the long hill to the station. From the top of Bay Road, if we had time to stop, we could see right across Lavender Bay and Milson's Point to the magnificent new Harbour Bridge and the city beyond. Once, when I was quite small, we were taken out at night to see this view, and the great, mysterious spread of lights, flickering or still, yellow or red or blue, strengthened my dawning wonder at the size and majesty and attraction of the world around me. The cinema we visited on this first occasion was the State, and to a couple of little girls from the country (the notion that Gosford itself might one day be termed a city would then have been absurd) 'stateliness' was an apt word. It was so vast, and so adorned with artificial lamps and gilt and plaster carvings and rich upholstery and curtains, that I could only have seen it as a real palace. To add to the splendour that was — literally, I think — breath-taking, a kind of fancy piano arose by magic from beneath the floor, and a smartly dressed gentleman performed upon it. For me there was a moment of panic when he sank out of sight, and all the lights went out, leaving us in cavernous, claustrophobic, midnight blackness.

I hadn't the faintest idea where movies came from, nor had I ever seen a stage play (our mother used to tell us, rather wistfully, of the pantomimes she used to see as a child, at Christmas-time). So what was there on the screen, when the double curtains had parted, and I had sunk back into my dress-circle seat, was as real as anything else I beheld with my eyes and heard with my ears. From start to finish, I was personally involved in the action.

It was a Shirley Temple movie, *The Littlest Rebel*, and had the extra attraction (if any was needed) of being a period piece, so that I contemplated with awe and envy the heroine's flounced and be-ribboned crinolines. The movie opened with a well-dressed ballroom scene, as in a junior *Gone With the Wind*. The story was not difficult to follow, nor did I mind that its progress was held up now and then while 'Virginia' (not 'Shirley' — I was not even consciously aware that somebody else was only *pretending* to be the heroine) did a little tap-dancing or sang a song. It had all the narrative ingredients I liked — excitement, suspense, runnings away and returnings home, a Cinderella reverse situation (riches to rags, with restoration at the end), a kindly, misjudged father, and (which may have caused some passing unease) a bravely dying mother. And even a military touch, but I don't think my brother was with us at the time. He would have been eleven, and on the threshold of that grand-sounding place, high school.

It was, in short, melodrama, as were most of Shirley Temple's earlier films. The later ones we saw either in Gosford's Valencia cinema, or the new and resplendent Regal, opposite the Union Hotel. We went always to matinees, with our mother, and — quite often — our father. He was unimpressed by American movies, and remained so all his life. They both enjoyed the British films of the late thirties and early forties, but until we were considered old enough to go to evening showings, they had to attend singly or not at all. Baby-sitters were unheard of, and I cannot remember the three of us being left alone at night until we were all well into our teens.

I'm sure both our parents suffered through most of Shirley's films, except perhaps *Captain January*, which was genuinely funny, and without the kind of slickness and brashness that my father and many of his contemporaries came to associate with all things American. What drove my mother to protest was the way in which standard children's books, such as *Rebecca of Sunnybrook Farm* and *Susannah of the Mounties*, were distorted almost beyond recognition to allow the star to do her usual showbiz routines, and reduced the rest of the characters to cardboard cut-outs. She agreed, under pressure, that this was hardly Shirley Temple's fault, and that the child did have some talent.

For me, however, it was all delight. Contemplating *Stowaway* and *Poor Little Rich Girl*, and the like, I was almost moved to abandon my literary career in favour of being a movie star — or, at the very least, appearing on stage. Our parents held out firmly against the tide of Shirley-mania, but it was pervasive. Shirley Temple books — square, fat and shiny-covered — took pride of place in the Christmas catalogues; by some means or other, I acquired at least one, and was able to read fulsome descriptions of what Shirley ate for breakfast, what clothes she wore (I was besotted with details of her vast wardrobe), what toys she had, and how she spent her very busy day. Shirley Temple dolls in all stages of cuteness appeared in shop windows, along with Shirley Temple frocks, hair ribbons and every other kind of accessory. And there were competitions for Shirley look-alikes, or so it was rumoured. I can't recall seeing any, let alone participating.

Our mother, with her lifelong tendency to run counter to pop culture, wanted us to be taught ballroom dancing, as a social accomplishment that would provide much enjoyment in later life. For the same reason she encouraged us to learn to swim and to play a bit of tennis — not competitively, but as true recreation and a means of meeting and joining with others. The 'others' I believe she saw democratically, but with hopes that the friends we made would have a broad range of interests, yet much in common with us. Which seems a modest enough social ambition. Unluckily, our enrolment in dancing classes coincided with the Shirley Temple cult, and we were expected to don tap shoes rather than learn the waltz and the schottische. This at once ruled our brother out of contention; there were one or two boys who came to classes and tapped and sang with the best of them, and may even have graduated to ballet shoes, but at the time Robert and his friends were engrossed with model aeroplanes and building a track for their billycart. Besides, they were too old.

So Dorothy and I went off one afternoon a week to dancing class in the Matcham hall. My sister had natural talent and a sense of rhythm, but I was deficient in both. However, I approached the whole thing with my usual optimistic confidence, and no doubt with starry-eyed visions of admiration and applause. These expanded when we were told we were to take part in a concert in — of all places — the Valencia theatre. This was the Shirley Temple dream about to come true. The wonder of it grew even more when our long-suffering mother set to work making three sets of costumes for each of us. There were green, pleated skirts and red waistcoats for the Irish Jig, blue and white outfits for the Sailors' Hornpipe, and a special rig for our own group, grandly and inappropriately known as the 'Matcham Ballet'. And, of course, the silver-frosted shoes with the taps underneath.

There were numerous rehearsals, which I hadn't bargained for. I saw no reason why success should not be instantaneous. We had to travel into Gosford on Saturday mornings, and struggle at dress rehearsals with those slithery geisha silk costumes. Worst of all, it was becoming only too evident that I was surrounded by talents superior to my own. Ringlets and ribbons bobbed on every second head, in time to agile tapping feet, and there were children who sang as well — songs such as 'If You Were the Only Girl in the World', 'I'm Forever Blowing Bubbles' and 'On the Good Ship Lollipop'. My rainbows were beginning to dissolve like imperfectly set jelly.

'That little girl on the end can't keep in time.' It was the verdict of the audience (my mother heard it, and was amused), and no doubt of the dancing teacher and some of my classmates as well. I didn't ever grasp the concept of keeping in time, when it came to dancing. Why was it so important, anyway?

Not long afterwards we left the dancing class. Eventually Dorothy, in particular, picked up the essentials of ballroom dancing at high school, where we had both 'frolics' and break-up dances as a matter of course. And I had to abandon forever the Shirley Temple dream of any kind of movie career.

But the notion of being some kind of public performer lingered on. I could still do recitations. These were standard at school concerts, and I was used to hearing poetry recited at home — or rather, declaimed. My father knew a lot of the works of Henry Lawson and Banjo Patterson, including the whole of *The Man from Snowy River*, and was also strong on excerpts from the poetry of Longfellow and Macaulay and similar British ballad writers. My mother, naturally, could reel off a lot of Walter Scott (especially 'Marmion') and Robbie Burns, with considerable amounts of Tennyson and Wordsworth thrown in, to say nothing of vast selections from Shakespeare. We all did our bit at school. Among my favourites were Arnold's 'The Forsaken Merman' (so sad and romantic and laced with orphans, though I didn't comprehend at all why Margaret should be so obsessed about that grey church on the windy hill), Noyes' *The Highwayman* (whereof the recitation of which could be suitably dramatic) and Browning's *Pied Piper*. I also fancied Vaughan's 'My Soul, There Is a Country . . . ' not because I was aware that I had a soul, but because mention of a place beyond the stars was irresistibly romantic and mysterious. The works of a few Australian poets were firmly impressed upon our minds and memories, such as Dorothea Mackellar's 'My Country', Lawson's 'The Bush Christening', and 'Bellbirds' by Henry Kendall. The last-named poet was our local product, so to speak; our father knew the Fagans, the family who had taken Henry into their home. He sounded especially romantic.

Once or twice I 'did' recitations at home, when my mother had visitors and Country Women's Association meetings. I think this was against her better judgment, but some sort of entertainment had to be provided, along with the afternoon tea. My standard piece was A. A.

Milne's 'Vespers', with piano accompaniment, and some restrained dramatic gestures. In my best blue linen frock, with white collar and the intricate smocking, which had cost my mother hours of eye-straining labour, I perhaps bore a passing resemblance to Christopher Robin, and we all knew most of the words from *When We Were Very Young*.

I suppose it was a time when children accepted without much question what they were told about themselves. Judgments were passed concerning academic ability, state of health ('Mary has always had a weak chest'), natural talent, physical appearance and behaviour, and many of these apparently arbitrary judgments could influence the course of a life. We seemed to be divided into sheep and goats quite early in our school career; those who gravitated towards the bottom of Second and Third classes seemed to be the ones who eventually would proceed no further than Sixth Class, and then leave at fourteen. Often — and tragically — there were children, too, who could have benefited enormously from secondary schooling, but who were kept back for financial reasons.

Both our parents fought against this kind of segregation and categorisation. We were not expected to brag about accomplishments, especially academic ones, or to crow over anybody else. What praise we received at home was equally apportioned; our mother felt this was especially important because while my brother and I tended to race ahead academically, Dorothy's talents lay elsewhere. She was far better than I was at all kinds of handiwork — cooking, sewing, knitting and drawing — and also every kind of sport or game. She took things much more seriously, too, while I was usually known as 'slap-dash'. As long as such a remark was accompanied by an affectionate smile, I stayed unworried.

The labelling was done outside the house. I expected the whole world to be friendly and trustworthy, and inevitably I learnt otherwise. Once, in First Class, a new and unfamiliar teacher slapped me for talking to a neighbour (I was in the habit of talking to classmates, anywhere, any time). I howled for hours, until I had to be sent home. I think what struck me with the terror of the *dies irae* was the thought that somebody actually disliked me enough to do violence to my person. It was my first realisation, too, that there were grown-ups one could be afraid of, and who called you 'naughty' for mysterious reasons, so that in order to be liked and approved of, you had to be 'good' — whatever that was.

Being labelled 'not good at dancing', or singing, was hardly so serious, for by that time I had my compensating pursuits, such as reading and writing, and coming top in class. And for a while we all had piano lessons, which I liked without being in the least prepared to spend all that time practising. My brother had had a teacher who actually came to the house and taught on our own piano, but by the time it was our turn, the only available tuition was at the Convent in Gosford. This had to it that sense of personal importance which I so enjoyed, for it meant leaving school on Friday afternoons to catch the Gosford bus.

The old Convent of the Sisters of Saint Joseph was a modest building indeed, tucked into a corner directly above the railway line, near the road bridge. Yet my lasting recollection of it, paradoxically, was of its quietness. And also, on a more material level, of the big old mulberry tree in the garden, where I browsed and ate berries while waiting for my lesson. Inside, it was cool and shadowy, and sometimes I heard the Angelus bell, and wondered what it was.

It was a rather daring step (more on my mother's part than our own), to be entering a Convent for any reason whatsoever. I should imagine our aunts had something to say about it. I may still have been, initially, rather in awe of the nuns in their black robes, after my infant encounter with them, but having discovered they were kind to me, and praised my efforts at finding Middle C, and gave me an interesting book with friendly observations on such things as crotchets and quavers, I let bygones be bygones, and even learnt that the other pupils, mostly from Catholic families, bore a striking resemblance to the rest of us. Dorothy was not so fortunate; her teacher happened to be a nun made of sterner stuff, and there were confrontations over scales and fingering that often left my sister in tears.

While religious sectarian attitudes were banned at home, and I had listened often to my mother's appealing descriptions of the Catholic churches she had seen in France — especially the Sainte Chapelle, which I later visited myself, with a feeling of delighted familiarity — it was impossible to miss the anti-Catholic murmurings and rumours that went on both in the community, and in my aunts' home at Waverton. (One of my aunts used to read excerpts from *The Rock*, out loud, while they sat on their verandah in the evenings. Playing about the garden, I overheard, and probably gathered the impression that all priests were villainous, and that if anyone was about to start World War II, it had to be the Pope.) The most mysterious, and therefore the most fascinating, whispers were to do with something called *'Turning'*. It was rather an anti-climax to discover, from my mother, that such an event was nothing more than a Protestant becoming a Catholic, usually in order to avoid a 'mixed' marriage. These were peculiar adult concerns, and of little interest to me.

I had already noted that at school, on Scripture mornings, a handful of children were weeded out from the rest, and sent off with a priest, who apart from being in black, like the nuns, drove a car and walked and talked like any other person. It seemed a rather cosy little group, enviable because they met outdoors, under a tree, or in the open-fronted weather shed.

I learnt just enough about the piano to be able to pick out a tune or two, spurred on by the desire to sing along (privately, by this time) with some of the Shirley Temple hits such as 'When I'm With You' and 'Oh, My Goodness!' I acquired a bit of Mozart for one exam, but it was painstaking. Our parents didn't have the heart to bully us into constant practising, especially in the case of Dorothy, who tried twice as hard as Robert or I did, because she set her own standards so high, and was devastated by what she perceived as failure. The musical talents our parents had were to miss a generation, it seemed.

But I rather regretted the passing of the mulberry tree, and the sights and sounds of the Convent.

At school, more interesting changes were taking place. A rise in numbers made it possible to acquire a third teacher, and Fourth Class was moved into what was always called the 'stone room'. This was the original schoolhouse, built in 1893. Its thick, solid, sandstone walls and window embrasures appealed to my incipient novelist's imagination; it was the nearest thing to an ancient castle-like dwelling that I had to hand. And I was still mindful of the adventurous doings of 'Fourth Formers' in school stories, even though we did nothing more exciting than the usual reading, writing and arithmetic.

Outside in the playground, there was sexist division. Boys ran about a lot, played marbles in season and 'Bobbies and Bushies'. My brother was inevitably known as 'Ned' because of our matching Irish surname;

there was quite a Ned Kelly folk-hero cult, which annoyed our father. He always maintained that Ned and company were a disgrace to the nation. Sometimes on P.T. afternoons we came together for games of rounders and Prisoners' Base, but cricket was understood to be a male preserve, though girls were allowed to field (which I found horribly boring), and — as an indulgence — to bat now and then. It was the heyday of the Ashes contests, and in our house, at least, you couldn't help but know the names, types and performances of every Australian cricketer, especially when the radio Test broadcasts began. Our father's memory for, and interest in, cricketing history was so keen that to the end of his days he could recall who opened the batting for any country in any match in any year, what were any individual's bowling figures, and who fielded and took the most catches in slips or at silly point.

The girls had their own games. A perennial was 'Mothers and Fathers'. This was entirely innocent, played in the shelter of huge old pines, whose needles gave us the material for building walls to divide our dwellings. 'Father' was always played by a girl, but, as I remember it, the role was rather tame; he mostly went out to work in the fields, came home and looked for his supper, then sat about with pipe and newspaper. It was 'Mother' who was the bossy and the fussy one, and hers the most coveted role. Naturally, she had a large family, to allow parts for all female members of the class, and smaller children were in demand as the babies. There was interminable housekeeping, carried out with pretend equipment, and a lot of bickering, some of which was real. It was not a very exciting game, but I loved it, because it could be made to resemble one of the family stories I both read and wrote. Or even — if the others could be coerced — a boarding school story.

We also built cubby houses in all sizes, from the miniature models of twigs and leaves and pebbles, to the grand affairs big enough to stand up in. Once these were finished, however, we reverted to the standard 'Mothers and Fathers' game.

It didn't occur to me that the boys might be having more fun. I was happy enough being a girl — or perhaps, more accurately, being me, who happened to be a girl. My strong maternal streak may have been partly conditioned, but it was also spontaneous. I liked to look after younger children (until they became too cantankerous), and enjoyed hearing news of the arrivals of new babies (though I still didn't know where they came from), and my interest in the composition of other people's families never died. I romanticised them, of course — and yet I knew the reality. I understood without having it explained to me in full that being motherless was an unhappy state for one young classmate, and that she bore what seemed to be an additional handicap by being Jewish. We all liked her because of her remarkable witty sense of humour. I knew that other children could die, and that parental grief was a real and moving thing, as when Gwennie's younger sister, thirteen months old, fell down the family well and was drowned, or when a schoolmate died of scarlet fever. And I understood what poverty was, while recognising by instinct the dignity with which it was endured. My mother taught me that it was good to try and put yourself in the other person's place, and to treat him or her as you would prefer to be treated. The capacity to identify with another was, in any case, useful to a budding writer. But I think I began to comprehend the difference between having genuine compassion, and being condescending in one's pity. One of my mother's favourite gospel verses was that concerning the Pharisee who thanked God he was not as other men; she should not abide self-righteousness.

VIII

Today, from my back door, I can look across the mangrove swamps and the channel that goes up by Bensville to the Broadwater, to the nearer villages and hills of Davistown and Kincumber and Saratoga, which in my childhood were on the far southern and eastern fringe of my landscape. I might have heard of the Davis family for whom the village was named, because my father was interested in local history, and the prolific Davises (one of whom also gave his Christian name to Bensville) were renowned shipbuilders in the years when the waterways were thoroughfares and carriers of timber, stone, shells for limeburning and every kind of merchandise. Until I went to high school, these were distant places, although I once went to see my father play cricket at a bush-rimmed oval in Kincumber. He wore a green cap, I remember. A long time afterwards, when my own eight-year-old son donned his first cricket cap, he at once took on an astonishing resemblance to his grandfather. They were both slow bowlers, mostly of leg spin.

Outside Gosford, and some of the more popular holiday resorts such as Terrigal and The Entrance, you could readily associate families and their names with the villages they came from. Beyond the Ridgeway, there were enough Davidsons and Cliftons (interrelated) at Lisarow to field two cricket teams; fittingly, they produced a Test cricketer in young Alan Davidson, a contemporary of ours in high school. Ourimbah had its Morrises, and a bit further south was the territory of the Pryors. In Erina, there were Burnses and Howards and some Gavenlocks. In between were fitted the more recent settlers, such as my parents, and many of their friends. These tended to divide into my father's associates from the Packing House, the R.S.L. and the Cricket Association, and my mother's women friends, scattered about the nearer hills and valleys of upper Erina, Wamberal and Matcham. These latter formed the nucleus of the Erina Vale Country Women's Association, of which my mother was foundation president. They met regularly at our house, and that I appreciated, because they brought such delicacies for afternoon tea, and later collected books for their modest library, which I raided. I thereby discovered that there was a whole fascinating range of reading matter outside the area of children's books. My mother may have groaned in spirit as I dipped into the works of Ethel M. Dell and Berta Ruck, but there were more solid offerings besides.

Most of my mother's closest friends were, understandably, British migrants like herself. Some had large families, some one child or two, and some none at all. The Country Women's Association gatherings helped to bring them out of various kinds of isolation (which my mother, I suspect, also experienced), cemented friendships and fostered considerable creative talents. Lurking in the living room with my slice of luscious sponge cake dripping with cream, I sometimes lifted my head long enough from a book to listen to the steady animated buzz of conversation coming from the verandah, in every accent from Highland Scots to West Country to Irish to South London to — as refugees trickled in, mysteriously — Yiddish and German and Italian. Almost imperceptibly, the stories I wrote myself

85

took on a kind of pre-war flavour in plot and character, but, for the time being, all was peace on the home front. It was not yet time for my mother and her friends to put aside their handicrafts — the making of layettes for the district's new babies, the quite beautiful embroidery and crochet work for selling at fund-raising stalls, and the painting and pottery — in order to make camouflage nets and knitted socks and parcel up fruit cakes for the troops. Nor was it yet time for outbreaks of racism, beyond the C.W.A. circle, when some of the good souls with European names and accents were called Axis spies and threatened with internment.

I always liked to go visiting with my mother, especially — of course — at afternoon tea time. Until she got an electric stove, in the late thirties, my mother wrestled interminably with the kind of wood-burning range and oven which most of the women in the community had been used to all their lives. Husbands and sons collected and chopped certain kinds of wood, the combustion of which seemed to guarantee perfect oven heat, so that sponge cakes, yellow with farm eggs, never fell below the proper — and marvellous — height and consistency. It was the same with pies and scones. Thus when there was an invitation to a real afternoon tea, you knew there was no danger of starvation. After that, you were free to explore house and grounds, and regain sufficient energy to walk home.

Our mother's kitchen tribulations could not have been too grim. I can remember how she demonstrated the Highland Fling and other Scots dances in the ample space between stove and kitchen window. Like most country kitchens, it was large and had a walk-in pantry stocked with jars of preserved fruit, product of the impressive machine known as the Vacola outfit. We also made lots of toffee and fudge and coconut ice on the old stove, usually for school fetes or parties, with a certain amount for home consumption, and much enthusiastic testing of toffee in cold water to see if it were setting.

Not all my mother's friends had children of my own age. Several families had sons and daughters at high school, or even university, and of these I was in respectful awe. There was always much talk of education and future vocation, as much for the daughters as for the sons, and this fitted in very well with our own mother's views and experience.

My school friends sometimes came home to play, but they were rather scattered about the district, and as they generally had to walk back before dark, playtime could be limited. Dotty lived way up on Mount Elliot, Lois at the Terrigal end of the Serpentine Road, and Eunice down at Matcham. (Eunice, too, was one of a big family, with names I found interesting. A younger sister — quite beautiful — was called Venus.) I was always on the lookout for new neighbours with suitable children for playmates. Only once did I bring home some children who were apparently *not* suitable, and I never found out what the problem was. They were four little girls who had but recently arrived at school, and to me they seemed quite charming. They wore matching frocks of red and white checked cotton (and I think they had shoes and socks, all four of them), and were shy and quiet. There must have been a skeleton in the closet somewhere, because our mother rarely turned a hair when we brought playmates home. (Even the seasonal matter of head lice was accepted with resignation — though not by us, when we had our hair scrubbed with kerosene.) After a brief, unexplained stay, my four new acquaintances and their elders left the district, and were heard of no more — a not unusual happening in the thirties.

Then, one Christmas holidays, I acquired a special friend — somebody outside the confines of school. Had I had the words then, I would have described the meeting as an 'occasion'. Down in the south-western corner of our valley was a farmhouse which, from its position on a cleared and fertile slope above a creek, its background of bush and its gabled windows, had a somewhat romantic look. (Later, I identified it a little with the 'Green Gables' of L. M. Montgomery's beloved novels.) One day its new owners — promisingly named McLeod, married to a MacQueen — met my mother (who probably admitted to having been a Henderson), and I was asked to come and play with their visiting niece. I'm sure Dorothy would have been invited, too, but she may have been too shy. I wasn't one hundred per cent sure about it myself, for there was always a bit of social strain about such encounters. And I knew already that Joan was a city girl, daughter of an Anglican minister, which sounded rather sophisticated.

It turned out to be a meeting of kindred spirits. We instantly found tastes in common — for food, books, playing with dolls, dressing up, inventing stories and talking. Especially talking. Joan's relatives moved away from the valley, but for many years afterwards she came to us for school holidays. I can remember hanging about the front verandah waiting for her to arrive on the bus, the first moments of renewed shyness after several months of separation, and then the gladsome genuine reunion. And the dizzy prospect of all those holiday weeks stretched before us, particularly if it was summer. For then we slept out on the verandah, under mosquito nets, and gazed at stars and moon and trees black against a western sky — and talked. Thousands of words must have been poured out into the evening air, until it was time to sleep and wake and start all over again.

The friendship was at its best when I was around nine or ten. So we talked, I imagine, about important matters such as our immediate past histories (going back as far as two or three months), what films we might have seen (like us, Joan went only to Shirley Temple matinees), storybooks we had read, adventures we had had or would have like to have had, and occasionally events at school. But children on holiday don't spend a lot of time reminiscing about such mundane things. I heard all about Joan's two brothers and her younger sister, and some of the goings-on in the Rectory. Once I visited the family when they lived in Woolwich, and was charmed to find the Rectory an old stone house with even a staircase and top floor. At the nearby docks I saw my first-ever overseas ship, and added one more dimension to my inner adventure landscape. It was an instinctive recognition of the wonder of 'going down to the sea in ships'. My initial awe concerning Anglican ministers wore off as I grew to understand that Joan's father was mostly a father like anyone else's, though from Joan's accounts he seemed sometimes absent-minded, and certainly very busy. My father could be both those things, too.

The regular activities of the Christmas holidays — shopping, trying to discover where the presents had been hidden, going to the beach, putting on concerts at one end of the verandah, collecting cicadas and going to the shop for iceblocks — became twice as absorbing when you had a bosom friend with whom to share. There was real enthralment in a darkened cinema, waiting for the beginning of the serial with the glories of *Wee Willie Winkie* or *Heidi* yet to come, when you knew you could relive it all on the way home, and into the evening, with your best friend (and then re-enact the whole thing, with improvised costumes, the next day).

We had our own invented pastimes, apart from the perennial games with dolls (families of them, who led a fairly routine sort of existence of getting up and dressed, going to school where they competed for prizes, going on modest excursions, and, naturally, dressing up again for parties and concerts). One year, it was a novel game of 'Selling Houses'. Rather ironically, in view of the real-estate boom that was to follow in the district some twenty years later, we set up our office in an abandoned shed at the top of the orchard (now vanished), and designed endless homes for presumably needy families. Neither of us was gifted architecturally, but it was a lot of fun, and fulfilled two of the prime requirements for any satisfying ongoing game — firstly, we had a special place in which to operate, and secondly, we had, for a time anyway, the importance of keeping it all a secret. It was *our* game.

Another favourite bore some resemblance to the activities of Ethel Turner's 'Ungardeners', and indeed we probably borrowed her idea. We set about transforming a patch of bush behind the little old weatherboard church which was in use, surprisingly, only on Saturdays, and then for the whole day. We turned it into a miniature Botanic Garden, with rock pool, arduously filled from buckets, moss surrounds, and transplanted bits and pieces, which, in the way of native plants, resented the interference and went into decline. Bush settings, also, were used for open-air concerts and as stages for imitation movie performances. The secret-garden project was to have been a closely guarded occupation, too, but was soon discovered by my sister, for one. Our mother thereupon suggested that we all three play together, which was sensible, but somehow the drama and the magic went out of the whole thing, simply because we had no secret any more. And I found a one-to-one, exclusive friendship so romantic and satisfying that I didn't want to share Joan with anybody.

There was a time when she stayed with us, not just for a few weeks, but for several months, and actually came to school with me. This to me was a great gift and good fortune, but the reason for her long stay may have been quite tragic, as her young sister was very ill with what turned out to be spinal tuberculosis. Although neither of us talked about it, and in any case such events were generally hushed up by adults around us, some thoughts of the young Ruth may have been in our minds when we invented yet another pursuit that summer. Imbued with the mythical principles of the stories we read, such as *Anne of Green Gables*, the 'Emily' series (my personal favourites among L.M. Montgomery titles), *What Katy Did* and even *Pollyanna* (whom I accepted initially because she was an orphan, but whose further adventures I didn't pursue), we decided to adopt two small girls who were newcomers to the school, and were living temporarily with their grandparents, which gave them, almost, orphan status. We walked with them to school, fussed over them, kept a benevolent eye on them in the playground, and spent weeks collecting small items in boxes to give them at Christmas. They were nice ordinary matter-of-fact little girls, and put up with all this good-naturedly, but I think we found their lack of enthusiasm rather dampening, especially when they received their gifts. Our combined reading of fiction had led us to believe that such philanthropic offerings were always greeted with cries of delight and devotion, preferably lifelong.

Perhaps we were also impressed, at the time, by the writings of Frances Hodgson Burnett. I was certainly acquainted with *Little Lord Fauntleroy*, and even more absorbed in the ups and downs of Sara Crewe, in *A Little Princess*. This was a riches-to-rags-to-riches story, which appealed greatly to my sense of the fitness of things. I would have had no objection at all to the magic discovery that I was in fact a high-born, long-lost heiress myself, and must have been in training for it at times, because my father occasionally called me 'The Duchess'. I had a talent for 'playing ladies', especially when there was anything like mundane housework to be done. He said I got it from his sister, my Aunt Jane, who loved to muse, regretfully, about the grandeurs of the life-style that might have been hers had the ancestral fortune not passed her by. I can remember, too, hunting through the drawers — including a tiny, exciting concealed one — of my Scots grandfather's old desk, convinced it held an ancient parchment revealing that our family in general, and myself in particular, were rightful inheritors of a castle, half a county and chests full of gold and silver, to say nothing of titles. My own written stories at this time had heroines with names such as 'Lady Genevieve', and 'The Honourable Priscilla', who inhabited an uneasy domain somewhere between Britain's moated granges, and the rough and homely landscapes of coastal New South Wales. But I was aware of the principle of *noblesse oblige*; like Cedric and Sara Crewe, my aristocratic heroines always remembered the poor clustering at their gates. After all, they had been there themselves.

There were more energetic pastimes for Joan and me, however, when we joined in with my brother and sister and some of their friends. Boys, at this time, were inescapable facts of life; we were not particularly interested in them, unless their pastimes looked inviting enough to lure us away from our own treasured pursuits. Robert had gone to high school at the age of eleven, and during term time could be heard talking of such erudite subjects as French and Mathematics and Latin (his favourite). A photo of him taken on the occasion of his entry into these realms shows him in his first wool suit, fair hair brushed to perfection, wearing an air of near-angelic solemnity. In no time he was bringing home at weekends and holidays his high-school mates, a lively, voluble lot whose carryings-on brought back to my mind the 'larks in the dorm' of my favourite school stories. One holiday period was spent making, with tremendous labour, a billycart track from beside the house right down to the orchard. It was a work of art, complete with banked curves and precipitous final slope, at the bottom of which we less skilful drivers invariably tipped over. Perhaps not surprisingly, my brother developed a passion later in life for car rally-driving, something handed on in turn to at least one of his four sons.

Like most of the boys' occupations, this one was exhausting. You had to wait your turn for the billycart, often while lengthy repairs were carried out on the vehicle, and, after the breathless, bumping zoom down the track, you had to pull the cart all the way back up, and take responsibility for a broken steering rope or twisted wheel. The same sorts of problems were encountered in games of cricket, when you stood forever at deep mid-on (a boring position near the back fence, beyond the woodpile), until some newborn Bradman struck a ball right into your stomach, and the rest of the field berated you for missing a catch. Joan didn't fancy cricket, and on the whole this was sensible, but I still had longings to share in my brother's pastimes, and also to have his approval.

By contrast, bushwalking and picnicking were popular with everyone. Best undertaken in autumn or spring holidays, these for me were real adventures of the storybook kind. The route taken was always the same, which added the extra flavour of familiar communal ritual. There was heady delight in setting out on the brightest of mornings, half a dozen of us, stopping in the orchard to collect a few oranges (and throw windfalls at one another among the broad glossy trees), then scrambling over the slip-rails onto the bottom road, which lay before us like a brand new trail. Usually our dog came too, for in spring, particularly, we were alerted to the danger of snakes, and Hoggy was a proven snake killer. He was a dog who had chosen us, rather than the reverse; finding himself, in puppyhood, the possession of a single male owner down in the Matcham valley, he had opted for a household with children, and came up the hill to bestow himself on us. A kelpie cross of such loyalty that he had to be tied up to prevent him following us to school, he was nicknamed 'Hoggy' because his previous owner's surname was 'Hogg' — and by one of those coincidences which caused us young ones to fall about laughing, the man kept pigs.

Our destination was Conroy's Mountain, that rugged spur of bushland constantly on view from our living-room windows. It was the eastern end of a ridge that ran westwards to the place where Erina Creek flowed into Brisbane Water. To reach it, you skirted the foreign territory of other people's farms, crossed the Terrigal Road, and began the gentle climb up the foothills, on a timber-getters' track criss-crossed with the shadows of tall stringybarks and bluegums. It was a point of honour to go right to the top, up where the sandstone rocks tipped at angles holding real caves, and you could look down into a tangled gully where fern and lillypilly and wild clematis and lawyer vine grew over some ancient eroded creekbed.

When the oldest of us — the boys in the party — were held to be trustworthy enough to light fires and put them out again, we roasted potatoes and cooked damper, which were always pronounced delicious even when burnt black and covered with ants. (The cries of picnickers stung by bulljo ants were all part of the ritual.) Afterwards there were elaborate and exciting games of the old 'Bobbies and Bushies' — although that babyish primary school term may have been no longer in use with the boys. The games owed more, by this time, to the tales of spying and scouting and counter-espionage that abounded in pre-war editions of *Champion* and *Magnet*.

It was the derring-do of fictitious members of the Royal Air Force, however, that most attracted my brother and his friends. There was a time when a family friend gave Robert a collection of model planes, so magnificent that we younger creatures were hardly allowed to touch them. They were biplanes, beautifully made of balsa wood and gauze, and powered by elastic bands that unwound and set the propellers whirring like the wings of wood pigeons. To our awed and surprised admiration, they really flew, although crash landings were common, and much repair work called for. To see an actual aeroplane passing overhead was so rare that we all rushed to look — especially Robert.

But in only a few years he was to have his bedroom walls papered with aircraft identification charts, and even I could tell the difference, from pictures, between a Spitfire and a Messerschmitt.

During Joan's longer stays, we went to Sunday School again. I think this was less from qualms on my mother's part about having an Anglican minister's child in the household than from a desire to support a fellow countrywoman who had set up a small non-denominational gathering in her own home. It appealed to me on several counts — I could go with Joan, as well as with other familiar classmates from school, it was not too far to walk, and it was informal and friendly. And we even had afternoon tea. I had grown to associate formal church attendance with a kind of unease, largely because until the advent of Mrs Grenfell's Sunday School, I had felt like a stranger in a strange land. During our Waverton holidays, Auntie Lil took us to the large and highly organised children's group at St Thomas's, and I was overwhelmed with shyness unless allowed to stick like glue to my aunt's side, and help hand out attendance stamps.

Our parents hardly ever went to church, and unconsciously I derived some of my own wariness

95

concerning formal religion from my mother, who had abandoned many of the Presbyterian beliefs intrinsic to her childhood and girlhood. My uncertainties about this God person extended into my reading; if in perusing a new book, I came across in the first few pages extensive references to Him (why did he have a capital letter, anyway?), I was likely to abandon the book altogether, or skip those bits, provided the story was compelling enough. When I heard Joan's family talking of God in any formal fashion, I was instinctively embarrassed. Jesus, however, was different. I loved the Nativity story, for it had all my favourite ingredients — an arduous journey, heartless rejection, travail followed by glorious vindication, mysterious signs and symbols, celebration and hints of even greater wonders to come. And, of course, a baby. I felt rather frustrated because the storytellers seemed to cheat a bit, in the manner of adult novelists — having described their hero's antecedence and birth, they omitted to tell the young reader anything at all about his childhood, apart from one puzzling incident around about his twelfth year. Thereafter he leapt straight into full manhood.

My mother said, probably with more emphasis as World War II took shape on the horizon, that Jesus was a wonderful, unique person who gave us all the ideal prescription for living. She supported to the hilt, and even more importantly put into practice, his principles of non-violence and turning the other cheek, his extraordinary non-critical tolerance and acceptance of others ('tolerance', and 'charity' in the Paulian sense, were two of her favourite concepts), and his advice to 'do unto others as you would that they should do unto us'. Her general view of Christianity was of an ideal that could indeed be made practicable, if only it were tried.

All this I could understand and comprehend, for on the whole my mother's attitudes and behaviour matched up nicely with what she was saying. About the harshest comments she ever made on the ways of others were 'So-and-so does talk rather a lot' or 'I don't think I have a lot in common with So-and-so'. And although she and my father could and did argue spiritedly on many matters, they were never personal quarrels, as far as we knew. When we squabbled among ourselves, she was always there to pour oil on troubled waters. One word we were not allowed to use, in personal terms, was 'hate', though we could express mild, and temporary, mutual dislike. Neither parent was given to swearing, beyond my father's occasional 'damn'; and while we visited freely quite a few households where the adjective 'bloody' was not only common, but called into use to make almost complete sentences, we didn't bring it home.

Because I envisaged my life largely in terms of story, with me as both protagonist and commentator, I always responded to narratives concerning real people (which included, of course, characters whom an author *made* real), so I accepted readily enough this Jesus my mother spoke of, and who seemed part of the gathering at Mrs Grenfell's on summery Sunday afternoons. It was rather like being at home.

IX

I sometimes think that what influences our lives and helps shape our thoughts and imaginations may be less the big events than the little things, the small, apparent accidents of time and place and the presence or absence of certain people. Especially does this seem true of the climate of childhood, where so many vital impressions are continually being formed. In our own growing years we seemed to have a natural symbolic sequence in which to develop, and it was truly a world of little things — small adventures, small excitements, small steps in learning and gaining experience and understanding. We were permitted to *be* children, and to amble rather than run at forced pace towards adulthood.

Until the age of seven or eight, my images of night, for instance, were shaped by candlelight. And while this could sometimes be frightening, it also encouraged the imagination to dwell upon mystery and magic and wonder. When our own ancestors had only lamps and candles to gather round in the evenings, especially the long evenings of winter, it must have been a great deal easier for them to believe in the supernatural, in both its aspects; and in the power of story, and the importance of literal togetherness. That feeling of family closeness by the light of a kerosene lamp is one of my own earliest memories. When we acquired 'the electricity', our world was suddenly larger and more explicit (for with it came the radio), more conveniently appointed, less frightening (for at a flick of a switch, all night shadows fled), and less mysterious, so that automatically you felt constrained to let go your belief in mythical creatures such as fairies and ghosts and Santa Claus. And even reluctantly abandon your hope that one moonlit night you would look over the verandah rail and behold, not your mother's garden, but a whole new enchanted world.

Simultaneously, reality came in, and you stepped out to meet it. The same effect was produced by the multiplication of motor traffic in the district. Nights had once been so silent, except for distant barking dogs and train noises and sometimes the sound which filled my five- or six-year-old inner being with unexplained dread — the clatter of horses' hooves. (I never knew who it was that rode by on those nights, although it was probably just some harmless enthusiast exercising his mount.) In the latter half of the thirties, especially in the summer holiday season, cars and motorbikes invaded by day and night, often at unheard-of speeds and with great recklessness, so that accidents, on the sharp curves beside and below our house, were quite common. My father and the neighbours usually went out to help, but we children were never allowed to look upon the accident scenes.

It was not long, however, before we were riding in cars ourselves, and that, too, was both loss and gain. Our parents could never afford a car, and did not seem to regret it, although I can remember how my mother, taken on a touring holiday by motorist friends, talked of the experience for a long time afterwards, saying how she had enjoyed the freedom and the leisureliness of it all. (She who had once been such a dedicated traveller saw very little of her vast, adopted country.) For us children, the excitement of buses and trains was sufficient; on the only occasion when I was driven to

Sydney in a car, I was extremely sick before we had even reached Kariong.

The family who introduced us to more enjoyable car travel had bought the farm where I had first met Joan, and were to be our friends for many years. The vehicle in question was a large, blunt-nosed, more-or-less-convertible Nash, with running boards wide enough to hold camping gear, picnic hampers and a few stray children (often employed to open and shut gates). The bus excursions to the beach became a thing of the past; now, on Sunday mornings, we watched from our own back window to see if our neighbours were getting the car out of the garage, and if all was well, we waited for it to come chugging up the hill, with triumphant three-note hooter noises. I'm not sure how we all fitted in — and around — the car, big though it was. Our friendly neighbouring family was an extended one; apart from their three children, the couple had living with them the wife's mother, sister and brother.

At first our own mother came too, rather anxiously when she saw us youngsters bestowed upon the running boards or dangling out of unglazed windows. As we grew older and better able to take care of ourselves, she came less often. We barely noticed it, of course, but for her the change was not altogether welcome. She must have silently rather rued the passing of the old bus trips, and the walking and the picnics with just the four of us. They had been leisurely, as walking itself is leisurely, and had their own small-family close-knittedness. Our chauffeur was a fast driving, impetuous and volatile man who liked to throw caution to the winds whenever he travelled. He was a South African, and he and my mother had some quite lively political arguments, mainly on the pros and cons of British colonial rule. I had certainly never met anyone quite like him before, but admired his dashing spirit of adventure.

Sometimes we went in the car to the movie matinees.

On the occasion I best remember, it was to see *Captains Courageous* — the acutely Americanised version which nonetheless had the stoutly British Freddie Bartholomew in the main part. I was about nine, and unaccustomed to any kind of dramatic tragedy beyond that vaguely mentioned in passing in Shirley Temple movies. So the impact of the death by drowning of the sailor Manuel (most heartily played by Spencer Tracy), to say nothing of the protracted funeral scenes and outbursts of weeping that followed, was disastrous. I was in tears before we left the cinema, and howled so much on the way home that the car had to be stopped so I could be sick at the wayside. Fortunately, my mother was with us. She was upset herself, because the Hollywood producers had taken such liberties with the Kipling story, which, she kept telling me, had not ended with Manuel's death at all. I didn't find that much of a consolation; hadn't I just seen, right before my eyes, the lovable Manual die an awful, lingering death?

My sister had had a similar reaction at the showing of *David Copperfield*, when she burst into tears at the sight of young David (Freddie, again) being beaten by his nasty stepfather. It must have been relief all round when Freddie-cum-Cedric triumphed so happily at the end of *Little Lord Fauntleroy*. The next melodrama we saw was *Beau Geste*, two years later. I found that sad, too, but in a romantic and non-too-harrowing fashion. At eleven I was beginning to distinguish — barely — between reality and fiction, at least in so far as it was presented on screen.

The coming of this new family to the valley was to broaden my social horizon. Of the four adults in the household, I loved best the gentle, funny, warmhearted creature called simply 'Auntie' — a name I soon adopted myself, as I also used 'Uncle' for her brother.

She and my mother were good friends, too, which for me set the seal of approval on this new, informal relationship. They were South Londoners, who had migrated to Australia *en famille* when the older sister married her Afrikaaner. Before they came to our neighbourhood they had toured much of eastern Australia, camping out and, by the sound of it, having a most adventurous time.

Betty, the oldest child, became a firm friend of my sister. Because they had, in their travels, missed some formal schooling, she and her two brothers were rather shy, and none more so than the younger, Johnny. He was between one and two years old when I met him first, and beautiful, with thick fair hair and blue eyes. With my enduring interest in young children, I found him irresistible — even if he did shriek, in the beginning, at the very sight of me, and at every other strange face. In time, Johnny and I became friends, and I was allowed to help mind him on occasions, which filled me with a sense of importance and of being needed.

Between Betty and Johnny was Ronny, who was in the same classroom as myself at school. I was now in the 'big room', shared between Fifth and Sixth classes, and scholastic life was becoming more serious. For one thing, our teacher was the headmaster, and for another, as we neared high-school age, there seemed to be more frequent and more ponderous visits by Inspectors. For the edification of the last, the more academically inclined pupils were somehow manoeuvred to the fore, so that the inspectorial gaze should fall upon tidily written and correctly spelt compositions, spotless maps, and meticulously ruled and lined-up pages of sums (preferably correct). And those called upon to read aloud just happened to be fairly literate. The tension of such occasions seemed to reach even, or perhaps especially, to the oldest classroom inhabitants, those who were waiting for fourteenth birthdays and some kind of freedom.

Ronny was not at his best in this kind of atmosphere. He was always an outdoors sort of boy, and in the classroom resorted — out of tedium and frustration, I suppose — to being an entertainer. He was forever making jokes, usually behind the headmaster's back, and that, combined with his lack of interest in reading, writing and arithmetic, landed him in much trouble. He was, in the parlance of the time, a 'wag', and indeed that was his nickname. We all loved him, and he became to me rather like a second brother. He and his father taught me how to ride a horse, which I thought especially adventurous, because the heroines in both my English and Australian stories were forever galloping about on lively thoroughbreds, exhibiting great skill and daring. Riding the neighbours' stolid, fuzzy-coated pony, however, was not quite so romantic; it was bareback, and unpredictably jolting and even rather undignified. Later, Ronny taught me how to shoot an air rifle, mostly at tin cans; he used it for the more serious business of attacking rabbits, but although I understood that rabbits were pestiferous creatures, I don't think I could have borne to see one actually killed. He showed me how to fish, too, off the rocks at Terrigal Haven, and while I appreciated the sport in theory, I baulked at taking the fish off the hook. In short, I played a female stereotype role, which seemed at the time to come naturally.

Also naturally, I sampled the household's books, and discovered several new treasures. One was Jean Webster's *Dear Enemy*, which, for obvious reasons to do with orphans and a romance, delighted me — so much so that I invented, on paper, an entire orphanage of my own, complete with details of what the orphans wore, ate and did in whatever spare time they had. It must have been rather dull, but not as dull as another of

103

my literary efforts at about this time. After the extravaganzas concerning lost heiresses, hidden treasure and secret passages leading to the cliffs, I must have acquired an uneasy feeling that fiction had to be more than riots of the imagination. As usual, I sought advice from my mother, who made the sensible suggestion that it might be as well to write about what I really *knew*. Thereupon I rushed to the other extreme and produced a kind of autobiography based only on my actual daily experiences. It was so dreadfully tedious that even the author shuddered over it. I reverted to orphans, and at the same time tentatively introduced some romantic interest. In neither case was I writing about reality, especially in the area of love affairs, because they were still a mystery to me.

Another of Betty's books that I pored over was Gene Stratton Porter's *Girl of the Limberlost*. I found it unusual and a little alarming, for in describing the conflict between Elnora (a name so similar to my own) and her mother, and the deep dark secrets of the mother's relationship with Elnora's father, the author was showing me a kind of adult world wherein people did *not* always behave nicely and suitably towards one another. It was a bit of a shock, reinforced by another book that I found in the shelves of the C.W.A. library. This was obviously no child's book at all, although it had child characters in it. Moreover, it was American, light years removed from the cosy, happy-endings world of Shirley Temple and company. As I remember, it told the astonishing — to me — story of a deserted wife, fleeing from a violent husband with her young children. Her sufferings were horrendous (one child actually died, in lurid detail). After that I went hurriedly back to children's books. By doing so, I tried to bury the suspicion that the adult world might be a lot less comfortable than I'd previously thought. Perhaps growing up would be better postponed for a while.

The year 1939 had for us a beginning that could have been called apocalyptic, if we children had ever heard of the word. Our mother, who *had* heard it, was anxiously watching events on the other side of the world, and remembering 1914, but we were scarcely aware of that. There came a day in January when the temperature broke all records, and the bushfires outdid even those of 1928, the year I was born. It was for us, whichever way we looked at it, a day of drama. My mother was helping staff a C.W.A. stall at Terrigal, and we children went along, with Joan, who was staying for the holidays. We expected to swim, but the strip of sand between Esplanade and water was too hot to cross, and the water, if we reached it, brassy bright and flattened by a searing westerly. Finally, we retreated into the café across the road, and ate as many iceblocks as the exchequer could afford. (In my recollection, they were all emerald green.) This was excitement enough, but when we reached home, it was in a haze of smoke, drifting from the ridges on either side. (There is no more evocative smell, for a country-bred creature, than the tangy scent of burning eucalypts.) By nightfall, we seemed ringed by fire; then came the southerly buster, bringing the flames back in our own direction.

In a fashion later recognised as belonging to the writer — the persistent observer and taker of notes — I hung about watching it all from the back window. I was not particularly frightened, even when our mother started to put things in suitcases for a quick getaway. I still had implicit faith in the adults around me to turn back the holocaust and rescue us unharmed. I could see my father, in silhouette against the flames, with his backpack and hose, and all the male neighbours, with buckets and sacks.

It was always less the real dangers that I feared than the imaginary ones. I was probably even rather

105

disappointed when the fire indeed was put out, and there was nothing to do but go tamely off to bed. At some later date I used the event in a story; it re-emerged, just a few years ago, in my book *The Seventh Pebble*.

In the late winter of that year, I was caught up in excitement of a different kind. Our new friends had an interest in amateur theatricals, which naturally attracted me, though I had almost put my Shirley Temple days behind me. It was decided that they would put on a show for the C.W.A., and it was none other than my old familiar *Snow White*. But this was no abbreviated classroom version with impromptu costumes. A year or so previously, we had all been to see the Disney movie in which the fairy tale had been refurbished in a way that was both wonderful and weird; indeed, the weirdness and the wickedness had made me rather uneasy, and it was well that the dwarfs were allowed to provide comic relief. It had a strong resemblance to old-fashioned pantomime, melodrama and all, but highly glossed and speeded up by the new Technicolor and animation techniques. These both added to, and subtracted from, the elements of folk tale.

It was decided that our *Snow White* would follow the Disney version — or as nearly as would be possible in a moderately size shed at the side of our friends' house.

Auntie, with help from her sister and Betty and a few others handy at needlework (which ruled me out), produced marvellous costumes, particularly for the dwarfs and the forest animals. They were complete with masks, which had the added advantage of providing face cover for shy and reluctant performers. (Johnny, I remember, was thus coaxed into being a small chipmunk, and Ronny, who didn't have much time for this sort of thing, could safely ham it up as a dwarf.) Uncle was in charge of the stage effects, lighting and music; he used, for the scenes with the Queen-Witch, part of Schubert's *Unfinished Symphony*, which I cannot hear, even now, without a faint, reminiscent shudder. Betty played the Witch with considerable dramatic talent, so much so that I, as Snow White, was genuinely scared myself, which may have marked the only occasion when my acting was spontaneous. Her face mask was evil personified, and the hand that held out the poisoned apple had claw-like, blood-red fingernails. It was none too easy to remember that it was only Betty in disguise.

It was a great success, but I was hardly done savouring the attention and the applause when my brother was discovered slumped in a wheelbarrow, his dwarf mask removed (I think he had been 'Grumpy'), and the skin beneath peculiarly flushed: measles! Those members of the cast who had not previously had it succumbed at intervals over the next few weeks, and that included Dorothy and myself. It was an extraordinarily delirious time in more ways than one. I was scratching about in bed when over the radio, just across the hall, came the tones of Neville Chamberlain announcing the outbreak of World War II. Even to me, not quite eleven and so absorbed in my own doings and dreamings, that speech had portentousness. Even more dampening was the stunned response of my mother and father; it was like a new kind of silence.

Until then, my chief grumble about getting measles was that it barred me from going to a holiday showing of the Shirley Temple movie *A Little Princess*. I think it was just as well. Even I might have baulked at witnessing my favourite Sara Crewe played with an American accent and bunches of curls. Sara had had, I knew, 'heavy black hair that curled only at the ends', and was a rather quiet, dignified child who would never have dreamt of tap-dancing in the common room. As my temperature rose, however, I was afflicted with a nightmare of a distressing kind, all the more worrying because it belonged less to sleep that to wakefulness. It also was thoroughly mixed up with the encounter between Snow White and the Wicked Witch-Stepmother, and perhaps, more remotely, with the ominous voices from the radio. Beside my bed was a glass of water, with beside it another receptacle containing dissolved bicarbonate of soda, that faithful standby for daubing on every kind of itchy spot from chicken pox to the bites of grass ticks. Sometime during the night I drank from the water glass, and immediately became convinced that I had swallowed the carb soda instead, and was therefore uncompromisingly poisoned. Unlike Snow White, I did not swoon away, but stayed awake wondering how long it would take to die, and trying to come to terms with the dreadful inevitability of it all. Presumably if you were poisoned, you stayed poisoned, and there was nothing anyone could do. The fairy tale solution — that of the arrival of Prince Charming with his magic kiss — hardly seemed feasible, even in my fevered state. I was not personally acquainted with any Prince, Charming or otherwise.

Eventually I abandoned all ten-to-eleven-year-old pride, and went to alert my mother. In a few minutes, peace was restored. There had been no phial of poison at my bedside; I had only imagined the carb soda was there, when in fact it had been removed. (My mother did point out that she was not in the habit of leaving deadly potions about for her offspring to drink, and that carb soda was not poisonous, anyway. As usual, it was a triumph of her native common sense over my runaway imagination.) I went back to sleep, and woke tremendously relieved to be still alive. Even my measles were better.

Yet, however induced, that midnight experience had its effect. For the first time, I had understood that death could actually happen to *me*, and not just — at a distance — to other people and to animals. I, who had been modestly renowned for my delight in such physical adventures as climbing rock cliffs, riding on the running boards of cars, and travelling at speed across paddocks on the drag cart behind the neighbours' horse, developed a new caution. I no longer wanted to be the child who was 'game for anything', though I knew that 'game' was an adjective of approbation. Perhaps that early connection between 'gameness' and courage derived from listening to my father and his talk of wars past and present; for him, volunteering for active service was a deed of the utmost bravery, as well as moral obligation and evidence of patriotism. World War II had hardly begun before he was making enquiries as to how he could re-enlist, although he was in his mid-fifties. And my brother, barely fifteen, was already having his own dreams of glory, much to the anxiety of our mother.

My tastes in reading were changing, too; I was less attracted to tales of girlish adventure, and more to stories wherein the characters' feelings were explored — however tentatively.

Not long afterwards, Auntie and Uncle and their mother moved away from the valley to a home of their own. They also had their own car, a roomy Nash sedan with interesting dicky-seats behind the driver. In this we toured about on their house-hunting expeditions — most enjoyable for me, because exploring empty houses and overgrown gardens and paddocks was food for the imagination. Finally they decided upon a place at Narara, and I thoroughly approved the choice. It was to become a holiday home of great delight throughout my early teens. It stood on a hillside, west of the station, with a bushy ridge behind it, and an old orchard bounded by humpy grey rocks where wild plum trees bloomed in spring. Indeed, it was the sort of place where spring seemed perpetual, and dew always lay upon the wide thick lawns on mornings of wonderful freedom and daybreak dreams. As my personal horizons expanded and my growing times unfolded, there could have been no sweeter or more comfortable a home-from-home than this. And because Auntie and Uncle were there, it was a place of cheerful, unconditional love.

X

At first the war remained something vague and anonymous on the other side of the world; it didn't affect us directly. A second cousin of our mother's died in the Battle of Britain and I sensed my mother's distress; but I knew the young David only from hearsay and a family photograph, in which he appeared as a round-faced, solemn child in white shirt and kilt. For a few months it was being suggested that my first cousins, Uncle Martin's Sheila and Ronald, should be sent out to Australia to escape the conflict and the bombing, and this was excitement indeed; they were about our own age, and I had always wanted to meet them. I went so far as to plan where they would sleep, and what I would talk about with Sheila, in particular. From *her* photos, she was a jolly-looking little girl with two enviable attributes — long curly hair and a school blazer. However, they lived in Edinburgh, which was largely out of reach of the blitz, and in any case their parents — understandably — didn't wish to be parted from them. I met them both on a visit to Scotland years later. Sheila grew into a very tall, graceful young woman, adept at Scottish country dancing; Ronald, ginger-haired and possessing his father's keen sense of humour, became a forestry officer. Uncle Harry's two children I never met, but my sister has visited her cousin Doris at her present home in the Shetlands, which place seemed inaccessible to me because of the hazards of

111

transportation. I am not at all 'game' when it comes to small-aircraft flying or ploughing through stormy seas somewhere near the top of the world.

My father's enquiries about enlistment came to nothing, in 1940, but the model aeroplanes and the identification charts multiplied in my brother's room. Via the radio, names such as 'Dunkirk' and 'Dover' and 'Coventry' drifted in and out of my mind, in the same way as 'Ypres' and 'Bullecourt' and 'Passchendaele' had done a few years before, when my parents had talked about that other war. Shirley Temple movies mysteriously dropped out of sight, to be replaced by *Mrs Miniver* (only remotely related to Jan Struther's gentle and thoughtful book), *The Pied Piper* (a wartime orphan-story, which I loved) and *Journey for Margaret*, wherein the dramatic talents of a child called Margaret O'Brien greatly impressed me. But she was American, and our parents preferred the British wartime movies, which matched their own natural tastes for understatement. And at that time America was neutral, which in the eyes of most British-born folk amounted to being uninterested.

My own affairs remained absorbing. In Sixth Class I sat for an exam called the 'Primary Final', and another for a high-school bursary. I think it was the latter which involved a novel kind of test labelled peculiarly 'I.Q.'. It seemed official and important. I cantered happily through all the sections devoted to words ('Apple is to orchard as rose is to . . . ?'), and numbers in sequence, but was baffled by spatial designs that had to be reproduced and completed. Finding direction from any position in space has been a perpetual minor problem. I always had to think at least twice about left and right, clockwise and counter-clockwise. I was, however, generally full of confidence. The formal academic requirements of the Primary Final held no terrors; we were practised in rote learning. Parsing and analysis I had first met in Fourth Class, and I have never forgotten it, to the extent that even today I hesitate to split an infinitive, and confronted with a dangling participle, I always look anxiously about for its companion subject. As for verbs and objects, adjectives and adverbs, I was like a fish disporting itself in its natural element. And by this time, of course, I could write a rapid composition on any topic from 'A Rainy Day' to 'An Imaginary Journey in Africa'.

I passed the bursary exam, I.Q. and all, but was disqualified when my parents' income was found to be marginally above the limit. (This was rather a surprise to them, too, but the fact that my father owned property other than his farm put him theoretically in the 'landed gentry' class.) I was unworried. I knew I was going to high school anyway. The Sixth Class year for me was all quite romantic. The world about me was growing again; for the first time, our school competed in a district sports carnival. We had our own banner, and wore white clothing with green and gold sashes, and marched with dignity, more or less, around Gosford's Waterside park. There seemed to be thousands of children present, with banners proclaiming that they came from such far unknown pastures as Ettalong, Ocean Beach, Booker Bay, Wyong and Tuggerah. It was borne upon me that from these important ranks would come some of my contemporaries at Gosford High, then the only secondary school between distant Sydney and utterly inconceivable Newcastle.

At the end of the year we had a farewell 'frolic' in the Erina hall, the scene of all those over-and-done-with fancy dress balls. I had a new dress of blue-flowered voile, and danced with a boy called Kevin. It was accepted that we were partners for the evening, which gave me a happy feeling of social conformity. We hardly spoke to one another afterwards, but that didn't matter; each had, at the time, fulfilled the proper role for the other.

Then came the last prizegiving, and the last walk home down the hill from school. It was one of those sweetly sad occasions to be mulled over and stretched out (for twenty-four hours, at least). My chief regret was that Dotty wouldn't be coming with me to high school; we had been friends for a long time, and I truly loved her. She was quiet and shy, and a good listener who was not put off by my more inflated and extravagant notions. Inevitably, we saw less and less of each other in our teen years.

But it was Christmas-time, and Joan was coming to stay. I could now choose from catalogues, or simply by desire, whatever book I wanted for Christmas, and that year it was Dickens' *Martin Chuzzlewit*, guaranteed to keep my nose to the reading grindstone for a week or two. Of all the sets of adult books on my parents' shelves — Austen, Scott, Meredith, Thackeray, Dumas and the whole of Shakespeare in individual red leather volumes with engraved frontispieces — I was attracted most to a modest collection which belonged to my father, maroon-coloured books with thin paper and very small print, but with titles such as *A Tale of Two Cities, The Pickwick Papers* and *Oliver Twist*. I went first to *A Christmas Carol*. It was an early Chapman and Hall edition, with a lone illustration depicting Mr Fezziwig's Ball.

'Marley was dead, to begin with. There is no doubt whatever about that . . . ' I was hooked, from the first line, and never mind the small print. Here, indeed, was a real story to rivet the attention. In spite of the ghosts who made such regular appearances, I was not frightened. Perhaps I was beginning to discriminate

114

between the good ghosts and the bad ones; not long afterwards, for instance, I was more than a trifle uneasy about the ghostly visitation in *Wuthering Heights*. But then I found Emily Brontë's novel perplexing altogether; all that brooding passion on the moors was beyond my comprehension. Even when I saw the movie, with Laurence Olivier and Merle Oberon, I still couldn't quite grasp what all that twisted bitterness was about.

Having claimed, so to speak, *A Christmas Carol* for my own (for years I re-read it each Christmas), I went on to adopt *Oliver Twist* and *David Copperfield* and *Great Expectations*, with increasing enthusiasm. I thoroughly approved of, and identified with, each of the protagonists in their chequered childhoods; they were all boys who these days might be termed 'spunky'. I then encountered Little Nell, and obligingly tried to relate to her as well. My attention strayed, however, to the more robust characters, such as Dick Swiveller and The Marchioness. I felt it right and proper (I had a sense of obligation towards the writers of stories, as if I was somehow bound to try and appreciate their efforts) to shed a few tears over Little Nell's death, but they were of the crocodile variety. It was a relief when my mother agreed that Nell was an unreal creature; Dickens, she said, was not at his best when presenting heroines, but some of that was lip service to the sentimentality of his times. His readers and listeners expected those tedious Doras and Nells and Florences to wilt away to early demise, virtuous to the end. But I did have some genuine compassion for Little Em'ly, sensing the social problems at the back of her catastrophe, even when I wasn't too clear about the nature of her lover Steerforth's iniquity. And Dickens was kind enough to allow Em'ly a new life in that refuge for outsiders, Australia.

I moved on to *Dombey and Son* (finding that Dombey

115

Senior was an even more intimidating father than Captain Woolcott in *Seven Little Australians*), *Nicholas Nickleby* (wherein the horrors of Dotheboys Hall led me to revise my opinion of boarding schools), and then to *Martin Chuzzlewit* in that 'summer in between' at the end of primary school. I rejoiced in Dickens' power to tell a story, and especially his inexhaustible capacity for creating character (heroines excepted). At no time, however, did I have the temerity to think that I could imitate this awesome novelist; my own tales remained centred around the doings of ordinary girls and a few boys (put in more or less as standard requirement), in the style of Ethel Turner and L. M. Montgomery. The book I chose as school prize that summer was Louisa Alcott's *Jo's Boys*, and equal favourite was L.M. Montgomery's *Emily Climbs*. This latter book was given to me by my father, which in itself made it special; he usually left present-giving to our mother and aunts. In the stories of all three of these 'writers for girls' I sensed that while the main characters grew up in theory — even to near-grandmotherly age — in practice and at heart they remained young girls. Jo and Anne, Emily and Meg, and Mary Grant Bruce's Norah maintain their youthful romanticism to the end; their truly adult feelings are just hinted at or hidden, and their lives unfold much as they expected, according to their girlhood dreams.

Of all this I heartily approved. This, I thought, was not merely life as it was dreamed of, but life as it really *was*, and would be.

That summer before I started high school was to have been, in my expectations, a season of rainbows. In later life I took some memories of it, changed it about, added and subtracted characters, and produced a children's novel called *The Summer In Between*. Not surprisingly,

116

it has a dated feel; at twelve, I was still very much a child, and a country child at that — more like 'Anne of Green Gables' or 'Emily of New Moon' than an almost-teenager of the 1980s. The word 'teenager' was still rarely used.

The realities of my own 'in-between summer' were mixed. Joan was coming to stay, and I saw no reason at all why we should not resume our hallowed holiday activities, such as writing stories and plays, and even reorganising our families of dolls. That Christmas one of my aunts gave me the most beautiful doll I ever had; remodelled from one that had belonged to an older cousin, she had a porcelain face of cherubic picture-book sweetness, blue eyes with sweeping eyelashes, and long brown hair that could be plaited, brushed and combed. I think I still have her somewhere. Restored again, she would be a collector's item. My own daughter was not impressed by her, having a fancy only for the sophisticated Barbie dolls of her own generation.

For me, Patricia Anne became rather like the ominous 'Last Doll' of Frances Hodgson Burnett's *Little Princess*, wherein the heroine is about to clash head on with the harshest and most doleful of mid-Victorian facts of life, and dolls and such fripperies are to be put aside forever. My one experience was hardly as melodramatic as that. I had simply failed to allow for the fact that Joan, being some months older than myself, had voluntarily given up doll-playing as childish. Worse than that — she actually preferred my sister's company to mine.

'But why can't you all play together?' was the sensible parental cry, in tones varying from the patiently reasonable to the exasperated. But it was my first experience of being on the outside looking in, watching Dorothy and Joan with heads together, whispering in the night, and indulging in unexplained giggles. Even the

117

magic of the new doll wore off too fast.

It must have ended, as these things usually do, in compromise. We had still our outings to the beach and to the film matinees. That season's Shirley Temple offering was *The Blue Bird*, a version to make author Maeterlinck turn in his grave, but it was all right by me. Joan, who had begun to notice such things, said Shirley was being put into the kinds of dresses that would hide her newly developing female shape, but that I couldn't swallow. *Shirley Temple* growing up? And I still in my blue-flowered voile with the sash and the Peter Pan collar? That latter accessory was peculiarly appropriate.

Joan was to remain a friend of both Dorothy and myself for some years to come. Her father, the minister, was moved to the church at St Peter's, and I went there to stay on at least one occasion. It was an unlovely spot, in the flat wasteland of the city's inner-west, but I liked the solid old roomy rectory, and even the cemetery full of tumbledown memorials was quite fascinating. For all my fears of things that went bump in the night, I have never had a horror of graveyards. The headstones make interesting reading.

And while I enjoyed Joan's company still, as we rode the trams into town and the ferry to Manly, I was suddenly aware — and pleasingly so — of the attractions of her older brother, Alan, a handsome boy with dark eyes and black byronic curling hair. It was like a sideways glance of recognition, an acknowledgement that growing up might hold a whole other-world of relationships.

As that summer of the last doll progressed, however, and January drew to a close and Joan went home, the disappointments were forgotten. It was time to go to high school.

XI

In 1941, in our district, going to High School — which I mentally put into capital letters, because it was so in the school stories I read — was both occasion and adventure. Adventure, because we had to travel out of our home territory to get there, and occasion because we had to have special clothing and equipment signifying that we belonged in a new and important milieu. Today, when there are high schools all over the Coast, in places which once were villages with two-teacher primary schools, the sense of adventure may well be curtailed. Children don't have so far to travel. My own five miles by bus were as nothing in comparison with the distance covered by some of my new classmates. Colleen came from Morisset by train (her father was superintendent of what was then generally known as The Asylum — now the Psychiatric Hospital), having first had to cover several miles to the station. The journey, with waiting time, must have taken two hours each way. Others came from outlying settlements, such as Kangy and Kanwal, Kulnura and Dooralong, and as far south as Hawkesbury River. Quite often the traveller in question would be the sole ex-pupil of his or her primary school to go on to high school at all.

Surveying myself in the dressing-table mirror in the corner of our big lino-covered bedroom, in my new uniform, school case at the ready, I gave no thought whatsoever to costs. Education was free — wasn't it?

Travel was subsidised. But looking back now, I can understand why some parents couldn't afford to send their children to high school, and defended their choices by maintaining that all that secondary education was a waste of time, anyway, for a boy who would 'go on the farm' or a girl who would help at home until she married. And my mother may have thought that as children had to wear some kind of clothing to school, it might just as well be a uniform, and though the outlay might be considerable, the outfit could be made to last a long time.

I had no objections. Didn't the girls in the stories I read always wear uniforms? Ours was the standard model — box-pleated tunic in either summer or winter material, white blouses, tie in dark and light blue, black stockings (later reduced to white socks, in summer) and black shoes (the most expensive item, of the 'sensible' lace-up variety). I even had a white panama hat, but that was becoming optional. It was war-time, after all. My mother made the blouses and summer tunics, and knitted the winter jumpers, and some of my articles of clothing were hand-me-downs from my sister, but, even so, our parents would not have found it easy to equip all three of us, then together in secondary school. Extras such as exercise books and sandshoes and raincoats were expensive. In primary school, chaff bags were used as hoods and capes, unless the rain was torrential, in which case a lot of children stayed at home. Not us, however — I had, I remember, a stout gaberdine coat that had been my cousin's, then my brother's. Our mother had been reared in Scotland, where a small thing like rain did not come between you your education. And then there was *the* suitcase. Mine was a modest but status-raising affair, especially impressive when later I pasted our class timetable inside the lid. It was not, however, that most desirable of all models, a Globite. Globites were shiny, tough, roomy, could withstand the occasional kick, and made the best seats in bus queues. By the time my parents could afford to buy me one, they had been superseded by military-type haversacks.

I set off that first morning with a sense of importance that was breath-taking. Dorothy, then in Third Year, was with me on the bus, but Robert, in what was to have been his final year, rode to Gosford on his enviable Malvern Star bike. As it turned out, he was too young for the demands of Fifth Year and its attendant Leaving Certificate, and went back for another go, which allowed him the privilege of being dux of the school. When congratulated on this, our mother always felt obliged to explain that it was only at his second try; her desire to be honest and fair and to apologise for any apparent taking of advantages was a characteristic I inherited. But at the time I was very proud of being sister to the dux, and had dreams of emulating him. 'Dux' was such a fine-sounding Latin word and, like him, I loved Latin.

Gosford High School was big — not only in size, imposing with its triple-storeyed, brick facade, and its huge, two-level, inner quadrangle, but in numbers. There must have been some thousand pupils, and that first year intake ran to ten classes. It was a pyramidal arrangement; from some three hundred or so in the early years, there was a tapering off until only fifty or sixty remained in Fifth Year. It was a good school. Under the headmastership of H. G. Stoyles, who retired at about the time I started, it had flourished academically and in terms of *esprit de corps*. His deputy, Mr Thomas, was in charge when I arrived, and saw particularly to the boys' side of the school; the girls were under the keen eye of Miss Moore, nicknamed 'Winnie'. She was an excellent and dedicated headmistress, and hers was the face I stared at on that

121

first morning, as we stood waiting like a flock of sheep by the eastern gate, ready to be allotted to our ordained classes.

One of the books set as English text later that year was Horace Annesley Vachell's *The Hill*. I loved it, and now I think that its story of intense, idealised friendship between adolescent boys may have planted a seed which grew into the theme of my *A Candle for St Antony*, with other, later experience and observation mixed in. Just recently I have been reading *A World Apart*, by Daphne Rae, wife of a master at Harrow, setting of Vachell's novel, and came across the words of a school song, forgotten for over forty years:

Five hundred faces, and all so strange!
Life in front of me — home behind . . .

It might have been a far cry from ancient Harrow-on-the-Hill to the sunny summer playground of Gosford High, but I knew the feeling. Unease and shyness crept in as I realised that almost every face in the crowd was unfamiliar. Those few I did know from primary school were marshalled off. My friend Lois disappeared in one direction; my good neighbour Ronny went early, into a group called '1H', or even 'J', where he was to study agriculture and spend much time in the outdoors, down beyond the back fence at the school farm. I could have envied him, for a little while.

Finally, those of us who were left became, by an instant process of labelling, '1A'. My mother might have deplored this kind of categorisation, which a year or two before had pronounced my sister to be a '1D', giving her an immediate inferiority complex — but all that mattered to me that morning was the sure knowledge that I belonged *somewhere*. I might have had a horrible fear lest I be stranded forever by the gate, with no label, no classroom, no identity. As it was, I could now pick up my suitcase and follow on behind the person who was to be our class teacher. His name was John Gralton, and he took us that year for both English and History. A gentle, rather dreamy man, a Catholic in a non-denominational school system, he liked the coastal district so much that he stayed for the rest of his life, farming near Lisarow. One of his friends on the staff was Mr McBride, a Science teacher with a large family, beginning with Mary and Joseph. Joe was in our year at high school. There was then no Catholic secondary school; those children who had been to the Convent for primary schooling mixed quite happily, as I recall, with the rest of us — except on Scripture mornings.

I already understood that the lions of our year and class would be, initially at least, from Gosford Primary. It was big and busy and had lots of smart kids. My mother had already warned me not to expect to shine perpetually in such company, but I don't think I believed her. It was alarming, therefore, to discover that John (whose father was head of what was always called 'The Boys Home', at Mount Penang) and Pat (*her* father owned the Terrigal Bus Company) and Lois and another Pat, all seemed quicker with their answers (especially in arithmetic) than I was. Perhaps even more worrisome was their camaraderie — they had the confidence of old acquaintanceship.

But there were others, like myself, who were 'singles'. Barbara, from out near Chittaway Point, sat near me and became a friend; like me, she was a reader of storybooks. Gwen was from Wyong, an only child and a bouncing extrovert. And Daisy came from as far afield as Merriwa in the Hunter Valley; in term time she stayed with an aunt at Lisarow. Girls sat on one side of the room, boys on the other. Except in times of academic rivalry, I took little notice of the boys. That was to come later.

If I had any doubts (other than those to do with my pride) as to whether I would like high school, they were dispelled that day during our first library lesson. I had never seen a real library before. The Stoyles Library was, by any standards, large and impressive and well stocked, and, most importantly, it had a librarian of surpassing enthusiasm and love of books. Phyllis Bennett communicated with me the moment she held up a shiny new novel with a vivid cover, and invited us to look inside. This was accompanied by the famous Phyllis Bennett smile, wide and sudden and infectious. Books, she was saying, were for discovery and enjoyment, and I couldn't have agreed more.

With hindsight, I can see how events and people and places were all coming together to encourage me in a literary career. It began with having literate, articulate and bookish parents, for whom reading was as much a part of life as breathing. Moreover, they *talked* about books, about ideas and language and characters, and both could be critical of what they read — sometimes in opposition. Later, I always had good English teachers, and access to books of all kinds. These head starts may not be the first cause of the writer's creative urge, but they certainly provide the environment in which that urge can flourish. I have noticed similar processes in the growth of my older son, who from a young age was attracted to music. In high school, at a time when his musical talents could have been swamped by the demands of more academic subjects, he came under the influence of a very skilled and zestful young music teacher who encouraged Alister and some of his schoolmates not only to play instruments and sing in the choir, but to listen to and appreciate various kinds of music. When time, place, people and natural gifts are thus all in accord, we can indeed be called blessed. Nor, these days, do I see such integration as merely 'come by chance'; it all seems much too meticulously planned and provided. And we are not capable of creating our own gifts, though we do have the responsibility of helping to develop them. Even there, I see it more as 'response to' than earnest and onerous duty. It may be that in this sense any creative activity can be truly named vocation or calling. That aptly describes the kind of insistent inner urge to sit down and write a new book at a particular time.

I was conscious of little of this when I first browsed in the high school library, with so many new impressions crowding in. But for sure I had the writer's ego. Left to choose from these imposing shelves, I went first for the set of Dickens' novels, in uniform dark-blue bindings, and took down *Barnaby Rudge*. I genuinely wanted to read it, along with the others I had so far been unable to get hold of, but I also wanted to be seen as a literary child. I displayed the same kind of one-upmanship later in class, when textbooks were handed out, and I was able to say I already had my own copy of *Heidi of the Alps* and *Wind in the Willows*. In a word, I was a show-off, but my new classmates were kind enough to forgive it.

As if the bounty of the library were not enough, a group of us girls formed our own storybook-lending circle. Four or five participants listed all titles they had at home, and then we exchanged books. There was the added interest of 'playing librarian'; later in the year we enjoyed helping out at the library desk. One book I borrowed from a friend became an all-time favourite, rousing all over again those earlier desires to be a juvenile scene-stealer — Noel Streatfeild's *Ballet Shoes*. Reading not so long ago a biography of this English writer, I noted that her fondness for depicting children who shone in personal performance probably came from her own childhood insecurities and longing to be noticed. I understood the latter, if not the former. The works of Dickens took a bit of a tumble while I revelled

125

in the successes of the Fossil children — especially Pauline, who was a gifted actress at the age of eleven or so. Here was my kind of glamour. For a time I was absorbed in a new make-believe game wherein I invented a 'stage academy' of my own, and listed all the details of play productions, casts and reviews; all written in a private exercise book, once homework had been disposed of.

I didn't find homework too arduous at that stage. For English I did book reviews and compositions (not yet elevated to the status of essays) and looked up word meanings and broke up sentences into clauses and studied conjunctions. For History, I copied out notes on ancient people as a preamble to the real stuff — the history of Britain. I was well prepared, for my father had a stack of magazines, collectively called *The Story of the British Nation*, which said it all, and moreover were amply illustrated, beginning with fur-clad club-wielding Celts and Picts and Scots, and proceeding to an especially touching cover-portrait of the Princes in the Tower, velvet-clad and fair-curled, clutching each other in dignified apprehension.

At about this time my parents and brother, Robert, and friends were enjoying history with a difference — Sellar and Yeatman's *1066 and All That*. I liked its wit, and it encouraged in me a salutory kind of budding irreverence. Not all academic subjects, it seemed, had to be taken in deadly earnest.

But I would certainly have had difficulty seeing the fun-side of Science — especially Physics. Chemistry at least had entertainment value, as when the teacher demonstrated the properties of mysterious elements such as magnesium and phosphorus. But Physics held no magic whatsoever. I could barely understand it. Like Arithmetic, it seemed to be concerned with endless calculations of a dull and repetitive nature — filling tanks, measuring walls, balancing weights (what is a fulcrum?), estimating volume and mass of this and that. I copied it all down in my fine new Science book, and learnt it parrot-fashion.

The boys, of course, were expected to be interested in such things. But not all my preferences were on sexist lines. I found Algebra quaint but interesting, and I liked Geometry. It had the neatness and order and the 'Q.E.D.' satisfactions of my beloved Latin, and allowed for in-jokes by all the class wits (there were many) to do with Archimedes and his bath.

Our Latin teacher was a character. Later in life I found that almost everyone who had learnt Latin could recall vividly the idiosyncrasies of his or her teacher. Perhaps a certain kind of eccentricity went with the territory. Even in the forties, Latin was losing its importance as a subject, and was compulsory only in 'A' classes. Thus its teachers operated in a restricted field, and were themselves in the category of *rara avis*. All the more reason, then, for being fiercely devoted to their subject, and determined to drill it into the heads of their pupils at all costs.

Mavis Chandler was rumoured, among the senior students in general and by my brother in particular, to go into stupendous rages and throw chalk and blackboard dusters about the room. As Robert was a star student, however, he remained a favourite. I remember her as being on occasions bitingly sarcastic, but fair. And I developed a fondness for declensions and conjugations and irregular verbs and ablative absolutes. It was all so tidy and concise. The perambulations of Julius Caesar around Gaul became a challenge, not historically, but as some kind of impressive and fascinating word puzzle. By way of introduction to the background of those exotic Roman imperial times, we also studied the Graeco-Roman myths and legends, my favourite being the tragic tale of Orpheus and Eurydice, closely followed by that of Proserpine and the king of the underworld. Years afterwards, gazing at the stars and planets on a summer night, I remember too my first acquaintance with Orion the Mighty Hunter, the Seven Sisters of the Pleiades, and the classic gods, such as Venus and Jupiter and Mars, who rampaged through the pages of our book of Virgil, displaying the most un-divine jealousies and partialities.

Nobody suggested that the study of Latin was a waste of time, being quite impractical when related to any kind of job in later life. It was a language, after all, and though our minds boggled at the thought of people actually talking in it, it was still made up of words and phrases and sentences that could be translated into more or less comprehensible English. I liked big words, and found that a knowledge of Latin was a great help in working out meanings of the more ponderous ones. Simplicity of style, in my own writing, was something I came to appreciate much later, helped along a bit by university study of Anglo-Saxon.

French I enjoyed, too. Actually being able to read a *story* in another language was a triumph and delight. In our first half-yearly exam, French was my top subject. And so it should have been. My mother was fluent in it, with the kind of authentic accent that I, as a born and bred Aussie, never managed to acquire in six years of study. My ear simply couldn't become attuned to the Gallic rhythm and inflexion, a problem which led to some mortification when I travelled in France in later life.

She would have liked us to learn German, too, but that wasn't possible in our country high school at that time. Much of our study was based on the 'this or that' principle; in any one class your range of subjects was limited, so that you could do French but not geography, two Maths but no Art, and so forth. As a concession to the practical side of life, we girls did a year's sewing (most laboriously, on my part) and the 1A boys dabbled in Manual Arts. Unlike Dorothy, who was popular in the household because of the delicacies she cooked in the school kitchen and brought home, I knew Domestic Science only by hearsay. And I envied her her ability to draw, if only because a skill in art would have allowed me to illustrate my own stories.

I was so preoccupied with the setting down, the understanding of, the translating and utilising of words, words and more words, that it came as a surprise to me one day in an English lesson to encounter the music of them. Called upon to read Rupert Brooke's 'The Fish', I found myself plunged, with the poet, into a new 'cool curving world', where I for once forgot to listen to myself performing, and was carried along with the movement of words and images I didn't pause to dissect. It was my first real experience of the magic and mystery of poetry for its own sake. I grasped that it was not only possible, but often desirable, to apprehend meanings without understanding every word and every concept.

So it was significant that at this time I was also introduced most pleasantly to music, not as primarily performance (although I did sing in the First Year choir — not amongst the sopranos in First, or even Second part, but Thirds), but rather as appreciation. Our teacher was young and keen and beautiful, blessed with the first name of Liocadia, which name I mentally added to my collection. There must have been a taste for the unusual in the family, for her young sister, then at school with us, was called Zoe. She was a lovely child with fair hair and grey eyes; that, too, was registered, as befitting for the heroine of my next story. (I still collect names and physical appearances, for later use.) I adored the music teacher for a time, romantically and uncritically; it would be a few more years before I adored the male teachers instead just as romantically and uncritically. My beloved 'geese' had always to be the finest of 'swans'.

In our music classes we made acquaintance with Verdi operas and Beethoven pieces and more Gilbert and Sullivan. Halfway through the year we were taken to Sydney to attend one of the Bernard Heinze series of schools symphony concerts in the Town Hall. It was a tremendous occasion. Not only did we have the fun of travelling there and back in a cheerful, fully uniformed, comradely group, but we also had the privilege of standing up before the entire audience and being applauded, because we had travelled all the way from Gosford. It should really have been our teacher who took the bow. The actual concert programme might have come as anti-climax had it not been so well presented. The major work was Haydn's *Surprise Symphony*, which appealed to me through its lively tunefulness. Today Haydn remains one of my favourite composers.

Of a more serious nature were the half-yearly exams. I came fifth, and that caused some chagrin. The boy John came first, and I marked him down as chief rival. Actually, I rather liked him, and was sorry when the family moved away from Mt Penang not long afterwards.

There were no recriminations at home over exam results. My mother's stand against competitiveness, academic and otherwise, remained firm. It was unfortunate that she had at least one child who temperamentally was a perfectionist; Dorothy had her own drive to succeed, and took everything seriously and to heart. There were tears and outbursts over homework not done to her satisfaction, and bitter disappointments when — as the world had it — she failed in anything.

130

In her Intermediate year she had to begin wearing glasses, and this too was in the nature of total disaster, for she was at an age when appearance and dress had assumed great social importance.

Inevitably, we were confronted with double standards. At home we were taught, at least tacitly, that it mattered a great deal more who you were than what you did or how you looked. Acquiring an education was necessary in order to have work in later life, to be sure, but, said my mother, the person who had what others might call a lowly job had every bit as much worth and dignity as the university professor, the doctor (whose profession then was held to be very close to the top of the tree) or the schoolteacher. This practical socialist Christian doctrine appealed to me in theory; at high school, however, I was continually being reminded that the majority opinion was otherwise. Winners were applauded, losers were often ignored. And as I grew, it became more and more apparent that, on the social scene, 'winners' were those who were good-looking, adept dancers and above all attractive to the opposite sex. This became particularly obvious a year or so later, when the Great American Invasion took place. But my mother figuratively polished up her armour and renewed her own battle.

XII

I was not about to embark on my teens without treading the boards one more time as Snow White. Goodness knows I should have been expert in the part by then, but this — the third production — was going public. We were to perform in the Narara hall, all proceeds to the Red Cross. At much the same time as the attack on Pearl Harbour, I was visiting our friends on the Narara farm for rehearsals.

We could hardly fail to notice the gravity of the times, if only because our elders wore preoccupied and anxious frowns, were periodically glued to the radio, and discussed friends and relations in the Services. My father planned to try enlisting once again; my cousin Ted was about to join the Army, and brother Robert, though still at school, joined the Air Training Corps and made numerous lovingly painted and mounted models of fighters and bombers. Yet the war still seemed distant. It was only occasionally that we saw newsreels in the cinema, and there was no television to bring explicit horrors and violence into our living room. I glanced at newspapers, but rarely read them. It was not until 1946 that I waited impatiently to have my turn at the *Sydney Morning Herald*, because that year Ruth Park's prize-winning novel, *The Harp in the South* , was published as a serial. A few years ago, when I met Ruth herself at a Children's Book Council dinner in Brisbane, it was in special recollection of that 1946 novel, one of the first, in my experience, to arouse some understanding of and compassion for the struggles of ordinary, benighted 'outsiders'. It may even have set off echoes which helped call into being my own novel *The Seventh Pebble*. It had all the greater an effect through its uncompromising realism; my mother warned me that it was rather 'sordid'. In 1946 I still preferred to believe that life more resembled a rose-garden than a back street in a Sydney slum.

At the end of 1941 I looked upon the whole matter of the war in a romantic light, as epitomised in Rupert Brooke's 'The Soldier'. My mother knew otherwise, but refrained from forcing home the harsh facts. I was too young yet to read the works of the later World War I poets, such as Wilfred Owen and Siegfried Sassoon. My reading was still mostly children's books, or Dickens, or the adult novels of children's book writers such as Noel Streatfeild. My prize for coming first in the end-of-year exam was Elizabeth Powell's *The Old Brown House*, which I loved. It had everything, for me — orphaned heroine (with red hair), an adopted family, and, a rarity in those days, a setting that was recognisable and quite familiar, in parts of Sydney. I still read as many 'Billabong' books as came my way, though my favourite Mary Grant Bruce novel was still *Anderson's Jo*, whose heroine is yet another orphan, faced with the extraordinary dilemma of having two fathers. Searches for father-figures seemed a very common theme in my reading matter; another favourite was Jean Webster's *Daddy Long-Legs*, wherein the mysterious 'provider' is both father-figure and, in the satisfying and obligatory happy ending, lover. Other fathers, actual and adoptive, who attracted my attention were the bachelor child-minder in John Habberton's *Helen's Babies*, and the much more alarming and realistic father in Hugh Walpole's *Jeremy and Hamlet*. I heard recently the theory that this 'search for the father' (with its variants, such as a quest for 'roots' and ancestry and family) is indeed the basic theme of all novel-writing. It would seem to have deep underlying spiritual as well as psychological origins.

Meanwhile I was happy enough dressing up as Snow White, until at some juncture it dawned on me that out there in the hall was a large audience of mostly strangers. I was scared. I didn't forget my lines or movements about the stage, but I was, alas! more wooden than animated. Self-consciousness stepped in to put an end to a less than promising dramatic career. I made but one more appearance in a straight play, in Fourth Year on stage at the Valencia theatre, in a chilly little piece called *The Spell*. I was utterly outshone by my friend Nancy J., who came from the charmingly named Tumbi Umbi, then a rural village in some of the loveliest foothills of the Coast. Nancy could do what I could not — fling herself wholeheartedly into a part. She was meant to frighten the audience, and she did. She frightened me, too. Such abandonment was almost embarrassing.

In the next few years, however, I did enjoy some drawing-room Gilbert and Sullivan. Auntie and Uncle had all the D'Oyly Carte Company's recordings, played on the old-fashioned wind-up gramophone, and we had much delight dressing up and miming parts of *The Mikado, Ruddigore* and *Patience*. Dorothy and our friend Betty joined in, with some of the young people from the Narara district. One of these was a handsome young English-born fellow called Sandy, whom Betty later married. He is now well known as Sam Wakefield, author of *Bottersnikes and Gumbels*, and other books for children. My favourite part was that of Patience herself, opposite Betty's clever, languishing Bunthorne. I had heard, by that time, of Oscar Wilde, and had begun to appreciate satire. Indeed, I had tried writing some. As an exercise for Third Year English, I had produced a conversation piece describing in biting terms a group of less than charitable ladies gathered for afternoon tea and a little war-work. It was mostly imaginary; I had no conscious intention of poking fun at my mother's C.W.A. friends, nor their tireless efforts at fund-raising and camouflage-netting and providing of good things for the Comforts Fund. John Gralton commented at the bottom of my piece that it was 'clever, but lacking in the milk of human kindness'. My mother backed him up. I learnt that satire could be funny (mine wasn't) without being cruel, and that in writing, as in any other area of life, consideration of human feelings was very important. In a word, there had to be compassion.

If this concept needed reinforcement, it soon came in a very real sense. An old friend of my parents, living at Wamberal, was at this time most ludicrously suspected of being an Axis sympathiser, because he was of Italian descent and name, and was threatened with internment. Horrified, my parents and other concerned friends got up a petition to have him exempted. I cannot recall the precise outcome, but the bitterness of the whole experience cut deeply into the community. It was frightening that feelings of intolerance and self-righteousness and anger at the 'outsider' (one, moreover, who had dwelt in peace and goodwill in the district for years) could be so suddenly and vengefully aroused. I remember the incident recently, when residents in a similar community refused to countenance the setting up in their midst of a halfway home for disadvantaged children in the care of a government department. Again, the chief reason was a righteous one; the residents feared lest their own children be 'corrupted', just as they had feared forty years previously that one Italian-born farmer could sabotage the war-effort. Such affairs all too quickly turn into witch-hunts. Similar prejudices had raged before the war amongst the religious sectarians — especially Catholics and Protestants — but with Australia more and more drawn into actual danger, those difficulties were somewhat overlooked in the common cause.

Both personally and collectively, 1942 was a dramatic year. The first term of Second Year began with a day's session of pasting shatterproof paper over all the school windows. We found it most hilarious. And next day, because uniforms were so liberally daubed with paste, we were allowed to go to school in mufti — a rare privilege in those days. I remember wearing, with pleasure, my new summer garb — a floral garment called a 'playsuit', with a divided skirt and rows of scarlet buttons down one side. My mother had made it, in the latest fashion. There were many new fashions that came in with the war — such as pixie hoods, and knitted boxy jackets, and the pretty dirndls which had some vague connection with our Eastern European allies. But even with my playsuit I wore stockings and brown lace-up shoes. Bobby-socks and open sandals had not yet arrived — at least in our household.

The new air-raid trenches down at the bottom of the playground were objects of curiosity — out of bounds save to the more daring spirits — until one afternoon when we were all marched out to take cover in them. Rumours ran from trench to trench, the favoured one being that the Japanese had invaded Sydney, if not also the Central Coast. For me, it was still like something out of an adventure story, and the facts, eventually relayed by teachers, concerning the air-raid on Darwin, seemed anti-climactic. In my 'this-subject-or-that' academic career, I invariably missed out on geography, and knew nothing of Darwin except that it was a very long way from Gosford. Nevertheless, I was mentally plotting a new story, in which the heroine would be caught in an Australian blitz.

One of the immediate consequences of that attack — the first ever on our native soil — was an ingress of new pupils coming from Sydney to the (rather doubtful) haven of the Coast, either with their families, or to stay with relatives. Our already crowded school expanded to bursting point, and I scanned the newcomers to assess potential as rivals at exam time. Having satisfied myself as to that, I found them all quite interesting, and even a bit romantic, because I'd read novels about the evacuees in Britain. However, nearly all of them went back to Sydney before the year was out.

Another newcomer at about this time remained, to our delight. She was no evacuee, but the daughter of our new local member of State Parliament, and she lived in — of all places — the Gosford Hotel, about which we were to hear some enlivening and entertaining tales. Margaret had a gift for humour, and for mimicry. One of her best party-pieces was an imitation of nuns at her previous convent school, for she was a Catholic. This became apparent in her first Latin class, when it was her turn to read aloud from our newly acquired *Caesar in Gaul*. Miss Chandler stopped her in midstream, and stared.

'Church Latin,' she said. 'Your pronunciation!'

I'd never known there was such a thing as 'Church Latin'. It meant, apparently, that 'c' was pronounced 'ch', instead of our customary 'k'. As nobody knew precisely how the original Romans spoke their own tongue, it seemed a truly academic question. But we were impressed that a newcomer could do things differently from Miss Chandler's way. It may have been a chink in the armour. Not long afterwards, I was temporarily put of the Latin class for talking.

Margaret became almost at once a welcome member of our class circle. We were a cohesive group, and as far as I can recall, without looking through rose-coloured spectacles, there were no outsiders. Nor did I have at that time one particular close friend, but rather half a dozen. We visited one another's homes when transport could be arranged, often for birthday parties. Over the years my horizons widened, around the Coast, from Wyong to The Entrance, and Tuggerah to Tumbi to various parts of Gosford. During 1942 we had our first big social occasion — a Second Year dance at the Sailing Club, and instead of going home from school, I went to a friend's home to change and eat and generally prepare for what was to me, at any rate, the equivalent of a Royal Ball. It must have been autumn or winter, for I wore a wool frock, burgundy coloured, with embroidery on the collar and waistband. My mother still made most of my clothes, but the following summer, after my father had joined the Army and our income had taken an upward turn with allowances and his permanent pay, Dorothy and I began to choose our 'best dresses', at least, from the Hordern Brothers catalogue — or even go to Sydney to shop for them — still at Hordern Brothers, where our aunts had shopped for years. I was eighteen before I saw the inside of any other department store.

Socially, we could have been described as backward. Our mother had certainly tried, within the limits of the environment, to teach us manners ('consideration for others') and something of the art of conversation, and general deportment and comportment. This was not to impress others, but to make life easier and more pleasant for ourselves as we grew older. Yet, like so many of our contemporaries, we were shy and reserved and self-conscious among strangers, and often with adults. That bane of the young teenage years, a fit of the giggles, was likely to assail us at the least appropriate times — as when our headmistress came to lunch. Our mother was looking forward to a bit of stimulating conversation, but we had to leave the table. At the same time we were genuinely innocent. At school I occasionally heard mildly titillating jokes, which I simply didn't understand, but within our own group, this was surprisingly rare. I was in little doubt as to how babies were born — my mother had told me about that, partly in explanation of what was to me the inconvenient and often painful phenomenon of menstruation, widely regarded as female affliction. But although I read novels such as *Gone With the Wind*, Marguerite Steen's *The Sun Is My Undoing*, and Ruth Chatterton's *Anthony Adverse*, my explicit knowledge of sexuality was nil. Even the above-mentioned novels didn't provide physiological details; heroes and heroines might be passionately attracted, babies born out of wedlock, and strong feelings generally ran amok, but I couldn't imagine what actually happened. And on this matter I didn't seek enlightenment from my mother. Perhaps I did not yet want to know. But one thing I did know for sure, and that was that I wanted one day to have children of my own. To that end I put up with menstrual cramps for which the only alleviation, other than the passing of time, was a hotwater bottle; I don't think we had as much as an Aspro in the house. Having babies, my mother said, was most painful, but worth the effort. After forty years, with three grown children, I still agree with her.

The Second Year dance was a success. I was no better at dancing that I had ever been, but I could at least pick up the routines of 'The Pride of Erin', 'The Canadian Threestep' and 'The Valeta', even if I couldn't always keep in time, and was likely to fall over my partner's feet in waltzing bits. (That the waltz is the hardest of all steps to perform gracefully seems to have escaped whatever dancing teachers we ever had.) By and large,

139

the boys had precisely the same problems. But a miracle had occurred. I attracted the attentions of a tall lad not in Second Year, but in Fourth. I'm not sure how Norman came to be there, but to dance with somebody you had to peer up at, and whose left hand in the middle of your back was large and heavy, and who could twirl you about in a masterful fashion was a new and pleasing experience. I don't think we went in for light conversation while dancing, as people did in novels, and as it turned out we had little in common. The problem was, as I soon discovered, that this Norman was also much favoured by my sister, Dorothy, and I was accused of having stolen him away.

It was the briefest of encounters. A day or so later, in school, a letter was given to me by my friend Daisy, who was some kind of relative of Norman's. It invited me to meet him on a Saturday afternoon at Lisarow. (When I look back, I find the touching thing about it was the careful handwriting, correct spelling, and general politeness.) To get to Lisarow I would have had to ride my bike an unheard-of distance up hill and down dale; moreover, it might have meant both deceiving my mother and risking again the wrath of my sister. Instinct may have told me what Norman's intentions really were, but I wasn't about to find out. I stayed at home, and probably read a book instead.

Meanwhile the American troops had arrived in Sydney, and a few of them even appeared on the Coast. Suddenly, it seemed, the radio airwaves were jammed and scrambled with the sounds of a whole new pop culture, the strident and sentimental noises of which drove my father, when he was home on leave, to cover his ears and utter all his favourite imprecations, such as 'Holy Smoke!' and 'Strike me up a gum tree', and another, which I've never heard since, and may have

140

come from his reading of historical romances, 'By my Halidom!' He used to go off down to the orchard to escape, for Dorothy and I found the new 'Hit Parade' quite marvellous. Simultaneously, our cinema screens were taken over by American movies that were far removed from the sagas of Shirley Temple. Names such as those of Betty Grable, Carmen Miranda, Red Skelton, Tyrone Power (who at least, in my father's view, had the grace to be of British extraction), Van Johnson and company became household words, and if you didn't get enough of them on screen, you could always catch up with the movie magazines. We went to the Saturday matinees, but — probably through parental influence — the films I remember best were those sturdy British ones such as *The Way to the Stars*, *The Demi-Paradise* and *In Which We Serve*, wherein war-time realism outdid chauvinism, and understatement took the place of sentimentality. And I still preferred John Mills and Robert Donat to Robert Taylor and Clark Gable. One American movie which did leave an impression, however, was *The North Star*, made to honour our unexpected new allies, the Russians. Another I genuinely enjoyed was *The Pied Piper*, because it had an interesting collection of war orphans, two of whom were played by a young Roddy McDowall and Peggy Ann Garner. I think *Journey for Margaret*, wherein Margaret O'Brien wept more tears than even Shirley Temple in her heyday, might have been rather too much. By that time I could distinguish between a story that was naturally moving, and one which was written for effect. Both British and American movies in war-time were often deliberately produced for propaganda purposes, but while the British strove to be subtle, the Americans seemed to prefer a sledgehammer. Yet, as our country was in need of their protection, we could only grin and bear their culture — or, my father would have said, lack of it. We could not foresee a time in the future when the

141

American influence in Australia would outweigh the British.

My father went off to join the equivalent of the Home Guard with some enthusiasm and a simple pride. Perhaps, in his mid fifties, he hoped to recapture the spirit of 1916, when the rallying cry to go to the aid of Mother England had real depth of meaning. He believed in what he was doing, all the more so because it was now his own country that was at risk. And perhaps he sought again the mateship and sense of solidarity that he had found before in the Army. My mother said very little. She must have mourned all through the blitz that devastated not only England, but parts of France and Germany that she knew so well, and worried endlessly about Robert, who would soon be eighteen and couldn't wait to join the Air Force. She refused, all her life, to glorify war, or even to claim that God was on the side of the Allies. It was not God who started wars.

Dad's second Army career didn't last long. Eventually he was sent to North Queensland, where he came down with dengue fever, and was invalided out. Meanwhile, with the help of my brother, my mother ran the farm, and was able to put some money aside to see us through our further education. Occasionally I helped clean the eggs and feed the chooks, but schoolwork had to come first. Meanly, I probably fitted in story-writing in the guise of homework, for I had discovered that it was both possible and desirable to invent characters who didn't remain children, but were allowed to grow up. I had only one plot — a group of children met and mingled in carefree idyllic setting (I was still heavily influenced by the novels of L. M. Montgomery, especially *Rainbow Valley*, and the 'Emily' books), then grew up, scattered, and were reunited in various combinations and permutations. Some of the action, what there was of it, took place in war-time, romantically of course, but occasionally I ventured to introduce historical background. This was vague as to detail, because I did not yet enjoy the necessary dull-seeming research. I was besotted with family trees. If I spotted one in a library book, either from school or from Dymocks' (the arrival of a parcel of black-bound volumes from the latter was a much looked-for occasion), I grabbed it and ran. One of my favourites was Clemence Dane's *Broome Stages*, a real gem because it combined family saga and romance with theatrical careers. I also liked Hugh Walpole's *Rogue Herries* novels, and Winifred Holtby's *South Riding*. The latter had no family tree, to be sure, but it had plenty of families. I devoured Eleanor Dark's *The Timeless Land*, gratified to find that even Australia could be used as setting for family-cum-historical stories. I took it as encouragement in my own literary career, all the more so because the author and I shared the same first name.

While my characters grew chronologically, they in fact lingered in perpetual early adolescence. I didn't know what to do with them after that. Looking back, I can see how they reflected my own ambivalence concerning this whole matter of growing up.

XIII

Between house and orchard there ran slantwise a broad pathway which had once been a track for horse and plough. Disused except for foot traffic, it had become carpeted with grass and moss, and was lined with saplings and old grey rocks. It rather resembled what in my British novels was called a 'ride', and at fourteen or fifteen I found it a romantic place. From the slip-rails at the bottom you could look across the orchard and a slope studded with blackberry bushes to the valley and the hills and the sky. I was there one evening contemplating all this, as a southerly moved across from the ridges, when Robert saw me and wanted to know what I was looking at. Receiving no intelligible reply, he said: 'It's because you're an author. They're always mad', and passed by.

I took it as a compliment.

Perhaps I didn't wholly take for granted the homely beauty and peace of my surroundings. Mooching about gazing at sunsets and stars and a rising moon, hearing the distant beat of surf on hidden beaches, and enjoying the scent of roses and orange blossom borne on the breezes, I was aware of both longing and vague dissatisfaction. Some years later, in my last term at university, I came across some lines of Louis MacNeice's that I never quite forgot:

> *The sunlight on the garden*
> *Hardens and grows cold,*

144

We cannot cage the minute
Within its nets of gold . . .

I would have kept all those moments of recognised beauty in cages for ever — and still would. But I also instinctively recognised impermanence. There was something I wanted to hold onto, which was slipping away.

My reading took what seemed like a regressive turn. While I had enjoyed fantasy as a child, my natural inclination had still been towards the 'real life' family story. Now I re-read *Peter Pan*, and came upon those magical books of Eleanor Farjeon's — *Martin Pippin in the Apple Orchard*, and *Martin Pippin in the Daisy Field*, And I either bought for myself, or had given to me, a set of J. M. Barrie's plays. I especially liked *Dear Brutus*; the scenes between Dearth (a significant name) and his 'dream-daughter' in the mysterious wood haunted me for a long time. The ending is equivocal. The reader doesn't know whether in fact Dearth reformed and went on to have an actual daughter called Margaret, or whether he fell by the wayside. I clung to the former resolution. After all, in the stories I'd read in earlier years, it was customary, if not obligatory, for black sheep to turn white.

I knew nothing at the time of Barrie's own psychological difficulties, and wouldn't have cared, anyway. I was still in that blissful state — something akin to that of Eve in the Garden of Eden — when I'd never heard of Freud. A few years later I had some brief acquaintance with his works, but I didn't believe a word of it.

Perhaps it was just this that constituted our innocence and ignorance. Nobody peered closely at teenagers to dissect their complexes. Rather, they were seen to be 'going through stages', and if one particular stage

145

seemed extra sticky, there was always the consoling belief that they would 'grow out of it'. More often than not, we did. Feelings were not much discussed in our household, not because we were assumed to have none (my sister was quite capable of shattering that illusion), but because *nobody* talked much about personal feelings. We were of British stock with Aussie offhandedness superimposed. And good manners alone forbade too much dwelling upon 'I', 'me', 'my', in conversation. Until the last few years of her life, I only once saw my mother cry — and my father, never. The one occasion upon which my mother did break down (for thus it would have been described) was so astonishing to my sister and myself that we backed off in total disarray.

My mother knew I nourished poetic feelings about sunsets and clouds and — more dangerously — people, for such things I could share with her. And we could discuss any book, including a Barrie play, both as literature and from the point of view of ideas therein. We could hardly talk about my deeper feelings, however, when I couldn't even define or articulate them. Indeed, they were, in a pantheistic fashion, of a spiritual nature, and she probably recognised that. At about this time she agreed to let me go to pre-Confirmation classes, though she had reservations concerning formalised religion.

The classes were held at first in the little weatherboard church where we had attended Sunday School, and I found them boring in the extreme. The question-and-answer arrangement of Anglican doctrine seemed to bear no relation to my everyday or my inner life (although in the latter there were certainly more questions than answers), and what I enjoyed most was riding to and fro on my bike. But at about this time I formed a friendship with a fellow confirmee, and this *was* to have a lasting effect.

It was Julia who lent me the *Martin Pippin* books, as well as all the Montgomery titles I'd not yet read. Her family lived in a valley below that landmark, Brooks' hill, bane of our walks home from Wamberal Beach. It was a pretty spot, still resounding to the calls of bellbirds, and through the bush and the clearings Julia and her friends had labelled various places in the manner of *Anne of Green Gables* — though with different names. In its own way, this coastal landscape must have been every bit as beautiful as Anne's Prince Edward Island; it is the power of the imagination, in any case, that invests the surroundings with a special loveliness. Casual observers may find them dull and ordinary.

Imagination was something Julia certainly had. She was artistically inclined, and produced delicate pen-and-ink drawings to go with her stories. I had known her since early primary school, and her mother was one of the first members of our C.W.A.. That there was deep tragedy in Julia's life was only too evident to all of us; every skin surface had to be protected from the sun, so that she wore always a wide-brimmed hat, long sleeves and stockings. Nor could she swim and sun-bathe like the rest of us. She had a congenital skin condition, all the more accentuated because her parents were first cousins.

Because I rarely heard this spoken of in terms of morbid pity and curiosity, I simply accepted that Julia was Julia. I stayed sometimes at her home, and enjoyed it. Not only did she have so many storybooks, and shared with me a fondness for make-believe, but also there were many creature comforts to gladden my heart — such as home-baked wholemeal bread with blackberry jam, and a deep open fireplace to sit about on winter evenings while Julia's mother read to us from, in particular, a most exciting adventure story to do with the lost treasure of the Incas. Her father, who was deaf,

147

played for us on the piano accordion, one ear pressed close to the surface of the instrument to follow his own tune. We slept out on the verandah, which, unlike our own, was partly enclosed and could be used as bedroom all year round.

On one occasion Julia and I rode on our bikes to Wamberal to watch the sun rise, leaving in the dark, and tramping over the sand to the beach in a silence touched only by the drumming of the surf. It was very beautiful, and I think I went home and wrote a very flowery description of it. Later, after Julia had died, I put it into a poem, and gave it to her mother.

Julia was about seventeen at her death, and I had been visiting her not long before. She was spending all her time, by then, on the bed on the verandah, but she had kept her fighting spirit and her imagination. I was touched by it, but not overwhelmed. The family had strong religious beliefs — Julia's aunt was an Anglican deaconess — and it had been with Julia that I was confirmed at the church of St Mark in Terrigal. Julia and her family believed that one day they would all be reunited in a place of perfect healing, and there they would be forever.

I took this to my mother. Did she believe that, too? She hadn't been certain of it since her Presbyterian girlhood, but she freely admitted that such a faith was a wonderful gift, enabling many people to bear suffering that otherwise would have been intolerable. Nor did it matter whether such faith was formally labelled Anglican or Catholic or even Hindu or Buddhist. As for immortality — she had given some thought to it and was rather drawn to the Chinese concept (which is also, in part, like the ancient Jewish) of immortality being ensured through the begetting of children, who in turn had children — so that a little of oneself stayed alive through the generations. Allied to this was her belief — to which she held through two world wars and various personal griefs — that mankind was not doomed, but that over the centuries was gradually and stubbornly improving, though often at the rate of one step forward and another backwards. Imbued early with this hopeful philosophy, I was able many years afterwards to perceive the drift of the writings of Teilhard de Chardin, though some of his scientific propositions left me confused.

What of death itself, then? At ten, in feverish imaginings, I had for the first time associated the thought of death with myself, but now I was thinking also of the death of people I loved. My mother pointed out that death can thus fall hard upon those left alive in this world. In the personal sense, she found comfort in the thought — indisputable, however one looked at it — that death promised an end to all pain, physical or otherwise, and total forgetfulness of previous miseries. Perhaps because I was rarely conscious of being at all miserable, I found this a bit perplexing. I didn't realise till much later that the extent of Julia's sufferings (she died from cancer) had been carefully hidden from me.

At about this time, I became suddenly and explicitly aware of my own identity. I had hardly gone through fifteen years unconscious of who I was; mostly I'd been happy being myself as reflected in the view of parents, brother and sister, and of other relatives and friends. I could recognise myself and my place of belonging. Now my recognition came from somewhere within. It was Christmas-time, and I was sitting in the back seat of my Narara friends' Nash sedan, waiting to go on some short journey. I was at the age when Christmas gifts, apart from books, consisted mostly of clothes, and had only just begun to appreciate it. One garment I had that year was of a new fashion, a white cotton short-sleeved sweater that soon came to be called a T-shirt — another tribute, perhaps, to American culture. With it I wore a green checked scarf. I gazed at the reflection in the rear-view mirror, and was not displeased. This, I thought, was *me*. It was not just perception of appearance (to which we were bidden to give little more attention than was sartorially necessary), but awareness of unique individuality. It seemed to hold all manner of promises and possibilities, even beyond my long-stated ambition to be a writer. With it came a sense of future enlargement of horizons, and that desire to set forth and travel which had been in me ever since I had first distinguished the sound of distant train-whistles.

It was the end of my Intermediate year. I passed with three As in English, French and Latin, and Bs in the two Maths and Science and History. John Gralton was disappointed that I had not done better in History, but no doubt I hadn't worked hard enough. I found the study of British colonial expansion, of battles and the Industrial Revolution and the growth of parliamentary representation all rather dull. It had ceased to attract since the succession of the Hanoverian rulers, at which point story and romance seemed to go out of the picture, and dreary facts make an entry. Australia featured only as an appendage of Britain, and as nobody ever bothered to fight over us as over Canada and the United States, we seemed relatively unimportant and lacking in heroes.

By contrast, English had been plain and pleasant sailing. That year we had studied *Twelfth Night*, and our appreciation of it had been boosted when we were taken to see a performance of it at Sydney's Theatre Royal. We discovered that it was very funny. Quotations from it, such as those referring to 'patience on a monument' and music being 'the food of love', became class by-lines, and Malvolio was a general favourite. There seems to have been a strong dramatic streak in many of us, and some, such as Margaret and Nancy J. and Lester and Bill (for boys had come more and more within our orbit), had a ready wit that may not have won them marks in exams, but greatly entertained the rest of us.

In poetry I was beginning to find some kind of answer to spiritual yearnings. 'Beauty is truth; truth beauty', attracted eye and ear as lantern and bell. Keats, for me, became poet of the year. I could be 'silent, upon a peak in Darien' with the best of them. Our landscape might be lacking in nightingales, Grecian urns and autumn harvests, but the sentiments of the Romantic poets were mine by adoption. They no doubt appealed all the more because the poets seemed to be mostly handsome and afflicted young men; at that date the least popular of the group was Wordsworth. Time reversed that choice. In Third Year I seem to have overlooked what is now a favourite sonnet, 'Surprised by joy — impatient as the wind . . .'

It certainly turned up the following year in *Palgrave's Golden Treasury of Songs and Lyrics*. My mother, who had sentiments but no sentimentality, was good at doing send-ups of Wordsworth's more maudlin offerings, such as 'We Are Seven' and 'She Dwelt Among the Untrodden Ways'. On the whole she preferred Robbie Burns, a poet of the down-to-earth kind, whose livelier verses were not on our reading lists. Other immortal ballads which she liked to quote in mock horror were Tennyson's 'Come into the Garden, Maud' and Longfellow's 'Excelsior', complaining of the latter that she had never been able to make out what precisely the hero was up to, struggling through the Alpine snows with his incomprehensible banner. She gave me what alone I could not have acquired, especially at fifteen, and that was a sense of literary proportion and economy. And also, a certain irreverence for established institutions, including Victorian poets.

We studied no Australian poetry at all. I had heard of Christopher Brennan and Hugh McCrae and Douglas Stewart only because their works were discussed in the

151

Bulletin, which my parents both read. As far as we knew in high school, our native poets were memorable only for such pieces as Dorothea Mackellar's 'My Country', a ballad or two by Henry Lawson and, of course, because we lived in the Gosford district, Henry Kendall's 'Bellbirds'. Inevitably the British emphasis in all things literary influenced my writing; the similes and metaphors we were encouraged to use were for me, at any rate, heavily derived from the northern hemisphere.

Third Year had delights other than academic. I went to National Fitness Camp with my friend Beryl. We had known each other since the first days of high school, and went through the entire five years together. She came from Tuggerah, then a small settlement on the flat lands between the northern railway line and the Lakes, and was the youngest of a large family, all the daughters of which were educated right through to Teachers College level. In the Tuggerah district there were three families surnamed respectively Hand, Legge and Foote — regarded as hysterically funny until you got used to it. I was to meet up again, many years later, with one of the Footes — Hazel — when she had become the dedicated and innovative children's librarian at Blacktown, in Sydney's west.

I hardly think it was the fitness part of the projected camp that attracted me. I was no athlete, though I had tried to adopt a suitably keen attitude to team games, particularly hockey, for two reasons. Firstly, it was the game so earnestly and vigorously played by the heroines of every school story I'd ever read ('Oh, I say! A spiffing goal! Do buck up there, Priscilla!'), with the possible exception of Louise Mack's Australian school story *Teens*, and, secondly, my father had given me my very own hockey stick, of which I was inordinately proud, not only because the only other girl I knew with

152

such a distinction was Nancy S., the best hockey player in our year, but also because it was my father who had given it to me. I felt I had to live up to it. But far from scoring spiffing goals, I was placed at full back, where I alternately shivered in the cold and stiffened with terror when an entire pack of the opposition bore down upon me and my fellow back (generally much more stalwart than I, fortunately) with sticks raised suspiciously high ('Not above shoulder level, girls') or slashing at the ball with devastating intent. Unlike Dorothy, who was in all her House teams for basketball and swimming and things such as tunnel-ball and captain-ball, I was lacking in team spirit. Later, in summer, we drop-outs were allowed to play vigoro down at the old show-ground, which was fun because nobody took it seriously. Before that, however, we had to pass your life-saving tests to prove we could actually swim. This involved rescue and resuscitation exercises, and diving for bricks, carried out in the Gosford Baths, which were then decidedly murky, and infested at times with sea-lice. That I actually passed could have been due to an error on the part of exhausted examiners; all in all, it is fortunate that I was never called on to attempt a rescue of anyone drowning at sea.

What attracted me to the proposed camp was more a desire to be part of a group adventure away from both home and school. I had already tried being a girl guide; as there was no local pack, I had to be a 'lone guide'. And long before you reached the stage of qualifying for camping, you had to know how to tie a lot of knots and do a bit of cooking and know where the Southern Cross was. For all my musing upon the stars, I didn't know one from another. So the girl guide venture was short-lived. My mother prudently had refrained from buying the uniform, having predicted the outcome.

You needed no uniform or knot-tying for National Fitness Camp — just garments such as shorts and tops and jumpers. (Jeans were unheard of, and females who wore trousers, other than those in the Land Army, were considered 'fast'.) Then there was all the excitement of an early morning train trip to Sydney, and a long bus ride to Mona Vale, which northern beach suburb was quite new to me. The place we stayed in was romantic enough, even for me. Called 'La Corniche', it was a great creamy-coloured, two-storeyed mansion set on a headland with a magnificent view of shore and sea. It has long since been demolished. I regarded my two weeks there as the equivalent of a stay in an especially delightful boarding school, complete with larks in the dorm, chats over communal meal tables, and any amount of lively (all female) company. True, we did have team games and gymnastics and the like, but we also had campfires and singing and much rambling over the beaches and headlands, ostensibly studying the basics of geology, topography and marine life.

I enjoyed it so much that I went to a second camp later in the year, rather against my mother's better judgment, for the end-of-year exams were drawing close. She was right, but for a different reason. I didn't like the second experience nearly as much as the first; it was held, not in a romantic mansion, but in a collection of bare huts on the shores of Lake Macquarie. And the feeling of congeniality and camaraderie had fled. With the poet, I had sought to cage another minute, and inevitably failed. It seemed unfair that such intense spontaneous enjoyment could not be repeated *ad infinitum*, at will. I began to recognise, by instinct, what nostalgia was, as I also knew the keen leading edge of anticipation.

The desire to experience Life (of course, in my thinking, it had a capital letter) with this kind of intensity and romantic enhancement was to remain with me always. But I was not alone in it. My sister had it, too, and took her disappointments even more to heart. While her reaction was open and angry and immediate, mine was more subdued and withdrawn. I tended to brood, or go off in what was usually termed 'sulks' — though not by my mother, who encouraged me to bring the matter out into a kind of philosophical discussion. And I had the extra and precious gift of being able to 'write things down'. My own magic moments might have passed, temporarily, but I could always invent stories wherein such experiences were relived through my characters.

One of the poets we certainly did not encounter in high school was George Herbert. At fifteen or sixteen, pagan though I was, I would have approved of:

True beautie dwells on high; ours is a flame
But borrowed thence to light us thither.

XIV

Ours was a generation wherein, once we had passed through the first year or two of high school, educational opportunity loomed large. Our parents had survived the Depression, and made plenty of sacrifices to ensure that we would have our chances to take up secure and well-paid jobs. Those (decreasing in numbers) who would stay on farm or orchard had, by contrast, to leave school early and educate themselves — if they chose. In 1944, of course, it was taken for granted that eighteen-year-old boys would enlist in the armed forces; revolutionary was the fact that quite a few girls did likewise. My brother, Robert, was already in the Air Force, training at Tocumwal and Narrandera. He didn't qualify as a pilot, to his own disappointment, but was accepted as air-crew material, and went on to become a wireless operator, thereby following in his father's footsteps — though in the air instead of on the ground. To our parents' relief, he went through the system too late to see active service in World War II, though one day he would see enough of it in Malaya and Vietnam. His decision to stay on in the Air Force, as choice of career, was not favoured by our mother, but, as usual, she made singularly little fuss.

Dorothy had passed her Leaving Certificate, and gone to Sydney, where during the week she lived with our aunts and attended the Metropolitan Business College. For a short time, my parents considered sending me to

156

the Presbyterian Ladies College as a boarder for my last two years of secondary school, but it proved too expensive. It had naturally appealed to me as romantic and adventurous, but no doubt the reality would have been too crushing. When I did finally live away from home, three years later, I was overcome by homesickness for the first month or so, and that at the ripe old age of seventeen.

I was happy enough, anyway, at high school. Fourth Year had a feeling of prestige. From five Intermediate classes, our ranks had dwindled to two. Of those, some pupils would complete the year and leave at sixteen, generally to go to work in the banks or similar commercial enterprises. (Amongst these was Alan Davidson, assisted by my father among others, to get a job in a Sydney bank so that he could play cricket at grade level, and eventually graduate to state and national representation.) Some of the girls would take up nursing; the better the educational qualifications, the greater the chance of being accepted into one of the big city hospitals. Several of my classmates who went on to Fifth Year had their sights set on Teachers College, where, if you lasted the distance, you were guaranteed entry to one of the most secure jobs of all, even if it meant being bonded for five years or more. One boy (but certainly at that time none of the girls) was aiming for the highest, medicine, and — determined, hardworking fellow that he was — he succeeded. As for myself, I too hoped for university entrance. That I eventually got there was due less to my own perseverance than to the encouragement and dedication of my parents and some exceptional teachers. My ambition was still to be a writer; I accepted, however, that studying English at tertiary level could be useful, and that I might even have to do something as mundane as earning my living in ways other than literary — at least to start with.

157

That parents, and sometimes other family members, had to put up with certain hardships and sacrifices in order to educate the children was taken for granted. And I'm sure many parents do it still. Every parent seems naturally to hope that the child's lot in life will be better than his or her own. It's like an instinct. And, just as naturally, the teenage offspring are largely unaware that any great parental sacrifice is involved. For the most part, my own parents forbore to remind me that my extended education was costly; only afterwards did I realise it would have been impossible had my older brother and sister not been off my parents' hands already. Dorothy finished Business College and went to work in the head office of the Rural Bank in Sydney's Martin Place, where she made new friends and had the kind of social life which included going to balls in what was to me a most enviable long frock. At high school we still made do with ordinary dances, called 'socials', in the Masonic Hall.

Self-sacrifice is something looked on rather askance in the liberated atmosphere of the eighties. It can be decried as a sort of martyr syndrome, damaging to self-esteem and self-realisation. The plain truth is that anyone who has children is going to have to give up something, just to make room for the newcomer. It would never have occurred to my mother, for instance, that this meant loss of her own identity, whatever it might have done to material comforts. She kept her individual tastes and pastimes and philosophies, her claim to her own life as something valued and valuable, her place in a community. She always maintained she had chosen to have children, and didn't regret it. If at times her life was physically hard, and economically a bit precarious, then the same was true of almost all her friends and neighbours. In her own way, she was one of the more liberated of women; refusing always to follow trends or to adopt any attitudes that she had not carefully thought through for herself. In her old age, her ability to draw upon inner resources of intellect and experience and a practical kind of imagination stood her in good stead.

I didn't consciously seek to model myself upon my mother, but I did share with her a deep longing for personal fulfilment. At sixteen, I saw this in terms of getting a university education, travelling ('the world is your oyster' was one of her sayings), writing books and, at some future date, getting married and having children of my own. That there were other kinds of fulfilment was a discovery reserved for much later.

Fourth Year brought new subjects and new teachers. My early interest in Geometry having died a natural death, and not being replaced in my affections by that peculiar study called Trigonometry, I chose to do the least exacting of scientific subjects — General Maths. (The Powers-That-Were sternly insisted that we could not ignore Maths altogether.) That left room, after English, French, Latin and History, for one more field of study, so I took Economics. I found it utterly dull, the laws of supply and demand being as seemingly irrelevant as the study of triangles, and slithered by through learning by rote bits of a textbook quite without charm. That quality, however, was later supplied by a handsome new male teacher, whose appearance at least brightened up the classroom.

Then there was the new French master. It was understood that I would do French honours in Fifth Year, as well as the English variety, so I was expected to put some extra work into both subjects. Rex Crawford became a kind of idol to me for those two years, especially in the honours class, which consisted of from one pupil to a maximum of three. This was élitism indeed, and I revelled in it. How many pupils now, under a completely different matriculation system, get that sort of heady individual attention? I had it, also, in the tiny English honours group, and in the Latin class, where Nancy J. and I exchanged banter with Miss Chandler over the translating of Cicero's *Pro Milone* and the tragic affair of Virgil's *Dido and Aeneas*. With Rex Crawford, I learnt how to write French essays using the idiomatic phrases looked for by Leaving Certificate examiners, and struggled with *Dictée*, trying to guess where the punctuation marks ought to go. Even though I joined the *Alliance Française*, my pronunciation remained obstinately Australian. I was to meet Rex Crawford again many years later, when he became headmaster of North Sydney Boys High School, where my two sons were pupils.

It was probably my new English teacher, however, who had the most lasting effect on my career. Her name was Thelma Schardt. The staff photo of 1944 shows her staring away from the camera with a quizzical expression. She was brisk, emphatic and challenging, and it was the challenge that I needed. English to that point had been for me as the proverbial breeze. It was a matter of reading set books, learning bits by heart, writing character sketches, and, in one's own writing, using various literary devices and a sprinkling of imagery to dress up ideas and descriptions. In a word, my writing was largely derivative. And in my reading, I admired novelists such as Galsworthy and Dickens, and backed off from any but the more entertaining of contemporary ones. Miss Schardt (we knew, because we made it our business to find out, our teachers' first names, but never used them in class) insisted that I read, for instance, the novels of Virginia Woolf. I was, to say the least, baffled and astonished. I couldn't decide if *The Waves* was a novel at all. Novels had recognisable plots, orderly progression and characters who *did* things, instead of making all their thoughts public and thereby interrupting what story there was.

160

My teacher said my tastes were conservative. She was right. My later encounters with Huxley and Joyce and Lawrence were more in the nature of duty than honest appreciation, though I learnt to analyse and dissect them as required. Forty years later, I still count among my favourite novelists Galsworthy, Henry Handel Richardson, Martin Boyd and Tolstoy. Perhaps it's because all deal with interesting families, with characters both memorable and identifiable, and also because they are classic in form. Shape in novels has always appealed to me, likewise the ancient unities of time, place and plot. And I like a sprinkling of that truly witty humour which distinguishes, for instance, the immortal doings of the Forsytes. I think I felt, even at sixteen or seventeen, that Virginia Woolf's characters were taking it all a bit seriously, and that the result was rather depressing. In fact, I was neither budding intellectual nor academic; I was wary, too, of all that seething emotion. As antidote, I delighted in my first year at university in Stella Gibbons' *Cold Comfort Farm* — the origin of an irreverent catch-phrase — 'Something nasty in the woodshed'. My mother, for one, was of the opinion that novelists should beware of exploring their 'woodsheds' too obsessively. Or explicitly. I can imagine what she would think of some of the TV and movie offerings of the eighties. But I think she would criticise them on the grounds that they are simply boring, un-literary, and ill-balanced, as much as on any moral basis. Her morality was of the kind which forbears to take any action which would harm others, and she would support, I'm sure, the concept of responsibility in entertainment.

In our general English class we studied *The Tempest* and *Hamlet*, and all forms of lyric poetry. Several of us were appointed to the editorial committee for the school magazine, *The Bellbird*; I have a photo of this sedate group, girls in tunics and blazers, white socks and black

161

shoes, the boys in sports jackets, long trousers, shirts and ties. There is hardly a smile among the six of us, but we didn't in fact take our duties too earnestly. Fourth Year was understood to be a social year, before the harder grind of the Leaving Certificate. We moved about in a large group, within which boys and girls paired off in a series of combinations which gradually became settled for the rest of our time in high school. Very few lasted beyond that.

Our gathering place after school was the Tourist Milk Bar in Gosford's main street. One of the few remaining landmarks of the forties, its interior has been redecorated, while its long enclosed shape is the same. In 1944 it was modern indeed — chrome-shiny, with upholstered booths seating six (or even eight, with an agreeable squash), and potplants and mirrors. You could watch, and listen to, your chocolate or caramel milkshake (or malted, if you could afford it) being blended; and on hotter days, perhaps after the boys had played a Rugby League game at Grahame Park, you could opt for an icecream soda, usually in a vivid shade of green. We were a generation consuming large amounts of then barely mentioned cholesterol — eggs and milk for breakfast, homemade butter on sandwiches at lunchtime, cream on dessert at dinner, and quite often cocoa for supper. Fortunately, there were oranges and various summer fruits in abundance, too. One of my out-of-school tasks was making the butter, a laborious process when the cream refused to 'come', but satisfying when you reached the stages of shaping the firming substance between two wooden pats. Milkshakes, too, were part of the ritual of going to the movies either in afternoon or evening; less pleasing was the ride home on the 'picture bus', generally packed to the doors.

162

My accepted male partner at this time was Bill. Son of the school Science master, he became boys' school-captain and one of the stars of our talented and successful first-grade football team. Tall and lanky and with a shy but cheerful grin, he had a natural humility and gentleness that made him one of the most pleasant of companions. We went bikeriding at weekends, and he came back to our home for supper. We danced together at socials, of which the biggest and best was Fourth Year's Farewell to Fifth. It was a genuine boy-and-girl friendship, and not at all passionate. We were both too shy. He went on to study Pharmacy, and years later we met in a South Coast town where he had his chemist's shop. Both married by then — to other partners — we renewed our acquaintance briefly, as comfortably and practically as when it had begun. It has always seemed regrettable to me that high-school friendships, so close and enjoyable at the time, do not usually endure for a life span. This was especially so when we grew up in a country town, from which many of us departed in search of careers.

All-girl friendships were equally important. It was with Beryl that, early in our final year, I had one of the happiest holidays of my growing time. Before Christmas, to earn pocket money for the occasion, I worked in a Gosford store, selling handkerchiefs, scent and scarves, feeling quite grown-up and independent, even when the hours seemed long and my feet hurt. Beryl's uncle had a guest house on the Myall Lakes, and we were to spend a fortnight there in January.

My geographical horizons still didn't extend beyond Sydney in the south, and Wyong in the north. The journey to Legge's Camp, then, was adventure indeed. First we took the train to Newcastle, staying overnight with one of Beryl's married sisters. Always somewhat uneasy at sharing a house with strangers, I was no great dinner-table conversationalist. I was also in the grip of the old anticipatory excitement, which became evident next morning when I succumbed to travel-sickness on the bus trip to Bulahdelah. It was the perennial problem of reality breaking in on the romantic imagination.

But once Uncle Harry (a lean, tough, silent man, a pioneer of the district's development long before 'tourism' was even a word) had met us in his car, and driven us across paddocks and through the summer-morning expanse of eucalypt forest and paperbark scrub, and the roof of the guest house arose at the edge of the lake, I sensed not only recovery, but discovery. By lunch time, any traces of either home sickness or the travel variety had fled with the early mists dissolving on Alum Mountain.

It was a remote place. The track from near Bulahdelah was the only access road, and all other traffic was by boat, north past Violet Hill (could there be a lovelier name?), east to the coastal fringe, or south via Lemontree Passage to Tea Gardens and Port Stephens. The two-storeyed house, with wide verandahs, stood on a little rise above the she-oaks and the jetty; there was around it not so much a garden as a small park with shrubbery and woods and reedy glades soft with pine needles. Every path seemed eventually to lead down to the shore, where crabs scuttled over pebbles, and the water was cool and clear as crystal — for there was nothing to make it otherwise.

I had brought with me a few books as preparatory reading for the English honours course. Of them I remember nothing but a few poems. I can recall encountering for the first time Gerard Manley Hopkins' 'Inversnaid', but this hardly seemed appropriate ('What would the world be, once bereft of wet and of wildness?') because we seemed to have no 'wet and wild' weather at all. Other so-called modern poets in the collection were English ones such as Robert Bridges and Alice Meynell and old acquaintance Rupert Brooke, but it was an Irishman who gave the greatest satisfaction. Sitting in a boat moored at the jetty one lazy summer afternoon, I came across Yeats' 'Lake Isle of Innisfree': 'For always night and day I hear lake water lapping with low sounds by the shore.'

It was a triumph, to find a poem that matched a mood and a setting. But sometimes I got it back to front, chose a likely looking poem and then tried to summon up the appropriate mood. This proved to be especially hazardous later, when the poems were centred on romantic love. It was as if I thought it obligatory to experience as soon as possible this enticing feeling the poets wrote of in such delicious images.

I have read somewhere that of all sensory stimuli, the one with the strongest power of association is the olfactory — the sense of smell. Certainly, the scent of the bush, for instance, on a warm summer afternoon is one many Australians would associate with the climate of childhood, and all its outdoor delights. It may be a cliché that, when overseas, Australians can be cast into deepest nostalgia when they smell burning gum leaves or wattle blooming, but it is also true. I find it equally true, however, that what the ear encounters, from early childhood onwards, can evoke all kinds of spontaneous recollections. The sounds of pounding surf are now to me less appealing than Yeats' 'lapping of lake water'. The association probably began when, as children, we spent so much time swimming in and playing around the Wamberal lagoon, but it was intensified at Myall Lakes, and met again throughout the years until in 1980 I enjoyed the sounds of lake water on the western shore of the Sea of Galilee, both in calm and in storm. It's a harmony, too, readily rediscovered a few metres from where I now live, among inland tidal waterways.

The other sound redolent of both then and now is that

of the wind in the she-oaks. It is at its sighing, singing best when the summer wind blows — the nor'easter that is both salty and fresh, and a welcome visitor on a hot afternoon. More vigorous is the noise of the big pine trees, of which so many grew around another guest-house of loved memory — at Blackheath, in the Blue Mountains, where in the sixties and the early seventies we took the three children for the August–September holidays. Then it was usually the west wind, and for the now-grown children the sound of it in the pines has always spoken of clean-swept late winter mornings, of exploring bush trails and riding pack-ponies in the Megalong Valley.

Beryl and I pottered about the nearer stretches of the lake in a rowing boat, sometimes fishing, but more often gently investigating the little coves and headlands, or diving off the boat for a swim. On other days, we were taken for excursions on Uncle Harry's launch, as far afield as Mungo Brush and Tamboy, then a tiny fishing village between lake and sea. We crossed the sandhills and gathered shells on a great empty ocean-beach, and looked south to a place called Seal Rocks, which after a much later visit in the seventies, became the 'Chapel Rocks' of my book *The October Child*.

It was a sociable time, too. Staying at Legges's Camp was a family with several girls and one very small boy, called John. At two-and-a-half he was a delight to me, and I became a kind of informal nursemaid. Entertaining young children appealed to me in my teens; at home I had still played, until I was about fourteen, with Betty's and Ronny's little brother, another John. I liked the ease with which you could enter with them into places of make-believe, and let imagination roam free. These two were particularly charming and amiable children, and no doubt I romanticised their childhood as I had done my own. In my later student days, when I did some baby-sitting for the remarkable sum of five

166

shillings an hour, I discovered that by no means all young children were sweet, innocent and well-disposed towards oneself. It came as a shock. Even the stories I wrote rarely featured any kind of villains. The worst things the young characters ever did were disobeying parental instructions for a brief period. Nor were they ever really ugly, or fat, or spotty, even in adolescence. They were allowed to be poor on occasion, but it was a most genteel sort of poverty.

On a superb January late-afternoon we went by boat to Violet Hill, climbed its grassy slopes, and came back down for an evening meal by a driftwood fire. At twilight the wind dropped, and the quiet and the peace were deep as the lake itself. A few people fished from rowing boats, but there were no outboard motors to shatter the calm. I knew we would soon be going home, and I would have taken it all with me, if I could.

J. B. Priestley — whose *Good Companions* I read that same year, and whose plays, such as *I Have Been Here Before* and *Dangerous Corner*, I later found fascinating — says that in recollection, our personal experiences are enhanced; in retrospect, we know a keen joy that is not so much memory of an actuality, as a distillation of it. Such 'improved' re-living of experience might, he thinks, be part of an eternity where, of course, linear time, or any time, does not exist. Perhaps, too, my own capacity to enjoy, and to mourn, as much in recollection and anticipation as in present actuality is related to all this. Certainly the child who could be breathless with imagined glimpses of a forthcoming fancy dress ball or school picnic, and then afterwards try to recreate the wonders in play, grew into the sixteen-year-old who, going home from the Myall Lakes holiday, grieved because it was so implacably over.

But present actuality had other charms. During those

167

same holidays, I stayed for a few days with Nancy S. and her cousin Judy at Nancy's parents' beach house at Terrigal. Set on the little promontory between the ocean shore and the mouth of the lagoon, with a front verandah from which you could gaze north to the then-untouched cliffs of Forrester's Beach, and south to Terrigal's Haven, the Skillion, and beyond, it was made all the more delightful by the presence of two British sailors to whom Nancy's family were offering hospitality. Briefly and mostly in silence, I adored the older, quieter and less extroverted of the pair. His name was Thomas, and in recollection he seems to have been in his late twenties. By contrast, Bill, coming to visit on his bicycle, was a mere boy.

He remained a faithful one, however, all through that year, the last of high school.

XV

It was a year, as we were more than once reminded, of both privilege and responsibility, and not only at school, but at home. There, however, the responsibilities hardly weighed upon me. During the week, I was the only child still at home, and it was understood that I would spend most of my time studying. Always at my most receptive in the mornings, I used to get up early and work on the verandah, with birds and cats for company. Our dog, loyal friend of our childhood, had died of old age, with the minimum of fuss as if wishing not unduly to disturb us. Across the yard, among the peach and plum and nectarine trees, the hens clucked and pottered, but they, too, would soon be gone. Both my parents were nearing sixty, and plans were already afoot to give up the farm and build a new, smaller house further up the hill.

At school, matters other than academic absorbed our interest. Who would be prefects, who boys' captain, and who the girls'? I was gratified to be made a prefect, if only because all my friends were, and we were granted the dizzy privilege of a prefects' room — a small apartment on the top floor, into which, from time to time, we managed to smuggle those others of our year who were not regarded as prefect material. We were, in fact, a free-and-easy and cohesive group, all aware (how could we have been otherwise?) of the grave importance of getting our Leaving Certificates, but happily enjoying our position — literally and figuratively — as 'top of the school'. I was not one to take prefects' duties too seriously; it was fun to wear the badge, and stand on stairways to make sure (theoretically) that lesser beings didn't proceed two steps at a time, and try to organise the bus queue (an absurd assignment). It was more pleasing to feel, occasionally, on less formal terms with the staff, even when they carried on about setting examples to the rest of the school, and demanded more decorum in the prefects' room.

I hadn't really thought I wanted to be girls' captain until I didn't make it. Then the loss of status and apparent worthiness seemed keen — for a week or so. Prefects were chosen by schoolmates, but captains by the staff. What essential ingredient was lacking in me, then, that the teachers found me wanting? Could it have been my ineptitude at all forms of sport? (When I travelled with school teams, it was either as reserve or scorer.) However, I became vice-captain, which was a nice compromise, all the more acceptable because not only was my mate Bill the boys' captain, but my friend Nancy the girls'. Nancy, her cousin Judy, Beryl and myself became a foursome; a group within a group.

Nancy had a steadiness and a reliability which I lacked; hence, perhaps, her appointment as captain. Leadership quality is elusive, an attribute of spirit and personality as much as of mind and intellect. It commands respect, and is quite recognisable even when beyond definition. Mostly, in our day, it was summed up in the one word: 'character'. Maybe today it might be said that such an individual had 'got it all together' — which, after all, is a simple statement about integrity. It would have been obvious to me that, in any life-threatening crisis at school (a most unlikely possibility), the rest of us would have turned to Nancy for help. They would hardly have looked to me; I might have had the ability to select a gerund instead of a gerundive, or give a definition of 'meiosis', but making practical snap decisions has never been my forte.

With my perpetual curiosity about other people's families, I was impressed by Nancy's. Her father and uncle owned Gosford's biggest hardware store. Now run by a cousin and other relatives, it is still flourishing. There were during my childhood and adolescence the usual uncharitable and envious rumours of racial origins and so forth; the older members of Nancy's family were often referred to as 'the Jews', a pejorative term used of anyone with a faintly Semitic appearance. Such nonsense, said my mother sturdily; it didn't matter where their forefathers came from (our own, for instance, had probably been at one time living on handfuls of oatmeal in Scotland, or digging peat in the wilds of Ireland), but what did matter was that Nancy's grandfather had made good in a new country, and founded a large family wherein the menfolk provided most diligently for all their relatives, who were scattered around the district.

I enjoyed visiting Nancy's home on the hill opposite the railway station, as well as the holiday house at Terrigal, but I can't recall being particularly covetous of either. I still preferred being a country-dweller, rather than a 'townie', and as to the rest, Nancy was ever-generous in sharing with us the holiday accommodation, and even the two saddle horses she owned. And I liked her mother, a gentle person, who in that last year of school encouraged her daughter's friendships all the more because of her own incurable illness. She died the following year of cancer, in the same form that took Nancy's own life when she was only forty. Almost impossibly, it seemed, Nancy's twenty-year-old son, Michael, likewise died of cancer, some six or seven years after his mother. Nancy's husband, Cedric, the likeable Englishman who had been one of the sailors entertained at the Terrigal house, was left with one daughter and — one imagines — a lot of shattered dreams.

It is a truism to say that in our lives we cannot, and do not need to, see around corners. There were no real shadows as we scrambled, struggled, laughed and played our way through Fifth Year. If there was any special quality in my friendship with Nancy, it was my unspoken sense of her strength — a rather quiet solidity that reminded me, I suppose, of my mother's, just as they had in common a keen sense of humour.

There are some of us who seek consistency and reliability in others throughout our lives, and, if we are so blessed, find it just when we most need it. Such relationships have no sexual component, but for most of my life I have found such strengths more often in fellow-women than in men. It's as if one being seeks its complement in another, a process which has much to do with the longings of the spirit. We live now in a time and place, however, where such loves and longings are regarded with suspicion or derision — as I found to my cost when I used such a theme in *A Candle for St Antony*.

Every now and then there was a serious side to my 1945 experiences which had nothing to do with the studies I was closely pursuing in order to win a university scholarship. (It was never a question of *which* university — there was only one, Sydney.) We were not yet past the second term when America dropped the atom bomb on Hiroshima. Amid the first loud rejoicings that now the war with Japan would soon be over, and our servicemen and women (especially the prisoners-of-war) would come home, there were murmurings that disturbed me. Probably they came mostly from my horrified mother, with here and there a dissentient voice among the school staff. It was also by

172

instinct that I grasped the magnitude of the event, though not until much later did I understand that my own generation had come to the end of something. For sixteen years, in spite of the shadows of two world wars, we had lived without the knowledge that humanity had the sure means with which to destroy itself; and now nothing would ever be quite the same again. I have the deepest sympathy for today's teenagers, so many of whom have to grapple with a kind of existential impermanence that was so remote from us in our relatively sheltered early youth.

'Halcyon days' — named for the fabled kingfisher able to charm wind and wave in order to breed in its floating nest — were reality for many of us, and in my own case this was largely due to the efforts of parents and other elders. I still believed that such days could last for ever.

There were celebrations in May and in August for the ending of the war in the different hemispheres. In May, I was staying with the family of our friends Betty and Ronny, in the 'Green Gables' house across the valley, while my mother was in hospital in Sydney. She had an operation for what was generally called — *sotto voce* — 'women's troubles', and it was the first time I remember her having any physical ailment at all. She seemed to have never been troubled even by colds or flu, and scoffed somewhat at my father's tendency to complain of a minor malaise of any description. Yet not long after that stay in hospital in 1945, she began to develop signs and symptoms of the rheumatoid arthritis that was to change the course of her life.

In August, all of us from the high school attended a thanksgiving for peace service in the Memorial Park, so beautifully placed on the little bluff overlooking Brisbane Water, from the old town wharf to the far line of the Woy Woy foreshore, and the crouched ancient shape of Lion Island, guardian of Broken Bay. We sang

Kipling's 'Recessional', with its own sad, still relevant musings upon man, war and God:

> *All valiant dust that builds on dust,*
> *And guarding, calls not Thee to guard —.*

Somehow, post-Hiroshima, it was not the spontaneous, relieved kind of celebration that it had been in May, when we had a holiday, and Betty and I wandered in Gosford's main street listening to bands playing.

Of course, there was rejoicing when the service men and women came home, and the prisoners-of-war were set free. I no doubt saw it all in the usual romantic glow, believing, I suppose, that they all took up their lives where they had left off, and lived happily ever after. Amongst those who would have returned to Sydney that spring or summer, was a man who some thirty years later wrote a book about his experiences in camps on the Burma Railway, and — as has happened with some writers throughout my life — became a kind of personal friend, although I never actually met him. His name is Stan Arneill, and the book is *One Man's War*. It's a first-hand account of survival, grief and that kind of gritty, dogged, simple and persisting faith which grows and triumphs through the worst adversity. He still marches on Anzac Day, in the ranks of that Eighth Division which is honoured, as it passes so depleted, by no cheers, but a deep silence.

Other thoughts on personal survival, triumph and tragedy must have been at least briefly aroused in me when I saw newspaper photos of the European concentration camps. Like the use of the atom bomb, they posed a threat I felt as an uneasy stirring beneath girlish, rose-coloured dreams.

But one dream persisted, and flourished. I was still writing, sometimes poetry (highly derivative, owing

174

more than a little to the works of Tennyson and Brooke, in particular, and conventional as to metre and rhyme), and sometimes short stories or descriptive pieces of an effusive nature. These had little to do directly with school English, where I dutifully constructed bits of metaphor and antithesis and hyperbole, wrote précis of this and that, and made up sentences to show the difference between words like 'ordnance' and 'ordinance', or 'deprecate' and 'depreciate' — most of which I've never forgotten. And, of course, we studied the set books (which, I'm afraid, I *have* forgotten) and wrote character studies and dissected plots. The Shakespeare play for that year's Leaving Certificate was *Macbeth*; we saw a performance of it as the Independent Theatre in North Sydney, and the prefects' room and adjacent corridor resounded to cries of 'Out, damned spot!' and 'Double, double, toil and trouble', while the boys had spirited sword fights with whatever came to hand. The play's violence — especially as reproduced on stage by Doris Fitton and company — seemed to obscure the fact that it had real historical background, which came alive for me only recently, when I read Dorothy Dunnett's superb recreation of the whole period and its people in *King Hereafter*. Indeed, I have always preferred to glean my understanding of history from imaginative reconstructions, and consequently scraped through Leaving History with a bare pass.

In English, the icing on my cake was still the writing of compositions, or essays if the topics were appealing enough. I had, however, become more anxious and self-conscious about it than in the carefree, scribbling days of childhood. I wanted to know if I was good enough to be, in future, a 'real' writer. Thelma Schardt was encouraging, as was my mother, but what of outside professional opinion? It was my mother who, sensing my doubts, sent a short story of mine to none other than the editor of the *Bulletin*, seeking not publication but comment. I have still a kindly letter from John Fountain, beginning: 'My personal opinion is that your daughter's work shows promise. She seems to have plenty of imagination and a nice feeling for language. He went on, very sensibly, to advise against trying to get anything published for at least the next nine years. In fact, I *was* twenty-five when I wrote my first full-length novel with a view (not fulfilled) to publication.

The short story submitted is in what was for me an unusually subdued style, with the minimum of florid description of landscapes. For the first time I concentrated on character, and human feelings, and brought in people who were, or were meant to be, adults rather than children. One of them was an Aborigine, which surprises me now, as I look back; I can recall very few occasions when I met Aborigines in our district. It's less mysterious that I should have chosen to write of any member of a minority group, however, because of my mother's championing of their rights.

With, so to speak, official sanction of my writing ambitions, I went into our last high school term with confidence. While I was still aiming for an Arts degree, I was allowed to look at other options, including journalism and librarianship. I remember going for an interview at the Australian Broadcasting Commission, as candidate for a cadet reporter's job, but I have reservations about journalism — quite rightly, I think. As my mother observed, the way of a female in the world of the media (then a little-used term) was hard; she was generally expected to confine her reporting to women's interests, which meant cooking, sewing, child-raising, and notes on local social events — hardly writing at all, as I saw it.

The last term was a heady mix of study, last-minute revision of essentials such as French idioms and irregular verbs, Latin prose 'handy hints', and bound-to-be-useful quotations from our English set texts, moments of panic, and much sentiment because we were all so soon to be separated and scattered like sheep. One final day before study-leave and exams was our recognised 'muck-up' day; modestly, we paraded about the school corridors for a while, then went for a picnic up to President's Hill, behind the new buildings that were to become Gosford Hospital. There was also an evening social, the traditional Fourth Year's Farewell to Fifth, held in the Masonic Hall. It was understood that you should have a new dress for this occasion, even if it was your only new out-of-school garment for the year. Mine (chosen from Hordern Brothers catalogue) was a silk floral creation with yellow trim. I had grown my hair that year, and for special outings wore it in two plaits tied up around my head. I considered this rather romantic (even though I had the kind of fine slippery hair that never stayed put), and befitting a future university student. In fact, it rather gave me the air of an austere intellectual, which I wasn't, and may have inspired the verse inscribed on my place card: 'Our whole dignity lies but in this — the faculty of thinking.' I have no idea where it came from, but liked its philosophical tone.

We paired off for the dancing, in our standard arrangements. With Bill I performed the Gipsy Tap and the Pride of Erin and the Destiny Waltz; the Gipsy Tap, especially, was something of a hazard with Bill's long legs covering enormous measures of polished floor. In the Progressive Barn Dance we occasionally danced with members of the staff, which was both alarming and adventurous. And there were some, male and female, to whom I was genuinely sorry to say farewell, like the trio who had had the greatest influence on my school career — the teachers of English, French and Latin.

The last dance was always a Jazz Waltz, with dimmed lights. And after that we sang 'Auld Lang Syne',

177

whereupon the more susceptible of the girls cried, although I wasn't among them. I did, however, try to feel suitably sad and solemn, unsure, as I was so often to be, of what was real emotion and what I was expected to feel. I had the fiction-writer's tendency, too, to see myself as part of the plot of a novel, while about one-quarter of me was standing back observing and assessing — taking notes for future reference. Nor did I really feel sad; what lay ahead seemed far too interesting and appealing.

We must have been well prepared for our final exams, as I can remember that the actuality was not as taxing as the trials had been. My deepest doubts concerned the General Maths paper; fortunately, I never knew how close I came to failing, but it must have been a near thing. Some of my answers to problems looked distinctly peculiar, even to me. Then I had the unusual experience of sitting for the two Honours papers either solo (for French) or as part of a pair (for English). I remember the extraordinary hush of the upstairs room in which we sat, with, far away in the distance as if I were already geographically removed, the sounds of the rest of the school going about its business. There was a sense, when it was over, of anti-climax, of exhaustion in limbo, a vague wonder as to whether, after all, we could have satisfied those anonymous authority figures who would actually (could it be possible?) peruse what we had so painstakingly written, and mark it accordingly.

Lethargy dispersed, however, when four of us took the fortnight's holiday we had been planning for months — Nancy, Judy, Beryl and I camping in the boathouse below Nancy's parents' Terrigal summer home. The boathouse was beneath coral trees beside the gate that led to the lagoon, and was furnished with bunk beds and kerosene lamps, while meals were usually taken

178

outdoors. Often for dinner we went up to the big house, but as a rule we had our independence, with the entire beach as playground, and even the two horses pastured nearby to ride as we chose. We swam and boated and walked; on one of our tramps, south almost to Macmaster's Beach, we discovered the big cave I was to describe eleven years later in my first published children's book, *Patterson's Track*.

There were young males staying at the house — Nancy's cousins and friends and visiting servicemen — and some mild frolicking in and out of ocean and lagoon seemed in order. But we were still shy as violets, and liable to fits of blushing and confusion, particularly when the males were adult. There was never any question of a male invading the privacy of our boathouse unless on the most practical of pretexts, such as wanting to borrow the boat or bringing food supplies. The light-hearted (mostly) diary I kept during the holiday records faithfully the details of almost every meal we ate; appetites were healthy after all that study and exam-taking. I note also the number of times the horses escaped from their various pastures, and how we sought them, bridles and lumps of stale bread in hand, along the then-leafy and dusty roads and tracks at the head of the lagoon. We would ride them home bareback, Nancy on her high-spirited and handsome 'Fella', who bit people, such as me, whom he disliked, and myself on the more amiable 'Blondie', who once decided to gallop and dropped me off on the way. Once or twice we rode over to Avoca on the old Tramway Road, which ended among bottlebrush and ti-tree on the sands north of Avoca Lake. And stopped, occasionally, to gaze at the bright summer ocean and talk, mostly of life; once of death and immortality. Later, I wrote a poem for Nancy (though I'm not sure if I ever showed it to her) recording the occasion in nostalgic style: 'We ask each other what death can mean, While loving life'.

Nancy did not yet know of her mother's illness, at least consciously. She knew, however, that there seemed to be no firm plans for her future career, while the rest of us chattered on about teaching (Beryl), or nursing (Judy) or university, for me. She had talents in both music and art, which the rest of us lacked; and in my diary I observe, somewhat priggishly, that while Beryl and I rapidly gave up on trying to sketch Terrigal Haven, 'Nancy persevered, the result being a most amazing painting, quite good, really'. She also went regularly into Gosford for her music lessons, while the rest of us lazed and lounged, and in the afternoon heat took the rowing boat up to the headwaters of the lagoon, punting about in the reeds or sheltering in the quiet under the road bridge. There seems to have been little traffic; it was still early December, and we were delightfully aware that for most of humanity, the school holidays had not yet begun.

One article of furniture that the boathouse possessed was a packing-case bookshelf. Released from the compulsion to read 'set books', we could indulge in novels to our heart's content. I also had with me a copy of Vera Brittain's *Testament of Youth* which my mother had recommended. I remember lying out on the sand dunes on a blue and white, nor'easterly afternoon, weeping over the doomed love-affair between Vera and her Roland. This wasn't fiction; this was real life. Nor was it hard to see why my mother found it such a compelling book, for it recalled so much of her personal tragedy, and echoed her own views on the nature of war and peace. What appealed most to me, however, at the age of just seventeen, was Vera's account of life in pre-World War II Oxford. It seemed the essence of all the wonder of the 'city of dreaming spires', and shaped my own dreams of university life. That, I told myself, was just how it would be — ancient stone buildings (though rare bouts of practicality told me that Sydney

University was less than a hundred years old), acres of books, stimulating lectures, endless intellectual discussion and, most of all, deep and congenial friendships, culminating perhaps in the meeting with *him*, the ideal male companion with whom I would share the rest of my life. Then, of course, we would have beautiful children, and I would still have time to write the Great Australian Novel.

Fortunately, at that stage one of the others would invade my nest in the sandhills and suggest a swim, a surf, a row in the boat . . .

I had some poetry with me, too — an anthology called *Other Men's Flowers*, compiled by Field Marshal Viscount Wavell. It was, and is still, an excellent book for dipping into, a favourite occupation of mine sternly discouraged in later English studies, when a writer's works were meant to be pored over in depth and at length. Wavell had a fondness for the poems of Chesterton and Belloc, Browning and Kipling; I approved of the two former, especially the extravagant rhythms and rhymes and images of 'Lepanto' (historically inaccurate, but who cared?) and the prancing evocations of 'Tarantella' ('Do you remember an Inn, Miranda?'). Years afterwards I borrowed the name of Belloc's companion for the heroine of a novel of my own, all the more inspired because it had its origins in a Latin gerund. I dodged most of Browning, and found much of Kipling dated and rather dull; I would return rather to Keats' 'Ode to a Nightingale' or Fitzgerald's 'Rubaiyat' (' . . . and Thou Beside me singing in the Wilderness . . . '). Now and then I would look upon the first poem in the collection, and be baffled:

> *But with unhurrying chase,*
> *And unperturbèd pace,*
> *Deliberate speed, majestic instancy,*
> *They beat — and a Voice beat —*

Most of 'The Hound of Heaven' I could barely understand, and I wasn't sure that I wanted to. What this Francis Thompson seemed to be implying was that all the good things of life — such as friendships and laughter and beautiful landscapes and even 'little children's eyes' — were not only transient, but perfidious — a horrific thought. Certainly, Keats and Wordsworth and Tennyson and company were given to melancholy musings too, but without specific mention of 'hounds' dogging their footsteps. Who *was* this mysterious creature who dared to say: 'I am He whom thou seekest'?

No more than in the following year, when in English One we studied the poems of Gerard Manley Hopkins, did I connect this with anything I might have learnt in Sunday School or Confirmation class. Nostalgic gloom was one thing, despair another, and few seventeen-year-olds in my own time were acquainted with the latter. More than thirty years passed before 'The Hound of Heaven', along with Hopkins' 'Carrion Comfort' and others of his 'Dark sonnets', The Book of Job and some of the Psalms became for me required reading. Then, too, I read of Thompson's personal life, tormented and alienated, and ceased to be surprised at his intensity.

Another book that was a favourite about this time was Axel Munthe's *The Story of San Michele*. I'm not sure what attracted me so strongly to this autobiography, although I can recall being fascinated by his accounts of the restoration of his seemingly enchanted villa on the Isle of Capri. The notion that some people in their lifetimes could create and dwell in an 'enchanted place' always had great appeal, especially as antidote to the likes of Francis Thompson, who seemed to be telling me so emphatically that there was no such thing as 'earthly paradise'. Places such as Munthe's San Michele, Thoreau's Walden, or even, in children's books, L. M. Boston's 'Green Knowe' or Frances Hodgson Burnett's 'Secret Garden' have now become crystallised for me as spiritual more than actual homes, for the essence of their specialness seems to be that, in fact and inevitably, one must sooner or later depart from them. The joy is in having been there, and in recollecting them, and their delight. Munthe certainly had his gloomy moments. I copied out some of his lines and kept them, I don't know why: 'Happiness we can only find in ourselves. It is a waste of time to seek for it from others. Few have any to spare . . . '

I didn't believe a word of that, as we packed up and left the boathouse, with Christmas ahead, then January bringing its exam results, and February with — I hoped — preparations for university. I was figuratively on tiptoe, ready to marvel, like Shakespeare's Miranda, at the 'brave new world'.

XVI

It seemed at first that the only brave new world I was going to encounter was the one giving its name to Huxley's novel. And that I disliked; novelists, in my opinion, were overstepping the mark in being thus morbid. It was worse than Virginia Woolf.

Reality classed once again with romance. To be sure, the university quadrangle was lovely, the copper roof of Fisher Library shone in the sun, and I liked the carillon. But I was crashingly, mortifyingly lonely, all the more so because the entire Arts Faculty premises were crammed with people. It was 1946, the war was over and the returned service men and women were flocking to the university on Repatriation grants. Not only were they all strangers, but they looked alarmingly old and self-assured. (Many of them were nothing of the kind, as I found out later.) As for students of my own age, they all seemed already gathered in chummy, merry little groups, hailing, no doubt, from city schools and proceeding to university en masse. Further, they gave the impression of knowing just where they were supposed to be, and how to get there. And most of them didn't carry briefcases like mine, but bore in their confident arms looseleaf binders and a textbook or two.

My mother had warned me that at university you were on your own, academically at least. Not here would I find familiar teachers to direct my studies every step of the way, and tell me precisely what to do for homework.

Such members of the faculty as I had actually met, during registration, were as remote as any gods of classic antiquity — especially Professor Henning, head of the French Department. He was forbidding. You were expected, he said, to be completely fluent in 'his' language to the extent of being able to think in it; otherwise you would be wasting your time, and that of the staff by implication. Such a stern lack of encouragement at once reduced me to a state wherein I was barely able to think in my native English, let alone French. My mother pointed out, however, that some professors were like that, jealously preserving the standards of their own departments, and that his bark was probably worse than his bite. There she was quite wrong.

I had, it appeared, done all the right things — earned my two honours, (first class in English, second in French), an 'A' in Latin, and three passes, which total was enough to win me both an exhibition and a modest university scholarship. I had just missed winning entry to the Womens College, which place I had visited and loved on sight. It could have been, I thought, Vera Brittain's Somerville, ivy-clad walls, sequestered garden nooks, cloisters, common rooms and all. I had a pretty vision of myself flourishing in these academic groves, amazing fellow-students with my wit, charm and creativity.

At that time I didn't give much thought, as, I later discovered, so many of the aforementioned fellow students did, to another advantage of being in College; it was handily placed near those other residences, St Paul's and St Andrew's, for the boys. (Wesley was known to be Methodist, and restricted, while St John's and Sancta Sophia, being Catholic, were more than somewhat set apart.) I was certainly not uninterested in the male half of the student body, but in the beginning I yearned for a solid support group of other girls, such as

185

I had known in high school.

When the Womens College dream dissolved, there remained the very important matter of where, in Sydney, I was going to live. My Waverton aunts were approached, tentatively, but, not surprisingly, in view of their age, they were not enthusiastic about having one more adolescent niece as boarder. Nor, I think, was I too keen myself. The Waverton house and garden had been a significant part of my childhood, a holiday home associated with outings to the Zoo and Manly and the Botanic Gardens, and playing with brother and sister and cousins in the park, but far from ideal as residence for a university student. As usual, my ideas were on a much grander scale, and the furthest thing from my mind (though not from my parents') was a consideration of financial difficulties.

It was through my mother's connections with the C.W.A. that a solution was found — expensive, but just feasible. That year the C.W.A. set up its own hostel for students, female only, in Bayswater Road, King's Cross, and I was accepted.

At first it seemed a far cry from the cloisters of the Womens College. King's Cross in 1946 was still, at least in some parts, fairly respectable, confined as it was among highly regarded areas such as Potts' Point, Elizabeth Bay and Darling Point. And Bayswater Road headed away from The Cross, down the hill past the Stadium and Rushcutters' Bay Park, to ascend by White City to the heights of Edgecliff and become the eminently desirable New South Head Road. The C.W.A. Club, however, was halfway down Bayswater Road, opposite a distinctly unappealing hotel, and the corner of the 'Dirty Half Mile', as King's Cross Road was called. Rather more stately was the old Belvedere, hidden among trees further down the hill, and behind us was St Canice's Church, in Roslyn Gardens. (It was a Catholic church, exuding mystery of a different kind from that of the peculiar hotel opposite, but equally unfamiliar.)

The Club was a tall, cream-coloured building, made up of several narrow terraced houses knocked into one, with four storeys descending from flat parapetted rooftop to the basement, containing kitchen and dining room. Each room, whether having two, three or four beds, had its balcony; front rooms, though noisy with the passing of trams and other traffic, were prized by some of us because of the views of lively goings-on — human rather than vehicular — in the street. From the roof, you could see the cluttered skyline of Darlinghurst Road in the west, lavish Darling Point in the east, Paddington to the south, and north, beyond the boats moored in Rushcutters', the Harbour itself.

Scenic attractions, however, had no appeal to me in those first days of adjustment. I had barely learned, at university, to find my way from the quadrangle to the (then brand-new) Wallace Theatre at the foot of Science Road, nor was I reassured, having found the Wallace in time for an English lecture, to discover that it seated a thousand, and every seat seemed to be filled. I think the first introductory lecture was given by Professor Waldock, the Department Head, but I remember nothing of it — I was utterly overcome by the horror of being lonely in a huge crowd. At some point I fell with delight upon my old friend Margaret from high school, her cheerful face as welcome as a lighthouse beacon in a storm at sea. She was in residence at Sancta Sophia, and introduced me to some of her ex-schoolmates from Loreto, Normanhurst. With them I tagged along gratefully, at least to the English lectures.

The subject which gave me the greatest difficulty, and most isolated me, because none of my acquaintances was taking it, was French. Its timetable, by comparison with those of English and Psychology, was demanding — in six sections, including such esoteric ones as Phonetics, and the inevitable, painful *Dictée*. In these two, I floundered early; the dictation was given by a Frenchman whose arrogance I so disliked that I was already a budding Francophobe — an attitude I still had more than thirty years later, when I travelled alone in France, and found most of the natives less than helpful in conversation. I always suspected that they had an inbred contempt for anybody unfortunate enough to be unable to speak the language. (By contrast, the Italians fell about laughing at my linguistic efforts, but did their best to help.)

Having survived a day of lectures, of hunting for books either in the library or the secondhand market, and of eating lunch alone in a corner of the Manning House women's dining room, I then had to negotiate the tram-ride back to the Club. I took the rattling old toast-rack model along Parramatta Road (one with some kind of a cross on its destination board was the right one), then Broadway and George Street as far as the King Street corner, where I transferred to the more elegant, enclosed variety of tram suitable for destinations such as Double Bay and Bellevue Hill, and alighted on the corner opposite the Club.

My fellow-residents were mostly, like myself, straight out of secondary school, but a few were elderly veterans of one or other of the women's forces. Among these was a lively, witty, sandy-haired person who indeed was not much older than I, yet seemed so because of her maturity. Lesley Rowlands went on to become the writer of the most successful *Why Can't the English?* and *On Top of the World*. I liked her, but at first was too shy to do more than smile tentatively in passing. Of more immediate concern was getting to know my three room-mates; sharing with strangers at such close quarters was alarming, to say the least.

It was understood that I would not be able to go home every weekend, because of the expense. At the end of the first week, however, I rang my mother and begged to be allowed to return there from Friday afternoon to Sunday evening. She agreed, of course; she probably even anticipated it. It was not easy to explain my desperate homesickness. I was experiencing for the first time that bewildering sensation of not belonging — all the more painful because my expectations had been so confident and exalted. Perhaps it was not possible for me to tell my mother of the seemingly trivial problems, such as my consciousness that I didn't wear the same clothes as the other girls. My dresses were either home-made, or the Hordern Brothers' models, and I had sensible lace-up shoes with stockings. At the Club, the girls wore pretty cotton frocks from David Jones or Farmers, and sandals or comfortable 'flatties'. And they all seemed to know one another, having been to boarding schools such as Frensham and Ascham. My father joked about this acquaintance with the offspring of the 'graziers', and that approach struck the right note, had I been in the mood to hear it. My mother, no doubt, tried to boost my threatened self-respect by pointing out how well I'd done academically, but I was aware now of the importance of social competence, and that I didn't seem to have it. I didn't blame anyone for this dreadful lack, but brooded over it. And, as usual, got it all out of proportion and perspective, those twin gifts which are often beyond the grasp of the average seventeen-year-old.

I think my father was rather indignant on my behalf, for he also pointed out that I 'wasn't bad-looking', either. We'd never been encouraged to think about our looks, because personality and character were what mattered, but I was entering a world where girls were forever washing and setting their hair, wearing make-up regularly, and being anxious about spots on the face. It

189

was gratifying, later that year, to discover from my peers that I was not unattractive. My most-envied attribute was an olive complexion that held a suntan for most of the year.

Reluctantly, I went back for the Lent Term. Probably both my mother and I were feeling that my going to the Club was turning out to be a mistake, but for different reasons. She foresaw that inevitably I would have financial as well as social problems keeping up with these particular Joneses, and there she was right. I was still of the airy opinion that money would be forthcoming when I needed it, in spite of evidence to the contrary. And all the other girls were constantly complaining of being broke; I had yet to find out that it was a relative term.

My judgments, of course, had been both hasty and ill-conceived. At closer inspection, my Clubmates turned out to be ordinary mortals quite like myself. There may have been some whose parents belonged to what in the forties was still Australia's nearest approximation to an upper class — the 'squattocracy' — but there were others whose families had struggled to send them to boarding-schools for the very good reason that no other secondary education was available. And there was Val, one of my room-mates, whose father owned a hotel in Mudgee, and who, like me, had attended the local high school. Val was forthright, practical, sensible and took no nonsense from anyone; a Science student, she provided a most-needed balance, as far as I was concerned. Janet, who had the bed on the balcony, was one of six children of a grazier from Oberon. She had her own responsibilities; three younger brothers were boarders at nearby Canbrook, and during the year one of them became ill with polio. Then there was Judy, who became one of my closest friends. She came from Wollongong, had been to Frensham, and was refreshingly short on pretensions, and gifted with a

190

sense of humour. In nearby rooms were Marion, whose
father was manager of the Port Kembla Steelworks, and
Joan, who came from an orchard and grazing property at
Narromine. In time, I made the not-surprising discovery
that we all shared the same feelings and uncertainties —
about ourselves, our studies, our attributes, and how to
get on with the opposite sex. In short, we became a
group, eating together, doing our assignments together,
talking, often late into the night, walking on autumn
evenings in Rushcutters' Bay Park beneath the huge
Moreton Bay figs, or down to the wharf at Darling
Point. Weekends became, instead of going-home
occasions, times for shared confidences over
laundry-tubs and hair-washing, and, in the warmer
weather, trips by tram to swim at Neilsen Park or
Redleaf Pool. And I had a couple of new dresses like
everyone else's.

No longer did I trail off to university alone. Indeed,
with that kind of callousness not unknown to the young,
I dropped those few acquaintances I had made in the
first weeks, and went to lectures and sat in the Quad
with the girls from the Club. I did, however, go to a ball
at Sancta Sophia, invited by Margaret. It was a solemn
occasion, for I wore my first long frock (which had
belonged, I think, either to my sister or my cousin, but
impressed me greatly for all that) and was partnered by
a Med. student from John's, none other than the younger
son of a family doctor at Gosford. Michael was a
pleasant young man, but the friendship didn't last. Med.
students, while socially highly desirable, were also very
busy and rather inaccessible, keeping mostly to their
awesome premises over on Missenden Road, far from
the froth and bubble of the Arts Faculty. It was almost
obligatory, however, for girl Arts students to be shown
by budding medicos through the Old Med. School, to
glance fleetingly at cadavers and things in bottles, and

then swoon away. I didn't achieve the latter, but certainly didn't linger.

Arts students were scarcely weighed down by attendance at lectures, though I continued to toil away at French in an ancient room somewhere beneath the Carillon Tower. Psychology One was a curious but not too demanding subject, largely taken up with something called Statistical Method — a little too mathematical for my taste, until we moved on to measuring one another's head sizes and intelligence quotients and personality ratings. (On one of these I was assessed by a Clubmate as 'emotionally unstable', which puzzled and worried me for a time. What on earth did it *mean*? Mature reflection tells me that we were all, to say the least, volatile as to feelings, unleashed as we were from the supervision of teachers and parents.) Centre of interest in the Psychology class for a time was a small group of sophisticated and well-dressed girls from a private school, who made a point of coming late to lectures and working hard at nothing. These were regarded as the social butterfly collection, filling in time doing Arts because it was fitting for young ladies so to do. Another fashionable course was Physiotherapy, but we had at least one friend at the Club who took this seriously and made a success of what has proved to be a most practical and caring vocation. A shamefully poor relation of all tertiary training grounds was Social Work; not even a graduate course, it was looked upon as the field of study for those, almost always female, who were a bit vague as to what else to do.

Although English was my favourite subject, I found much of it boring. Phonetics with Mr Mitchell and Old English with Miss Herring (we were aware that they possessed Christian names, but had to discover these for ourselves) barely raised a ripple of enthusiasm out in the back rows of the Wallace Theatre where we usually sat. I liked the substance of *The Canterbury Tales*, but couldn't appreciate the technicalities of Chaucerian language. Old English and Anglo-Saxon together were to become my *bête noire*, being obligatory for English Distinction courses. I could have done with some of Thelma Herring's undeniable devotion to her subject.

Professor Waldock's lectures on the modern novel were more to my taste, even if some of the books on the reading list were not. I began very slowly to appreciate the writing of Huxley and D. H. Lawrence, but shied away from Christopher Isherwood and James Joyce. *Ulysses* was in any case extremely difficult to get hold of, having been banned, so I read it, almost literally in snatches, in the library. Eventually I found in the same place all kinds of other novels that I *did* enjoy. I can remember one morning, probably when I should have been at a lecture, sitting in the hushed precincts of the Fisher reading Rosamund Lehmann's *The Ballad and the Source*, which haunted me for some time afterwards with its telling evocations of family relationships and childhood's 'paradise lost'. It may have been then that I also read Henry James' *Turn of the Screw*; I was still susceptible to ghost stories, especially those involving children. Both these novels have a quality not dissimilar to that of Joan Lindsay's *Picnic at Hanging Rock* — the peculiar desolation of innocence corrupted and destroyed. And it's interesting to notice that even at University I was attracted to novels with child characters, however adult they might have become in the course of the story. Yet had anybody ever suggested that when one day I did achieve my ambition of being a writer, I would write for and about children, I should probably have been affronted. Books for young people had no place whatsoever in the English syllabus; such a notion would have been ludicrous in the forties. Such juvenilia were left (one hopes) to the trainees at the Sydney Teachers College down yonder between Science Road and the Oval.

What writing I did outside course requirements consisted mostly of short stories and poems. The latter pursued doggedly themes of starry skies, murmuring seas, whispering trees and a pantheistic musing upon the Meaning of Life. There was emphasis on the glories as well as the dimly perceived transience of youth, along with a certain melancholy induced by rainy landscapes in university vacation, when one was supposed to study, but missed one's companions — a far cry, and an inevitable one, from the first 'I-can't-wait-to-get-home' feelings. If some of my longings were of a spiritual nature, I would hardly have recognised it. 'Spirituality' in those days meant to most of us (if we ever thought of it at all) formalised religious observance, and at seventeen and eighteen I avoided that. Indeed, Joan reminded me not long ago that I was in the habit of decrying her own faithful attendance at St Mark's, Darling Point, on Sundays; I rather fancied myself an agnostic, at the time. Perhaps it was in defiance of the chants and bells that sounded regularly from nearby St Canice's.

In the spring of that first year I fell in love. Hopelessly, as it turned out. It was bound to have happened in an atmosphere, both at university and in the Club, of youthful speculation about the whole matter of male–female relationships. Joan, I remember, was devoted (also hopelessly) to a lecturer who spent his entire hour reading aloud, in almost-solitary bliss, the poems of Gerard Manley Hopkins, while the rest of us were baffled and perplexed by the mysteries of 'sprung rhythm' and lines where words were transposed in ways totally unknown to the likes of Keats and Tennyson. (As for Hopkins' sentiments — what *could* he be getting at? Or whom?) A lot of the girls at the Club had boyfriends who came to the Club for weekend teas; one

194

of the latter was even in naval uniform, though about to do Law — a very handsome fellow indeed, called Laurence Street. At the university we communicated at intervals with a group of Arts–Law students including one Ian Sinclair, who was about my own age, and already had the clear and sonorous voice later to be much heard in both law courts and Federal Parliament.

It was Ian who played Cupid. It seemed that he had a friend who was admiring me from afar, and wanted to make my acquaintance. This extraordinary bit of information was passed on to me by a girl at the Club, as we were queueing in the dining room for our supper of mixed grill and vegetables. This was one of our favourite menus, but I instantly lost my appetite. It stayed lost for the next three days. Of course I knew by sight the student in question; we all did. His name was Warren, he had been to Scots College, and he was over six feet tall, and suntanned and handsome.

Here was the miraculous happening straight out of every romance I'd ever read. Enter the hero, the lover of my dreams; if I still thought of love as mostly romantic, with an occasional rather chaste embrace, I was little different from most of the girls of my acquaintance. That young men had other ideas I had yet to discover. It raised some puzzling questions, eventually. 'Young ladies', or 'nice girls', did not allow young men to take liberties with their persons, but what sort of rules did the young *men* have? I had an underlying feeling that to deny your swain his pleasures (and why, I wondered— incredibly as it might now seem — were these of such vital importance to him, anyway?) would be to risk losing him, a feminine dilemma which has persisted for centuries.

At first, however, this affair of the heart seemed to be all the poets declared it to be, gracious as the spring and early summer in which it flourished. On my eighteenth birthday, Warren gave me a copy of James Elroy

195

Flecker's *Hassan*, with inscribed on the fly-leaf the verses beginning:

> *We are the pilgrims, Master; we shall go*
> *Always a little further; it may be*
> *Beyond that last blue mountain capped with snow —*

We had recently seen a S.U.D.S. production of the play, and I found it quite acceptable that the hero and heroine chose 'one perfect day' of love together, as last concession before they were both gruesomely done to death. (Mature reflections tells me *Hassan* is a singularly morbid work.) 'The world well lost for love' was what it was all about — wasn't it? As for pilgrimages — no worries there, when you went hand in hand with the beloved.

We skipped lectures sometimes to go to the movies at the Union Theatre, watching shows such as *The Body Snatchers* and *Frankenstein*, which encouraged physical togetherness — out of genuine terror, on my part. I visited Warren's parents at their Vaucluse home, where I was practically mute from shyness, and roamed the Dover Heights cliffs after listening to Beethoven's Seventh Symphony, Warren's favourite. It was the first time that I encountered classical music as accompaniment to romance, and it led to an exploration of the works of the Romantic (what else?) composers. This was fortified, too, by my friend Joan's possession, at the Club, of an imposing gramophone with precious Thorn needles, whereon she played César Franck and Schubert (also Mahler, which I disliked), and by going occasionally to Symphony Concerts at the Town Hall. Brahms' First Symphony made a great impression. It was largely a matter of 'If music be the food of love, play on'. It was years before I began to appreciate music for itself.

University exams occurred, inconveniently, when romance was at its height. Though I had already set foot upon the primrose path by missing some lectures (mostly in English), by preferring idle chatter to hours of study, and by — alas! — taking up smoking because my friends did, and thereby running into financial difficulties, I still took final exams seriously — especially in French, if only from fear of the authorities. And there was much in the French One course I enjoyed, such as essay-writing, and reading and translating some of the short stories and bits of novels. The actual setting of the exams, mostly in the beautiful but stony Great Hall, I found rather daunting. I kept my misgivings to myself; early training and more than a little pride seemed to demand that. While my companions tore their hair and vociferously despaired and wailed of certain failure, I was somewhat admired for keeping my cool and my insouciance. Little did they know. I was as anxious about failure as anyone — perhaps rather more than some, for my academic future seemed to depend upon my retaining scholarship payments.

It was later that the taking of benzedrine — the only available 'upper' — became popular among some of my fellow students. I didn't need it; somewhere during the first hour of the written exams, especially in English, fear evaporated, and I reached a different sort of 'high'. The critical-analytical-logical approach to literature, be it poetry or prose, appealed to me, in a fashion not dissimilar to that experienced by the Med. students dissecting the cadavers. And what I couldn't recall of some works, I no doubt invented. The hieroglyphs of Phonetics I probably memorised the night before the exams.

With the coming of the long, summer vacation, the love-affair with Warren inevitably dissipated. It had, at least on my part, been too intense to begin with. I went home and wrote poems about it. They had titles such as 'Summer Love Song' and 'Day That Has Been', and much wistful reflection upon landscapes and seascapes. I bore Warren no grudge; I even felt, amid the gloom, that broken romances had a curious kind of satisfaction, as if at last one had 'been there', with the poets and classic heroes and heroines and the world's great loves.

I also came out of it as virtuous as when I began, which no doubt was a considerable relief to my parents, and didn't fall in love again for almost twelve months.

XVII

I remember very well the morning the exam results came out. Upon seeing them, I left the house and went down by the orchard to the sloping field above the dusty valley road, beloved in childhood. It was January, and blackberries were ripening. I sat somewhere in the shade and contemplated the facts. I had got a Pass in Psychology, and a Distinction in English. And failed in French. I had never failed in an exam before, and it was mortifying. Even the good result in English could not at first outweigh it.

My parents were remarkably understanding. I had passed in four of the six required papers, lapsing in Phonetics and — of course — the Dictation. Also, I had been given a 'Post', with a chance to reinstate myself. That month, my mother rented a holiday flat at Avoca Beach, and it was there that I renewed my onslaught on the French language. With the *dictée* I had my mother's patient help and guidance as to the finer distinctions of pronunciation, but what I really needed was an ear capable of picking them up.

It was a beautiful setting for summer study. The weatherboard flat, the front one in a building long since demolished, looked onto the south end of the beach, through a stand of pine trees. Cool salt air and the sounds of waves entered always at the windows, and near by were the tawny sandstone rocks and the tidal pools, and a tearoom called the Brown Jug, where we had afternoon tea with scones and jam and cream. (My appetite seemed to have been regained, broken love-affair and a Post notwithstanding.) For my mother, it was a rare and treasured break from ordinary surroundings. Avoca was a quiet place, with a few scattered holiday homes, one general store down near the lagoon, and behind the beach, steep little green hills where we gathered mushrooms after rain. Further inland, in the forest called Pickett's Gully, bellbirds never stopped singing. In that one small secluded area, all the loveliness of the Coast seemed encapsulated — sea and golden shore, olive-green lagoon, paperbark and she-oak and native palm, stout cliffs and sporting porpoises.

My father and sister came to visit at weekends. A photo of the occasion shows Dad, pipe in hand, dressed in suit, white shirt and tie; even at the beach in summer, he would not have appeared in casual gear. Shorts were what he wore on the farm, weather permitting, and even then with shirt and long socks. The notion of ever going out anywhere in a singlet would have horrified him. And we girls are in short-sleeved cotton tops and knee-length skirts, with hair rolled under in the 'page-boy' style that had become fashionable during the war. Jeans were merely curious garments worn by cowboys — and, daringly, their female counterparts — in American movies. We did, however, wear shorts sometimes — usually white, as if for tennis.

In February, never a favourite month at the best of times, for it was invariably humid and often wet, I went to Sydney to sit for the Post. As the Club was still closed for the vacation, I stayed with my aunts. The old Waverton house — actually a fine example of what is now called Federation architecture — seemed gloomy and shut-in after the breezy delights of the Coast. And the university, out of term-time, was empty except for a few staff-members and dismal semi-dropouts like myself. I was less than confident about the exams; as far as I could tell, I had done no better and no worse than I had the first time. In that assumption I was correct. I failed the Post.

My mother was indignant. She considered the entire French Faculty exam system unfairly rigid, and forthwith made an appointment to see Professor Henning and state our case. Marginal failure in one-third of the First Year exams threatened my whole university career. She said so. Professor Henning remained unimpressed and unmoved; exceptions to his Faculty rules were simply not allowed.

It was back to the Enquiry Office and the advisory service. I lost my scholarship, but was permitted to keep the exhibition if I could pick up an extra subject in Second Year. Four subjects made up a fairly heavy load, but there were some useful 'standby' subjects considered easy and undemanding, for reasons best known, I suppose, to their Faculty heads. One of these was Oriental History, famous for having the highest non-failure rate in the entire university. I took it up forthwith. My friend Joan, as it turned out, was also studying it, and took it a great deal more earnestly than I did. It had, however, a certain exotic fascination, and I even retained in later years a vague memory of the lists of the Mogul Emperors of India, if not much else. Yet even that was more than I remembered of my fourth subject, Modern History: I disgracefully crammed in what was needed for essays and exams, and promptly forgot the lot.

It was a shaky beginning to what became the happiest and most successful of my university years. When, today, I pass by Sydney University, altered though it is, I look upon it with affection, and it is largely 1947 that I am remembering. Mostly I see a particular corner of the quadrangle that we made our own — a sunny place, at least in the mornings, beside the stairs leading up to Fisher Library, and another set leading down to the depths of Anthropology, or was it Archaeology? Nobody we knew was attempting the latter study, but the former had become popular, and the names of Margaret Mead and the Trobriand Islanders came up sometimes in discussion.

What else did we talk about, so unremittingly? Psychology Two was a rich field, wherein the mysteries of Freud were dug around and the peculiarities of human behaviour delved into. We acknowledged that schizophrenia and manic depression might actually exist, and mused upon which of our acquaintances might be thus afflicted. We discussed books such as Forster's *A Passage to India*, and Eugene O'Neill's plays, such as *Mourning Becomes Electra*, a performance of which we saw at Doris Fitton's Independent Theatre. It went on for hours, and was very gloomy indeed. (Oedipus complexes were mulled over, too.) And we watched, avidly, the passing parade of fellow-students, to many of whom we gave nicknames, unaware of the honours that one day would be bestowed on such young men as the Mackerras brothers, Alistair and Charles, or that keen fellow involved both in the Students' Representative Council and S.U.D.S., whose name was Neville Wran.

The most inspired inventor of nicknames was our new Clubmate, Rosemary, who was living with us while her parents were overseas. Her father became Australia's leading paediatrician; I met him again in the seventies, when he was patron of the Autistic Children's Association. Rosemary was a funny, original, delightful red-haired girl, who, with her gentle friend Mary, became an essential part of our group, in lectures, quadrangle, Public Library, or in the coffee-shop we frequented at The Cross. It was called the Arabian; in its austerely dim recesses you could have a first cup of

coffee for sixpence, and the next two or three for
threepence each. (Such economy was important to
somebody like me, given to overspending on cigarettes
and sandwich lunches.) There, of course, we talked
some more. One evening I wrote some poetry there — a
deliberate send-up of the 'disenchanted' school of
modern poets featured in our reading-lists that year:
Auden and Spender, MacNeice and Eliot. That I even
dared to be satirical and irreverent on the matter of
sexuality surprises me now; perhaps it was merely that
at the age of non-quite-nineteen I still knew very little
about it.

Rosemary actually drove her own car. Having come
from a family that relied on public transport, I was
astonished that anyone my own age — and female, at
that — could be so independently mobile. Sometimes
we travelled to lectures in it, but as the year went on I
found a reason for returning to the trams. His name was
Jack, and he belonged to that rather elderly group of
Repat. students whom we watched from afar. He was,
in fact, about four years older than myself, and had been
in the Air Force; his upright, purposeful figure striding
down Science Road to English lectures was familiar to
us, and Rosemary, for a reason I never discovered,
nicknamed him Popeye. He bore no resemblance
whatever to the well-known comic-strip sailor, nor, as
my old photos show, did his eyes bulge. He did,
however, have a charming smile and a beautiful
well-articulated speaking voice, neither of which I had
failed to notice.

The height of our social ambition then was to be
invited to partake of coffee in the Union. I can
remember, on the first occasion I went there with Jack,
being suitably impressed by the atmosphere of this
all-male precinct. Manning House — the women's
quarters — paled in comparison. Then there were the
faculty balls, to which we went in parties, but on the

understanding that each had a particular partner. Jack wore his double-breasted Repat. suit, and I had two long dresses of a demure kind plus one of the angora boleros popular that year.

This was not the kind of breath-taking romance I had had with Warren. Jack and I held hands often, and when he first kissed me goodnight on the front steps of the C.W.A. Club, he asked my permission first, but physical togetherness was simply the natural accompaniment to a real friendship. We walked and talked a lot, drank coffee (Repin's was another inexpensive haunt), took study-breaks on the steps of the Public Library and wandered homewards under the giant fig-trees beside the Domain. Like myself, Jack had English as his major study, and wanted to be a writer — preferably Australia's answer to Hemingway, whose work he greatly admired. We both enjoyed, if that is the apt word, the novels of Graham Greene, though I was daunted by both their irony and pervasive haunting Catholicism. Jack was Catholic by upbringing; his father was a miner, and Jack had grown up in towns unknown to me, such as Kurri and Lithgow, reared by an older sister after his mother died. I must have been maturing myself, for I didn't see this kind of background as even vaguely romantic. He didn't talk of it much, but I gathered that it had not always been easy.

We all, Jack and his mates, Rosemary and Joan and Judy and others at the Club, worked hard for the exams that year, proving, if proof was ever needed, that mutual discussion and co-operation make study so much more palatable and profitable. I must have even paid more than passing attention to Anglo-Saxon, for I won a High Distinction in English, as well as scraping passes in my other three subjects. All seemed set fair for 1948 — the final year.

It turned out to be quite eventful, so much so that even

my study of English took second or third place to what I would probably have defined as a discovery of life. That year I began writing a novel, with Huxleyan overtones, wherein the characters had names like 'Fabian' and 'Dorinda', and were heavily into meaningful conversation, and not much else. I never finished it. There was no soothsayer to tell me that for the rest of my life I would write no fiction that had not children or teenagers as central characters; nor would I have believed such nonsense. There was no such thing as Children's Literature, especially in an Australian context. And the fact, still indisputable, that I felt ill at ease attempting to write of adult experiences and emotions would have caused the amateur psychologists amongst us to mutter about immaturity and arrested development. We were all trying so hard to be grown-up, intellectual and sophisticated.

I went no further with Psychology as a subject of study, but instead chose Modern Philosophy. We all knew by sight the Philosophy Professor, John Anderson, pacing around the Quad with his disciples, mostly male, and including his own son, Sandy, who was in our Modern Philosophy group. This appeared to be a subject to be taken seriously indeed, and for a time I enjoyed discussing Descartes' principle of 'I think, therefore I am', or Berkeley's 'The essence of material things is to be perceived'. It was quite in order to ponder for hours as to whether a tree in a desert actually existed if nobody saw it, and ever since I've found it an excellent topic of speculation in moments of idleness. The beauty of it all was that no definite conclusion was ever reached, which divorced it so emphatically from any branch of Science, which I disliked.

For English, we pursued among other matters eighteenth-century drama, and Shakespearean tragedy, which had as adjunct visits to the Tivoli to see the Old Vic Company presenting *School for Scandal* and

Richard the Third. With my friend Marion, I waited at the stage door to beam upon Laurence Olivier, hero since my movie-going days, and just as handsome in the flesh; and give flowers to the most beautiful lady we had ever seen, the exquisite Vivien Leigh. For a time I was stage-struck all over again. We still went to the cinema, often to the Savoy to see the French films which were suddenly so popular. My outright favourite was *Les Enfants du Paradis*, but if pushed I would have had to admit that some of the others were overlong and inexplicably doomful. The era of the great French comedies had not yet arrived.

We also discovered the novels of Evelyn Waugh, and with Joan I chuckled through *Decline and Fall* and *Vile Bodies*. Rather later I revelled in *Brideshead Revisited*, still my favourite Waugh book. Its intensely evocative vision of Oxford — 'et ego in Arcadia' — was a reinforcement of old romantic dreams, brought back yet again in the eighties, when I saw the B.B.C. televised version, with its haunting music and superb imagery. There is no doubt that the account of the friendship between Charles and Sebastian (a relationship which I did not accept as explicitly sexual, nor, I think, did Waugh intend it to be so) influenced my writing, years later, of *A Candle for St Antony*. Equally, that novel was affected by Brideshead's reflections on and of the Catholic faith, a matter to which my attention was being often drawn back in 1948.

In the first term of that year, my friendship with Jack had waned a little, and it was with one of his friends, Fitz, that I went on a weekend visit to Joan's family's cottage at Soldier's Point, on Port Stephens. Though we were a mixed party of male and female, the occasion was entirely decorous; we were chaperoned from nextdoor by one of Joan's relatives. Fitz was earnestly devoted to Anthropology, Joan's friend Neville was a lecturer in Economics, and another young man was a music student, so conversation — to say nothing of argument — raged on into the night, and was taken up all over again during walks along the shores of what was then the most delightful and remote holiday-cum-fishing village. It was not far, geographically, from the Myall Lakes of my sixteen-year-old experience, nor from the Seal Rocks, which I put, many years later, and in disguise, into *The October Child*.

Not long afterwards my relationship with Jack revived, and I moved into a milieu wider than that of the Club and the University quad and lecture halls. It was the era of the parties — important affairs in my own view, but to any casual observer no more than a gathering of assorted students in somebody's bedsitter, or a tiny three-roomed apartment, or even, occasionally, half a house. In memory the venues are all inner-city — Yurong Street, tucked away behind the Museum and the Grammar School and the neon-lit car salesrooms of William Street, or Margaret Street on the city hill below St Patrick's church, or in a terraced house in Victoria Street, Darlinghurst. A party happened when there were enough people, and a couple of bottles of wine or beer (with lemonade for the ladies), biscuits and cheese and conversation. Often we would walk home, through city streets of midnight quiet broken by the rattle of trams, or Hyde Park with the dark bulk of St Mary's Cathedral on the horizon, or along the byways of The Cross, where it was still relatively safe to wander.

Jack played the piano in a Pitt Street café to help finances; there, like Billy Joel's 'Piano Man' of a later generation, he provided whatever musical numbers the patrons wanted, but off duty he favoured the songs of Noel Coward, aided in the lyrics by a few of his friends. A favourite was 'Nina from Argentina', that celebrated lady who 'wouldn't Begin the Beguine when they requested it'. Genuine wit was appreciated by our group; a treasured book (which I still dip into) was

Thurber's *Men, Women and Dogs*. It's a great antidote to a tendency to take oneself too seriously ('What do you want to be inscrutable *for*, Marcia?' or 'Maybe you don't have charm, Lily, but you're enigmatic!'), and I'm constantly reminded of 'Thurber dogs' whenever I gaze upon my blue cattledog in her more reflective moments ('For Heaven's sake, why don't you go outside and trace something?'). We rejoiced, too, in those magnificent short stories, such as 'The Night the Bed Fell', and the one about the old lady convinced that electricity was leaking all over the house — to this day I have a suspicion that she may have been right.

I was now moving in a milieu of Catholics, some 'lapsed' (a new term to me) and some not. I observed them, so to speak, from a distance. On Sunday mornings, after we had stayed the night in somebody's flat (again, a remarkable innocent proceeding, where the girls had whatever was available in the way of a bedroom, and the youths slept on couch or floor), the sound of bells from St Mary's would intrude upon various slumbers, and a shape would stir, and mutter 'Eight o'clock', roll over, and go back to sleep. About an hour later the performance would be repeated, and so on until the more conscientious — or awake — ambled off to mass. I wondered why it was so important, but as Jack was not under such an obligation, I let it pass. I liked St Mary's; two of our friends were married there, 'behind the altar', because Geoff, unlike Maureen, was not a Catholic. I watched the ceremony with keen interest. Towards the end of that year, a kind of understanding had grown between Jack and myself that we, too, might get married. Undoubtedly, I was more enthusiastic than he, but my mother had no enthusiasm at all. Not that she disliked Jack — indeed, I think that of the few men-friends I invited home, she would have found him, with his literary ambitions, his love of books and music, and his humorous grasp of life's realities, the

208

most compatible. He was certainly the most mature. She believed, properly, perhaps, that at twenty I was much too young for marriage, and ought to embark on a career instead.

It was the cause of my first serious disagreement with her. Imbued with the romantic notion (so common among our generation of women) that nothing in the world was more important than true love, I would have eloped cheerfully with Jack immediately after the final exams, had the opportunity actually offered. It didn't. Somehow the relationship died a natural — but on my part, lingering — death. It had nothing to do with my mother's disapprobation; nor, true to her non-sectarian beliefs, would she have made any judgments on the basis of Jack's Catholicism, practising or otherwise. Jack himself moved away. As with so many of my friends, he was drawn to travel in foreign parts — without a wife.

I didn't see him again after that. He wrote and had published two novels, one set in Spain, one in Queensland, and both good pacey stories with traces of Graham Greene and Roman Catholic influences. Some years later, his name appeared under an article written for the Sydney *Bulletin* from Hong Kong, concerning the war in Vietnam. And then a war correspondent of the same name was killed in Saigon, one of a party of journalists caught in the crossfire. If that was Jack, his life — if not his writing — had certainly achieved the Hemingway touch.

Yet at heart he was a gentle man. When I remember 1948, I recall so much laughter, and such ordinary things, such as walking in the rain along Oxford Street past (and sometimes into) those old corner pubs which may not exist any more, and talking of books and people, and dreams and plans, and roaming on the waterfront in the Botanic Gardens or Circular Quay, watching the big and little ships go out. Or just sitting in a café, and talking — again. I remember St Mary's, too.

There were other events taking place that year, of course. In the early spring Joan invited several of us to her home at Narromine, and I had my first experience of the inland country life, on a homestead with broad verandahs, surrounded by paddocks and orchard ('Buddah' was famous for its oranges), with horses to ride, the shearing to watch, and picnics on the nearby hills. (I was irresistibly reminded of the 'Billabong' books of Mary Grant Bruce.) Unfortunately, while I was there I also had my first experience of appendicitis, for which later in the year I had an operation. Having had mostly robust health to that time, I resented the whole thing.

It was perhaps inevitable that exams and the associated studying had become simply an interruption to living. For most of my life I had been pursuing an education, and I was tired of it. I could no longer even pretend to an interest in Anglo-Saxon, and the writing of analytical essays on aspects of English Literature had definitely lost its charm. I was fortunate to get three passes, the minimum required for my degree.

Although preoccupied with affairs of the heart, I was still aware of the significance of leaving the Club for the last time. The narrow concrete stairways, the balconied rooms and the loftier apartments where we were allowed officially to receive male visitors, seemed suddenly so empty and forlorn — unless a few girlish ghosts waited in the shadows. As is the way with a twenty-year-old looking back on seventeen, I felt old and sophisticated (which I certainly wasn't) and awed. Serious undertakings lay ahead, such as finding a job. Friends were scattering in all directions. The Arabian Coffee Shop would know us no more, and the bells of St

Canice's, into which place Rosemary and I had once crept, trembling at our own daring, and expecting at any minute to be thrown out as impostors, to see what really went on at a Catholic mass, would chime on other ears.

Joan stayed on at the Club for the following year, and we kept in touch. Then she too set sail for abroad, where she had many adventures, some of a highly romantic kind. When my own turn came, I met her again in London. Rosemary married a doctor, lived for a time in Tasmania, and then, sadly, was widowed quite early, with four children. It seemed a fixed pattern, that we should, briefly, have post-graduate jobs, then marry and bring up our families. Nor did we question it to any extent. Val married a journalist, who later became editor of newspapers in Newcastle and Wollongong; Marion scored the greatest number of children — five — having married an engineer from her own home town of Port Kembla. Judy had a career in psychology, married, had children, divorced and remarried. Naturally, though one opportunity had gone, I expected to marry too. I assumed it would be just a matter of time.

In 1949 I went back to receive my Arts degree in the Great Hall. In borrowed gown and mortar board, I had my photo taken, in suitably grave academic pose. We celebrated afterwards, but it seems in recollection to have been rather a muted occasion. Emotions shared over three years of the student life could be neither prolonged nor recaptured — to my own regret.

The romantic and idealistic young creature who had entered university with such bookish notions and starry-eyed anticipations was far from dead. Looking back on those years, I believe I was let down quite gently during a crucial growing-up period. At least I was far from bereft of dreams.

XVIII

While my literary output for the next few years was to be confined mostly to poetry, I still wanted to be a writer. I have often been asked by young aspiring authors whether an Arts degree, or its equivalent, is of real assistance as preparation for such a career. Like most questions about the whys and wherefores of writing, it's not easy to answer. The bulk of my English studies consisted of reading, analysing and criticising the works of others; I picked up plenty of hints on style, characterisation and the construction of plot, but did singularly little creative writing on my own account. I developed preferences in reading, and in themes, but didn't always express them lest they fail to coincide with those of the examiners. Indeed, when later I began to write novels for children, much of my intellectual and academic knowledge of the novelist's craft had to be discarded and un-learned, because it had been assumed that the only reader worth considering was the adult kind, and of the actual relationship between writer and reader we discovered very little. No learning experience, however, is wasted on a writer. I both enjoyed and profited from three years of living in a world of ideas, freely discussed in an outpouring of spoken words. If nothing else, it gave me an ear for dialogue, as well as a taste for it.

It had been assumed at home that I would take up teaching, if only for the sound practical reason that an

Arts degree, of itself, was entry into scarcely any other profession. And, of course, my mother and grandfather and my father, for a time, had all been teachers. It had always been held up to me as an honourable and worthwhile vocation (a true calling) with the additional advantage of security. My mother did say, however, that time and experience were necessary to make a good teacher; I should not expect to find it immediately satisfying and successful.

In those days it was possible to obtain a teaching post in a private school without a Diploma of Education. You simply applied straight from university, and presumably learned your craft thereafter — a rather Dickensian principle of learning by doing. Privately, I was neither keen nor confident. I was, moreover, rather discomfited by a feeling of being once more at loggerheads with my mother. Teenage rebellion, now of early onset, for me had been considerably delayed; I had been willingly guided by her for most of my life, and didn't recognise my new emotion as inevitable self-assertion. I felt, without saying so, that this teaching business was not really for me, or at least not yet.

I applied for a post at a large Protestant day and boarding school for girls, in a city suburb. The city part I liked, for it meant I could keep in touch with at least some of my friends. And the accommodation problem seemed to have been solved when it was agreed that I should live in, and do duty as part-time housemistress. My salary was to be five pounds a week, with, of course, free board and lodging.

My mother heaved a sigh of relief at having got her last offspring satisfactorily launched on a career. My sister was still living with our aunts and working at the Rural Bank, where she enjoyed a mildly busy social life and many friendships. My brother, at about this time, was sent on his first tour of overseas duty with the Air Force, to Malaya; while there was more than a little trouble in those parts with border-country insurgents, it was the beginning of his lifelong interest in, and attachment to, the Western Pacific region, and the theatres of World War II, which he still visits, with family in tow, and about which he is currently writing a most detailed history.

Privately, I was dismayed at the prospect before me. The atmosphere of my new abode was, to say the least, intimidating, and the headmistress could have been most aptly described as being 'of the old school'. Highly qualified academically, she believed in strict discipline for staff as well as pupils, and I was to go in terror of her for the next ten months. When at the end of that time I left, I was still metaphorically glancing over my shoulder lest she be in full pursuit. At twenty, I was quite the youngest member of staff, expected to teach both English and History to a range of classes, in some of which the girls were only three or four years younger than myself.

It's alarming, in retrospect, to think that someone as utterly inexperienced as I was given charge of a roomful of adolescents and allowed to try and teach them anything at all. In History, I kept one precarious step ahead of them by memorising the evening before the set part of the textbook; fortunately or otherwise, I didn't have any budding geniuses in my groups to ask awkward questions on matters I had not yet covered. English was easier, with compositions to set and correct, and generally familiar stories and poems to discuss, but there was a large, tedious amount of grammar, for which nobody, myself included, had any enthusiasm. It was over this that I had an awesome confrontation with the headmistress, who found my work less than diligent. She was right, of course, but her uncompromising authoritarian attitudes reduced me to the depths of despair. I took refuge in poetry writing, proclaiming with the usual drama: 'Alone in a dry land, I long for my own people . . . '

In this I was probably influenced by the reading of the Psalms ('By the rivers of Babylon . . . ') which was part of the many church and assembly services I had to attend. I had no particular objection to this; I liked joining in the hymns, many of which were of the hearty, rousing, Nonconformist variety, and a few familiar to me from my own childhood. Indeed, one of the more lasting memories I have of those days is of Sunday evenings, when from the boarders' quarters came the tunes of Evensong, drifting across a lamplit garden, and rising among the old encircling palm trees. The building had a sternly medieval air, with crenellations and arched passageways and much stonework. In the winter term I had a room in the Tower wing, at the end of the corridor, which helped a little when I tried to hide sinful cigarette fumes. All around were the dormitories of fourteen-year-olds, whom I was expected not to corrupt.

What little I knew of the psychology of girls and children (the youngest boarder was seven) came from university studies, wherein we had measured juvenile I.Q.s, and from my own recollections of childhood and my reading. Such notions as I had picked up from those jolly English stories of boarding-school life were of no help whatsoever. The most prevalent emotion, if that's the right word, among the girls was undoubtedly boredom, and biggest excitement for much of the time was having some new main course at midday dinner. That didn't happen very often, either. On weekdays I was on table duty in the boarders' dining-room, which meant serving out food for some twenty-four hungry girls — a row on either side, a prefect at the opposite end, and beside me the youngest, often mute with homesickness. I certainly understood that. The food

215

was good, and well-cooked under the circumstances, but predictable — like the meal-time conversation, which was restricted to polite requests that the butter or the salt be passed to somebody's neighbour. Asking for anything for oneself was forbidden.

I had the greatest sympathy for the little ones, and for any who were clearly unhappy in their school environment. Most of the boarders were from the country, and their only outings were with friends or relatives approved by the authorities. Inevitably, they formed intense relationships with one another, relationships which were always in danger of breaking down, so that jealousy was rife. Sometimes they had crushes (that term was still in use) on staff members, including myself, and these I had to deal with as best I could, having no guidance on the matter. I hope, now, that I accepted their gifts and their shy smiles and letters with as much grace as I could have mustered. They were mostly pleasant young people, and I genuinely liked them. I had the added advantage that I could at least escape from school at weekends. If the girls' headiest excitements were to do with food and observing one another's brothers and male cousins from a safe distance, my own diversions and anticipations were bound up in Friday afternoons. Like Henry Handel Richardson's Laura, in *The Getting of Wisdom*, I almost flew down the long, shaded path away from the school and into freedom. And though I was older than Laura in years, and teacher rather than pupil, I was much the same age emotionally and socially.

One remarkable freedom was having five pounds a week of my own. I could buy clothes to suit myself, and books, and afford to have occasional meals in restaurants. Once on the city-bound train, away from the inquisitive gaze of schoolgirls so anxious to know where 'Miss Kelly' was off to, I indulged in romantic visions of the delights to come. Joan and I were into — of all things — a heavily Russian phase. Our gathering place was the Shalimar Restaurant in a Park Street basement, which for some reason was beloved by a group of White Russian exiles, whom Joan knew through a cousin who had married one. I recall the entertainment as being ordinary enough — dining and a little wining, occasional dancing, and much talk — but the emotional atmosphere was highly charged. Tempers tended to flare, especially when vodka was available, and violent arguments (domestic rather than political) often broke out later in the evening. It was all quite novel and interesting, and a far cry from the routine of a girls' boarding school. I met, among others, one of the descendants of the imperial Romanoffs, a man given, understandably, to melancholy moods and some nostalgia (though common sense now tells me that whatever recollections he had of past splendours must have been mostly secondhand), and an ex-naval officer from Vladivostok, called Victor. Victor was large and very handsome in a melting Slavic fashion, and for a short time we were mutually attracted. I even took him home once for a weekend, unannounced, which startled my parents considerably, and was less than a sparkling success. Victor had very little English. I was trying to learn Russian, but never advanced beyond a few words. The unfamiliar script was beyond me, as was the unrelenting rapidity with which it always seemed to be spoken.

It was all probably a kind of rebellion against the restrictions of student life and supervision, parental and otherwise, and also against my unsought separation from Jack. It was also an opportunity to observe a whole new world of human feelings, about which I had been till then largely unaware. Here before me were husbands and wives, friends and compatriots, who had no

217

inhibitions when it came to expressing every kind of emotion from undying devotion to apparent rage and hatred. I still believed that feelings could be ordered, and that they were either good or bad; you suppressed the latter, and pretended to the former. Not only had I imbibed this from upbringing, but it was also precisely how the girls were instructed in the school where I taught. That even marriage partners could be physically violent towards each other was an extraordinary revelation. The first time I witnessed it I was rigid with alarm, and just as astonished next morning to find that the two in question were on the best of terms, and behaving exactly as if the quarrel had never taken place. Joan and I probably put it down to unavoidable Russian temperament.

The interlude was inevitably short-lived. Joan was soon to go overseas, and at the back of my mind was the thought that perhaps I, too, would soon be moving on. In October I celebrated my twenty-first birthday, then a rather grand occasion marking official entry into adulthood. Somehow the secret leaked out at school, and I was inundated with gifts of flowers and chocolates from the girls. This I appreciated, but my dissatisfaction with the teaching life, and in particular the enclosed milieu of the housemistress, continued to grow. There had to be some other avenue. I began to write a novel in which the central character was a child, and a lone orphaned one at that. I decided to look for another job.

For the first time, I acted quite independently in my choice. It seemed to be on impulse that I applied for entry into the Commonwealth Public Service as trainee librarian — or a desperate attempt to escape my present environment. Deep down, however, there was some kind of instinct to tell me that this *was* a move in a desirable direction, though I didn't yet know what that particular direction — or desire — actually was. The position was well paid, and promised a year's training in

218

Sydney, with the guarantee of a job thereafter in one of the Commonwealth departments — probably in Canberra, a place I had never seen. (In my customary starry-eyed fashion I assumed that it would be quite delightful.)

My mother was disappointed that I didn't persevere with teaching, though sympathetic with my distaste for all the restraints of that particular school. I knew there were other schools, and different headmistresses, but I was simply not cut out to be a teacher in the normal educational mould. It was more than twenty years before I discovered a kind of teaching that had little to do with academic approaches and qualifications, and rejoiced in it.

I spent my last term at the school as overseer to the preparatory grade children, in a separate cottage in a far corner of the grounds. It had its own private entrance and exit, and a more homely atmosphere. Nor was it arduous to supervise the doings of a group of rather nice little girls, with another housemistress for support. Yet it was there, towards the end of my stay, that I had one of my experiences — rare, since childhood — of things going mysteriously bump in the night. Loud rappings seemed to come from beneath the floorboards, and once, coming back late at night from an outing, I saw a vague, white shape hovering about the vegetable garden. My firm belief was that some of the older boarders, celebrating the imminent end of the school year, were playing tricks, but, oddly, nobody ever mentioned it. Had they succeeded in scaring a teacher, they would have almost certainly managed to drop gleeful hints afterwards.

It was the last time that I experienced any kind of ghostly manifestations, for which I was later thankful. During my travels since, I have been in various places, such as ancient castles in Scotland and high-ceilinged, gaunt, turn-of-the-century mansions in New Jersey,

U.S.A., where the atmosphere was decidedly spooky, but in imagination rather than actuality. During my student days, and occasionally afterwards for a year or so, my friends and I had played the game of séances, where we put our fingers on top of a glass and watched it skid around a tabletop. Imagination, plus dimmed lighting and a bit of cheating, surely made a large contribution to the success of it, but there was enough mystery to keep us intrigued. Why, for instance, did the 'spirit' who came to our bidding turn out to be a Red Indian? (Only recently I read that this is usual in such sessions.) The other question was more practical — why did the creature never have anything really important to say? Most of its messages were the standard fortune-telling kind, all of which turned out to be quite inaccurate, though colourful. For the rest of my life I remained sceptical of every form of soothsaying, pseudo-prophecy and astrology, though I kept an open mind as to the true nature of the supernatural. 'There are more things in Heaven and earth, Horatio, than are dreamt of in your philosophy.'

The finale to the school year was the official opening of a new building, a grand and stately occasion. For weeks the entire school population had been rehearsing the school song and the Christmas hymn, 'It Came Upon the Midnight Clear', which even now I can't hear without a reminiscent shudder. Determined, apparently, to go out in a blaze of frivolity, I bought a new lime-green silk crêpe dress and the kind of capacious headgear known as a 'picture hat'. The effect, with a black academic gown over all, must have been extraordinary, and I don't think I ever wore the hat again, but I had made my point.

The headmistress gave me some sort of a reference, brief, and not glowing. Some of the girls, and a few of the staff, I farewelled with genuine regret. On the whole, however, I was light-headed with relief. Before my training began at the Public Library, I went with Dorothy for a fortnight's holiday at Austinmer, on the South Coast. Dorothy by then was engaged to be married, which gave her special status in my eyes, but on this occasion her fiancé was absent. Perhaps it was her final fling, as for me it was to mark the transition from slavery to freedom.

It was January 1950, and the guesthouse where we stayed was at the height of its popularity. Set below the crest of a grassy promontory between beaches, it had the wide verandahs, the shrubbery, the tennis-court and the big communal dining and recreation rooms that were standard for guesthouses built before the war, and not yet superseded by an outbreak of modern motels. It attracted young people, and they were there in plenty. A large, informal group formed, at least for the space of a fortnight; and the days were shaped into rounds of surfing, tennis, golf, hiking and, in the evening, card-playing or dancing or going to the pictures (which had not yet become 'movies'). We climbed the escarpment to Sublime Point, and hitchhiked back down Bulli Pass. I loved the beaches and the rocky headlands, and the looming mountain range, so much grander than the low-lying scrubby hills of my native coast. From the lookouts we could see as far south as Bass Point, landmark of our summer holiday many years later at Shellharbour, and important in the lives of two teenage sons. It was at the Austinmer guesthouse that I met my future husband, father of those same board-riding boys.

I also met a girl with whom I shared accommodation in Sydney during my library training. We moved from one room in a house at Middle Cove to a flat in Neutral Bay, and I travelled by bus to and from the Public Library. This imposing institution, which as students we had so often frequented, I now came to know, so to

221

speak, from the bottom up. As trainees, we spent some time hunting through the stacks for obscure volumes, memorising the intricacies of the Dewey System, and learning how to catalogue, classify and cross-index all manner of books. Any fancy I might have had about a librarian's work being pleasantly literary was soon dispelled. The only romance I found in all of it was in the study of Incunabula; I liked the history of book-creation, of illustrated manuscripts and lovingly tooled bindings. It was the beginning of an interest, to develop later in England when I became a children's librarian, in the honourable traditions of publishing and book production, and an appreciation of illustration as an integral part of the reader's experience — to say nothing of the visual and tactile pleasures of good binding, paper and print.

But we were being trained for careers in the Public Service, and our studies were mostly utilitarian. For the same reason, we knew that our small and exclusive group of trainees would be broken up at the end of the year. When our postings came out, three of us were consigned to Canberra, myself to some place, utter mystery to me, called the Commonwealth Public Service Board. With my friend Margaret, I undertook the longest train journey of my life, to that date, into the wilds of the interior, and to a strange settlement generally known, in 1950, as six suburbs in search of a city. In some ways, because by then my Austinmer man-friend had become a regular escort, and was still an engineering student in Sydney, Canberra seemed a place of exile, even a sort of Gulag Archipelago, but in actuality there was considerable enjoyment to be had in many aspects — the beauty of the encircling Brindabella Ranges, snow-tipped in winter; the glories of glowing autumn trees and the soft, lush greens of spring, the walks to the office in the mornings across the Molonglo River and along the stately avenues. And there was much friendship in the hostel where we lived, and plenty of laughter. On Saturday mornings we went for morning-tea-cum-breakfast to one of Canberra's few cafés, in the Civic Centre, and on Sundays played light-hearted games of golf on the very pretty Royal Canberra course. We picnicked at the foot of Black Mountain, or out at the Cotter Dam, climbed Russell Hill above Duntroon, or took an evening walk through the countryside to the beautiful old church of St John.

It was an interlude in which I wrote little, read a lot (often on the train, lurching its six-hour way from Canberra to Sydney for a weekend) and dreamed of marriage and travel and a satisfying future. I was in love with love, and on shopping trips to Civic or Kingston collected assorted items for the trousseau, or 'glory box', still obligatory for young women contemplating marriage. Most of my salary, however, was being saved to pay for my boat fare to England; it was understood that after our marriage we would go overseas. For a time, in mid-1952, the whole project was in jeopardy, when I became ill with what was finally diagnosed as a duodenal ulcer. I recovered, temporarily, and left Canberra two weeks before my wedding.

We were married in the Anglican church of St Thomas in North Sydney, where I had been christened. It was cold, in an early evening of June, and I remember that my bouquet trembled in unison with my shiverings. Three days afterwards, we set sail for England, on the liner *Orion*, where we had a cabin on 'H' deck. Two more dreams had come true — that of marriage, and that of travel, to a place my mother still called 'home'. And a third dream, of becoming a 'real writer', was soon to blossom. Almost simultaneously, a fourth would come alive — the dream of bearing children.

What, or who, shapes our dreams, and brings them to fulfilment? Mine seemed simple enough, and with one exception — that of writing — were shared with numerous young women of my generation. Looking back, I see that my mother, in helping to shape my childhood, also fashioned the stuff of which dreams were made. She who had travelled herself, spoke to us of the delights of visiting distant places. She who had always wanted children, and was perhaps more maternal than she was wifely (for, I think, few women are emphatically both), imbued in me from the time I first played with dolls that to bear and rear children was, on the whole, both privilege and pleasure. (She was also realistic enough to mention that it entailed a certain amount of pain, physical and otherwise.) Perhaps it was because I accepted that in order to have children you had first to be married — the alternative was unthinkable — that I was in such a hurry to get on with it. My mother, who herself had not had children until she was well into her thirties, was not altogether in favour of my marrying so young, but I was one of those creatures who, in her own words, 'wouldn't be told'. Besides, I saw no reason why I could not combine marriage and a career and children, and as it turned out, I managed to do just that. Ours was probably the first generation of women to attempt such a feat, in the fifties, for it was the generation of Germaine Greer, Betty Friedan, and Simone de Beauvoir, and the dawn of women's liberation.

Yet my mother was a liberated and liberal woman herself, refusing to be tied by conformist and conventional ways of thinking, or to be confined solely to a domestic world. Perhaps one of her best gifts to me was the notion that adventures of the mind and spirit and imagination can be just as joyful and liberating as adventures in the body. It is something to be both treasured and practised in middle-to-old age. Indeed,

224

when I had become older and wiser, we agreed that to enjoy a happy old age, you need to prepare for it all through your early life.

From my father I gained a certain romanticism, an interest in matters historical, and an Irish fondness for a good argument, although my mother had that, too, in the Scots genre. And from both, and the general atmosphere of my childhood, I gained a stability and, in spite of a Depression and wars, a degree of hopefulness. Browning says: 'We called the chessboard white — we call it black.'

On the whole, my parents called life's chessboard white. They believed in goodness and decency, and looked for these things in others, rather than the opposite. Their hopes for their children's futures centred on the principle of giving them a good education, without emphasis on heaping up too many material possessions.

Now, at the beginning of yet another New Year — 1987 — I look north from my back fence and see, hung with the mists of a damp, cloudy morning, those same humped, unpretentious hills that surrounded my childhood home. I have only to see them, and the child in me is alive again, playing in a garden, running along a summer beach, opening with almost breathless delight a new shiny-covered storybook, scribbling a story of my own, coming through the twilight into a warm, familiar kitchen. It was no idyll, but a real childhood, because we were allowed to be children, never pushed into growing up too soon.

One of the most precious attributes of the child should be a sense of wonder, a reaching out of imagination into worlds seen and unseen. Of all creatures, the child has the greatest capacity for the suspension of disbelief, so that what others call impossible could happen tomorrow, or even today. A child would agree, without knowing how to express it, with a remark by that great writer for children of all ages, Walter de la Mare, that it is a mistake to confuse reality with actuality, just as it's a mistake to think that the sun is not shining because there are clouds in front of it.

Our society encourages us to see our lives as linear progression, from birth through infancy, childhood, adolescence, to adulthood and what we call maturity. As adults, we are taught to leave behind the child in us, and concentrate on what we call serious and important matters, such as making money, succeeding in our careers, arranging our retirement. We call old people 'childish' when their minds wander, and treat them as if they had no minds at all. Yet it seems to me that by suppressing the child in ourselves, we run the risk of denying the best part of us. To be able to wonder, and to believe where we cannot actually know, gives us, not a 'head start', but a 'heart start', in a whole new world of the spirit.

'Except ye become as little children . . . '